OSLG

NOV 2008

THE ROMANOV BRIDE

This Large Print Book carries the
Seal of Approval of N.A.V.H.

THE ROMANOV BRIDE

ROBERT ALEXANDER

THORNDIKE PRESS
A part of Gale, Cengage Learning

Detroit • New York • San Francisco • New Haven, Conn • Waterville, Maine • London

GALE
CENGAGE Learning™

Copyright © R. D. Zimmerman, 2008.
Thorndike Press, a part of Gale, Cengage Learning.

Thorndike Press® Large Print Historical Fiction.
The text of this Large Print edition is unabridged.
Other aspects of the book may vary from the original edition.
Set in 16 pt. Plantin.
Printed on permanent paper.

LIBRARY OF CONGRESS CATALOGING-IN-PUBLICATION DATA

Alexander, Robert, 1952–
   The Romanov bride / by Robert Alexander.
      p. cm. — (Thorndike Press large print historical fiction)
   ISBN-13: 978-1-4104-1063-4 (hardcover : alk. paper)
   ISBN-10: 1-4104-1063-3 (hardcover : alk. paper)
   1. Romanov, House of—Fiction. 2. Kings and
rulers—Succession—Fiction. 3. Russia (Federation)—Fiction.
4. Large type books. I. Title.
PS3601.L355R66 2008b
813'.6—dc22   2008027786

Published in 2008 by arrangement with Viking, a member of Penguin Group (USA) Inc.

Printed in the United States of America
1 2 3 4 5 6 7 12 11 10 09 08

For L and P,
who continually teach me
what really matters

PROLOGUE

Solovetsky Islands, White Sea, USSR
October, 1936

"I know that when you get right down to it people are not that easy to kill. And as I'm sure you are well aware, murder's a very messy business, it really is. Oh, sometimes you get lucky with a single bullet, say, right in the temple. Or the proper angle of a knife shoved into a chest. But there's always a struggle, usually some screaming, and then there's always that mess — the blood, the splatter, the waste that comes falling out. Trust me, things get ugly even if you use poison. So, no, I can't say I ever enjoyed killing. I only did it for the revolution — because it was necessary to clean the vipers' den, because it was the only way to change things for the better, because there was no other way to move our country forward to socialism. As our great Comrade Lenin said — wait, now how does it go? Oh, yes: 'There are no morals in politics, only expedience.' Yes, that's what Comrade Lenin himself said. And I can't say that I disagree with that, not at all. In any case, how else were we to throw off the yokes of tsarist oppression and capitalism except with violence?" Pavel picked up a stick and started poking at the campfire. "But excuse me, I'm wandering . . ."

"No, no, Pavel, that's quite all right," said Vladimir, the other man, gray and worn, who sat on the other side of the fire, a tattered blanket pulled tightly around his black clothing. "I want to hear it all. It really is quite fascinating, you know."

Feeling the chill of the October night settle gently yet firmly through his ragged clothing, Pavel scooted closer to the flames. He wasn't a particularly tall man, and he'd always been trim, more so now than ever. Though he hadn't gone at all bald, his shock of once dark hair was rapidly graying, while the skin on his face and hands had grown as coarse and thick as crude, wrinkled parchment paper.

When he lifted his feet right up to the fire, Pavel felt the blessed warmth and saw it too as steam swirled from his muddy felt boots. It had already snowed this week but, glancing upward, he knew it wouldn't tonight.

No, it couldn't. They were so close to the polar circle, and the great northern sky was perfect, a vast blanket of deep blue, sprinkled heavily with stars and more stars yet. Indeed, it felt like the very last of all nights, and in a way it was, at least here, because by the first of tomorrow's light he would be making a change of lodging. He sucked in the night air, let the scent of the loamy soil and sweet pine wood fill his body and soul. *Bozhe moi,* my God, he thought, Vladimir and he had worked so hard, digging and digging for nearly a week, and now this was their reward, a glorious night. How had he made it this far, lived this long, outwitting first the tsar's secret police, next fighting for the revolution and civil war?

"I'm a lucky man, Vladimir. Do you have any idea why, eh?"

"No, tell me, Pavel, why are you so lucky?"

"Because I'm fifty and no men in my family have ever seen so many winters."

"Truly?"

"Truly. My father's father was born a serf and was crushed in the fields — trampled by his master's horse — just a year before emancipation. That was the year of 1860, and my own father was only two." Pavel shrugged. "As for Papa, well . . . his dream was to buy the land he farmed, but he died in misery of tetanus."

"And brothers?"

"Both killed in the war."

"Any sisters?"

"One, but she disappeared nearly twenty years ago, not long after the revolution broke out. Just where she is today, or if in fact she's still alive, I have no idea."

Tugging the blanket tightly around him, Vladimir suddenly started laughing. "I'm sure everyone in my family thinks I'm long dead by now."

Staring at the other man through the flickering yellow light and studying his grandfatherly face, Pavel couldn't help chuckling. Yes, he saw it quite clearly.

"You know, Vladimir, if you weren't so thin you'd make the perfect Father Frost. With your big gray beard and those twinkling eyes — yes, in spite of everything I can still see the spark in you — you'd be fit for any New Year's celebration."

"Perhaps . . ." Holding up his dirt-caked hands, he laughed and said, "But first I'd have to sit in a *banya* for a day or two to steam off all this filth."

The two of them sat at the crackling fire in silence for quite a long while, the darkness of the night seeping more and more densely around them. And Pavel found it wonderful. Such peace. Such quiet. If only, he thought, this night would never end.

Finally, Vladimir cleared his throat, and said, "So go on, tell me everything. I need to hear it all, you know."

"Well . . . well, my point is that she was really hard to eliminate."

Struck by the length of time that had passed since that fateful night — could it really be 18 years? — Pavel fell silent. And yet he could still see it in his mind's eye with such startling clarity. Yes, there she was standing in the cart, singing that hymn. And there he was shoving her along the rutted lane, leading her right up to the edge.

Vladimir asked, "Why was it hard? Because she was so beautiful?"

"True, she was astonishing — people would just stop and stare. Imagine, she was the most beautiful bride in Russia, married first to the worst of the Romanovs, and next to Christ. But no, it wasn't difficult because of all that."

"Then, because her sister was none other than our Tsaritsa — I mean, the former Tsaritsa — Aleksandra Fyodorovna? As part of the Royal Family, she must have been well guarded at all times."

"Well, you have a point. Before she abandoned society, she was flanked by the best

11

of soldiers. But, no, we could have gotten through. After all, we assassinated many other notables, including, you know, her husband."

"Then why? Why was that one so hard to do away with? Because she had taken to the cloth?"

Pavel shrugged. "Call it what you like, but she did seem to have some sort of divine protection. For example, while it only took us a few weeks of plotting before we blew up her husband, it took years upon years for her. That's how powerful she was."

"The soul is much mightier than the body, of course," muttered Vladimir. "So in those final days did she have anything interesting to say to you?"

"Oh, a great deal. She was under my direct watch, and we talked for hour upon hour."

"And what in the name of the devil did she speak of?"

"Actually, we told each other the stories of our lives, and the most interesting thing she told me was also the strangest."

CHAPTER 1
ELLA

Though of course I was the granddaughter of the doyenne of sovereigns, Queen Victoria, I did not grow up in luxury by any means, for our little Grand Duchy of Hesse und bei Rhein in Germany was not a wealthy one, having suffered so in wars, recent ones at that. Indeed, it was during such difficult times that my mother, Grand Duchess Alice, wrote often to England, begging Grandmama to send lint and old linens from Windsor and Balmoral, things Mama and her ladies could turn into bandages.

Actually, my mother's eternal want was by no means to remain cloistered within the cold confines of any royal court, but to go out amongst the people to see poverty and pain, so that her good intentions would never dry up. As if a heretic I heard her mutter more than once that it might be best if royalty itself were washed away. It was no wonder, then, that following the lead of her

13

good friend and mentor, Florence Nightingale, my mother took it upon herself to be out and about in Darmstadt, here, there, everywhere, visiting those in need.

One particular morn after our breakfast of porridge and sausage, she took me along, leaving my elder sister, Victoria, and my baby sisters, Alicky and May, at home. This was in 1878, and I had no idea where we were going in our dot of a town, for Mama had seen to the organization of the Alice Society for Aid to Sick and Wounded, which included the founding of many hospitals and homes for the poor. She was very progressive in these things, fighting for the good of the common people and even for clean water and proper bathing practices, something that riled many old-timers who cared naught for a weekly bath. Or a monthly one, for that matter.

However, whatever my mother's good intentions were that day, I myself wasn't full of enthusiasm. All of fourteen years of age, I would have much preferred to stay home and draw, or, if work I must, sew a frock or pinafore for a poor child.

"Don't dawdle, Ella," she called over her shoulder. "We haven't much time."

"But where are we going?" I asked as we quickly walked down a narrow cobbled lane of the Old Quarter.

"There's a woman in need, that's all I've been told — and that, young lady, is all you need to know."

Within a few steps we'd left the tangle of streets and come to a part of town I'd never seen before. The road was quite straight but quite unkempt, the small pitched-roof houses half falling down, the filth and waste running freely in the gutters. Children in rags, their faces smeared with dirt, ran this way and that like wild dogs. And when we rounded the next corner a man in torn clothing stared upon us. Had he, I wondered, recognized my mother with her dark hair, slim nose, and blue eyes as none other than the Grand Duchess Alice, or did he have evil thoughts? Of course my father, as ruler of our little Duchy, would have had a fit if he'd known my mother and I had gone not to visit the Alice Hospital or such, but instead descended into the lowest part of town, and were doing so not simply unannounced but without an attendant, let alone a guard of any kind. But that was my mother, a German princess by marriage but forever an English Protestant in her heart and ways. Oh, she was a stubborn woman, that one. Years later, whenever it was just my sisters and I at the tea table, the story always went round and round again how furious Mama had made Grandmama when she decided that she herself and not a wet nurse would feed us children.

Putting down her needlework for a moment, one of my sisters would invariably shout with a laugh, "And what did our dear Grandmama, Queen Victoria, call our dear mother, Grand Duchess Alice?"

"A cow!" we would all cry in unison.

"And what name did our dear Grandmama, the Queen, give for a name to her favorite Highland cow at Balmoral?"

"Alice!" we would all shout, roaring with laughter.

So that morning, already quite aware of my mother's determined nature, I brushed back a lock of my fair hair and took Mama by the hand and did not leave her side until we came to a tumbledown cottage. We stopped at a door, crooked and cracked with age, and my mother knocked upon it. When no answer came, she knocked again. Suddenly a child screamed in reply, and without hesitation my very regal mother, small in stature yet eternally energetic, put her shoulder to the door and plowed it open.

Before that moment I could never have imagined such grime, such stench, such chaos. It took a moment for my eyes to adjust to the darkness of the small room with its low ceiling, for no candles were burning and the fire had long since gone cold. Clutching an old wooden chair next to the sole table was a little girl, wearing a torn shirt and nothing below. Obviously something was quite wrong with her, for waste of a very nasty sort was dripping between her legs. The screaming began anew just then, not from this child but another, an infant, lying in some kind of cradle. My mother hurried over to the child, a boy of but a few months, who was likewise covered with his own waste.

Gasping, I breathed in, fully catching the stench. Feeling my breakfast start to rise, I grabbed my own stomach. I was just beginning to wonder whose children these were and what kind of mother could have left them so despondent, when I heard a moan and sensed a person stir against the far wall. It was then that something bloated and red began to reach out from a pile of rags. An arm covered with boils, I realized. Then came a shoulder, all scarlet and glistening with sweat. Finally a face, blotchy red and also spotted with boils. It was a woman, her hair stringy and greasy, her teeth all but gone, her face hideous and swollen. She looked like the ugliest witch from the fairy stories of my youth.

I stepped back and was about to run screaming.

Suddenly my mother took me gently by the hand and in English softly but firmly said, "Ella, my dear, you must learn to treat the sick and needy without hesitation or fear, for that is the true Christian way."

I gazed into my mother's small dark eyes and saw a ferocious caring and determination to help others. And so, taking courage from her and following her good Christian example, the two of us set to work. I was more than hesitant as I first occupied myself with kindling fire and boiling water. Soon my task was to clean the waste from the children and bathe them, which was by no means pleasant. Next my mother fed the little ones, which quieted them greatly, and then she made tea, and I watched with admiration as she fed this to the ill woman. Though this seemed to coax the woman out of her delirium, my mother was still concerned, and she sent a neighbor to fetch a doctor.

"But . . . but I haven't a florin to my name!" gasped the woman, her face so blotchy.

"You needn't worry about money, that will be taken care of," my mother said sternly.

"Your only business is to get better."

"And . . . and who are you? Why have you come to me?"

"We've come because our help was needed."

"But who —"

"Sh . . . just rest," soothed my mother without identifying herself.

By the time we left hours later, the doctor had come and gone and it seemed relatively normal in that little cottage, for we had scrubbed children and floors and all. Indeed, the little ones were fed and asleep, and the woman, whose husband had recently died in a mining accident, was resting comfortably.

As we stepped out onto the little street, my mother leaned over and kissed me on the top of my head, saying, "You did very nicely, sweetheart."

I took her hand in both of mine and kissed it, and then we proceeded back, chattering mostly in English, some in German, as was our custom. We returned completely unrecognized as mother and daughter of the ruling family until we were within steps of the Neues Palais, our dear home that Mama had decorated in such a very cheerful English manner, chintzes and all.

And that became not only the most treasured memory I have of my mother but one of the last. In a few short months our united family, which had always been bound with love, was torn apart by epidemic. Diphtheria came suddenly and mysteriously, first taking my baby sister, May, just four years old, whose loss alone nearly killed Mama. Indeed, it weakened her so that she, too, fell ill, and though the doctors kept the inhalers filled with chlorate of potash to ease her suffering, she was soon taken by the same disease. My own pain was quite unimaginable, for I was not allowed to look after my poor suffering mother in her final hours nor even to kiss her farewell — for my own safety, I was kept quite apart from my beloveds in their illness. Needless to say, grief overtook my father, and for years thereafter our palace was all but dark.

But then everything changed completely when I came to Russia as the bride of my father's first cousin, a Romanov — Grand Duke Sergei Aleksandrovich, son of Aleksander II and brother of Aleksander III — and it was at that time that I began to live a life of pomp and wealth beyond the reach of any other earthly kingdom.

And a mere nine years after my own royal marriage there I was in the Kremlin's

Cathedral of the Assumption, no doubt in my mind that the Russian Imperial Court was the most magnificent in all of Europe. My dear Grandmama had forever derided Russians for their extravagance, but Nicky's coronation, which was taking place right before my eyes on that beautiful day in May, 1896, was the most glorious spectacle I had ever witnessed. As I stood amid a sea of kings and queens, princes and princesses and countless diplomats, the sunshine streaked like golden spears into the smoky, incense-thick church, and the dresses and uniforms, the jewels and the sabers all sparkled and danced with light. Candles burned everywhere, golden icons of saints stared down upon us, and I dabbed a tear from my left eye. Before us an incredible event had just unfolded: young Nicky, twenty-six years old and the new husband of my younger sister, had by the grace of God been anointed His Imperial Highness Nikolai II, Emperor and Autocrat of All the Russias.

Nicky then ordered that the Imperial Crown be handed him, which he took directly from the hands of the very important Metropolitan Palladius of Sankt Peterburg. By tradition Russian tsars crowned themselves, signifying there was no man of any rank or priest of any import between Tsar and God. And with his own hands Nicky did exactly that, crowning himself with the great Crown, that blazing masterpiece covered in some 5,000 smaller diamonds, dozens of larger ones, brilliant pearls, and, of course, that magnificent uncut ruby — the world's largest of 415 carats — atop all. From that very moment, Nicky's only responsibility was to answer to God and God alone.

Next, in a surprisingly strong and steady voice Nicky commanded that the other insignia — the Imperial Scepter which held the famed Orlov Diamond of 200 carats and the Imperial Orb of gold — be given over.

The pale, grayed Metropolitan Palladius, dressed in blazing gold robes sewn with thousands of pearls and wearing atop his head a gold mitre decorated with diamonds and rubies, held forth the insignia as he proclaimed in a booming voice, "Take this Orb and this Scepter, which are the visible manifestations of the Autocratic power the Almighty gives You to rule over Your People and to lead them to Prosperity."

Nicky took the Scepter in his right hand, the Orb in his left, and seated himself upon his diamond-covered throne. A few moments later, he rose and passed the regalia to his aids. With tears in my eyes, I watched as Nicky commanded Alicky, my sister nine years younger, to come forth, which she did, kneeling upon a crimson cushion with a border of golden lace. With heart-stopping majesty Nicky then removed his Crown and touched it to the forehead of his beloved consort. Once the Crown was back upon his own head, he turned again to my sister and laid the regalia upon her — the Purple, the diamond-covered Chain of the Order of St. Andrew, and finally the Empress's Crown of some 2,000 diamonds. Immediately the choir burst into song, wishing the Tsar and Tsaritsa long life and long reign, 101 guns were fired into the sky, and it seemed as if heaven had opened and was pouring its divinity down to earth, such were the waves of glory and beauty and wonder.

Once Nicky had again seated himself on his diamond-covered throne and Alicky upon hers — Ivan the Terrible's, actually — we members of the Royal Family were allowed to approach the dais not simply to pay our respects but to pledge our fealty to our country and her Sovereign. Minnie — the Widow Empress Maria Fyodorovna — went first, a diamond crown upon her own head, her train stretching forever behind her, and tears by the bucket streaming from her eyes. Of course, this made me cry all the more, for we all knew that her tears were not only of joy and pride but surely of pain, for Minnie had lost her husband, Aleksander III, just over a year earlier.

Everywhere there were court gowns of gold and silver, jewels of red and blue and green, countless diamonds of the first water, and we proceeded by rank, everything being so strictly laid out. My own court gown, the train of regulation length — which is to say the length of nearly three men — was of creamy velvet embroidered with gold thread. And as I approached Nicky, I swept a curtsey as graceful as any ballerina. I could feel that dear boy's beautiful blue eyes upon me, his warmth, his love. Then I went to Alicky. So that she might be close by me, I had long prayed and done so much for her to find a husband in Russia, and I had succeeded beyond expectation, for here in my new land she had found the truest of love with her Nicky dear. Now as nearly everyone's eyes fell upon me to see would I kiss the hand of my younger sister, I took her soft fingers in mine and with real joy pressed my lips to them, and it was stunning and sweet, the love flowing between us. In a rush of emotion, I pledged myself entirely to her service and to that of our new Motherland. At that moment I was quite certain that no country was greater or brighter or more blessed than our beloved Russia.

That night, when the vast crowds gathered round the mighty Kremlin walls, their Empress Aleksandra Fyodorovna — my little Alicky — was led to a prominent bastion along the Kremlin walls and instructed to push down upon a particular button. Much to the joy and utter delight of Court and peasant alike, the miracle of electric illumination burst forth in the dark night as the thick walls and formidable towers of the Kremlin glowed for the first time ever with the dazzling magic of thousands upon thousands of electric bulbs. It was all glory, all power, and the future of our Holy Mother Russia seemed boundless and plentiful, stable and assured.

Indeed, none of us could have begun to think, let alone imagine, that this God-Anointed Tsar would ever, ever be pulled away.

CHAPTER 2
PAVEL

I was full of hope when I was twenty, and for a short while not only did I have a beautiful bride but we were wonderfully happy.

Oh, Shura . . . my Shurochka. She was the eldest daughter of the village priest, and she had such a big smile, such straight teeth, and such eyes, so blue. Beautiful blond hair, too, that at night she uncoiled all the way down to her waist. And, oh, what soft parts! A real sweet bee! She was the most beautiful girl in our village — we both came from the same small place, a mere crossroad at the foot of the Urals — and I had always wanted to marry her, knew that I would. And I did! Yes, we got married in the fall of 1904. September. She was just eighteen and I just twenty, and not three days after the ceremony — her father performed it — we fled the countryside. My grandfather's life had belonged to his master, and he basically died a farm animal, crushed in the mud. Years later, of course, my own father cut himself on his rusty plow and contracted tetanus . . . just heartbreaking. We had to hammer planks to the side of his bed to keep his quaking body from bouncing onto the floor, then we had to tie him down as his temperature rose . . . and next he passed from us. Granted, Papa was a free man but he left this world without so much as a single *desyatina* of land to his name, let alone a single ruble, and so I knew I would be leaving the province as soon as I could. To tell the truth, I didn't want to doom a son of mine to a fate like Shura's father, either — a poor priest with a big beard, totally dependent on handouts. No, the back of beyond of Mother Russia had not been kind to us, nor to anyone else in our village for that matter.

As my own dear babushka used to say, "Oi, things were better when we lived under the masters — at least then we didn't have to worry where we would find tomorrow's bread!"

And how did I do it, get the money for the train to the city? I stole it. I went to a nearby village and raided the hut of an old woman when she was out milking her only cow. But it turned out it was only enough for two tickets for me and my Shura to get as far as Moscow, which was a problem. Shura wanted to go to the capital. She wanted to go to Sankt Peterburg, the city of the tsars. *Da, da,* my Shurochka was the daughter of a priest and a true Believer, and she wanted to be nearer her Tsar, which was actually fine by me. Rumor had it that wages were higher in the capital, so I said to Shurochka, "Sure, let's go." But getting to Peterburg meant traveling through Moscow and then another night of travel, which was amazingly expensive, of course. And where was I going to get that kind of money, enough for two to travel so very far?

In the end it wasn't so difficult. I just had to steal more money. And this is what I did: me and a pal walked overnight to another village and snuck into three different huts. And that second time we made out pretty good. When the villagers were at church we stole a pile of money, and my half was enough for two tickets all the way to Sankt Peterburg and even enough to pay for our first few weeks in the capital. Oh, I didn't tell my Shurochka where I really got the money. No, she would've killed me on the spot. So I just told her my rich uncle in a nearby village loaned it to me. Even then she was hesitant, but soon enough she was all right, she was, when I told her that Dyadya Vanya expected to be repaid within a year, no more.

And so we packed bread and some dried fish, two meat pies from Mama, a few clothes, then kissed everyone goodbye and got a blessing from Shura's Papa, the priest, and set off. Oh, I'll never forget when, a few days later, our train pulled into the Nikolaevski Station in Peterburg. So many people! So many fine carriages! So many people on the streets selling meat pies and fruits and nuts and . . . and everything was, well, so exciting! The capital back then was amazing, a glittering heart of golden palaces right in the center and a great ring of smoking factories in the surrounding suburbs. At first it was so exciting because we were in the city of the tsars and we were young and, why, we had real . . . hope! *Da, da, da,* for the first time even I felt it, too, something good about the future. For the first time in the history of Mother Russia we were not bound to the land and our destinies were not controlled by our masters, and there we were, thousands of us flooding the cities, hope dangling right before us like a big carrot. It was unbelievable. I didn't understand it then, couldn't name it, but we were part of a new class of people, a new generation freed from serfdom, now able to seek a better life in the city, and we were known as *the proletariat.*

CHAPTER 3
ELLA

I suppose I first began to realize that things were beginning to pull apart in that autumn of 1904.

It was widely said that the mood of society had not been so bad in several decades, which I did not doubt. We were in that horrible war with Japan and as a consequence I was busy with my workrooms, organizing so many hundreds of women to roll bandages and pack medicaments. Determined to reach out to those in need, I even had my own ambulance trains to see after as well. However, this was Russia, a country ever so slow in awakening, which is to say I was shocked by the confusion, how poorly my instructions were obeyed and how such carelessness caused our help to arrive so slowly in the far east of the Empire. Heavens, there was such terrible, terrible waste as well.

Early that December, Kostya — Grand

Duke Konstantin — came to us for dinner. He was so distressed, as were we all, at the strikes and upheavals throughout the nation, and he went on and on.

"Good Lord in Heaven," said the stately man, who was widely known for his wonderful poetry, "it's as if a dam has suddenly broken, flooding our Holy Mother Russia with the utmost turmoil."

"You speak the truth," agreed my Sergei. "Russia has been seized with an incredible thirst for change!"

I looked upon my husband, so tall and thin, his narrow face so tight. It's quite true, Sergei had a very severe belief of the way things should be, an opinion with which I didn't necessarily agree. But of course I said nothing, for in Russia it was said that a husband was the head of a wife as Christ was head of the church. Upon politics I was therefore not allowed to comment, particularly amongst mixed company.

"Everything is being talked about with such squabble," continued Kostya. "The cities of Kaluga, Moscow, and Peterburg have unanimously adopted motions asking for every freedom. It's just absolutely awful. Revolution is banging on the door. Even a constitution is being openly discussed . . . how shameful, how terrifying."

Sergei nodded. "A constitution would be madness, sheer madness. I'm afraid our Russia is too backward for such reforms, that our people are neither ready nor mature enough for such things. The so-called parable of equality is just that — a simple story. Freedom and equality would only make the masses drunk and sick, and it would be the ruin of the nation, of that I'm quite sure."

"Absolutely," said Kostya enthusiastically. "Democracy is practical only in small countries like France or Britain, not in our huge Russia with our multitudes of different peoples, from Great Russians to Mohammedans."

Given Sergei's firm belief in the autocratic principle, it was small wonder that he did not approve of Nicky's steps, however tentative, to introduce reforms as the most stable course for Russia. But perhaps Sergei was right, perhaps it was as they said: God was Autocrat of All the Universe, and the Tsar was Autocrat of All the Russias. This was, of course, all quite contrary to what I'd been taught by my mother, who believed that liberalism was the best antidote to violence. Then again, this was Russia, an Empire ever so much more Oriental than Occidental.

With all this weighing on Sergei's mind, and fearful, too, that the government had lost its way, it came as no surprise that after fourteen years of service my husband submitted his resignation as Governor-General of Moscow. The two of us quite looked forward to retiring to our country estate, Ilyinskoye, where I planned to paint and read and host entertainments such as concerts and *tableaux vivants.*

Then we were hit by a terrible lightning bolt, two bolts, actually. First came the horrible news of the surrender of Port Arthur to the Japanese — imagine, and we had all firmly believed that Russians never surrendered! — and then in January came the awful strikes in Peterburg, which grew and grew by the moment, spreading all the way down to us in Moscow.

Lord, how painful it all was.

CHAPTER 4
PAVEL

After we arrived in the capital my Shura found work within a few days, which was of course good, even though the pay was so low, some 16 rubles a month, though that depended on her output. She found a job at a textile factory, not the big Stieglitz Works but a smaller one, and the trouble started when on her first morning there the manager, this fancy Mister Foreman with his squeaky big leather boots — and I was sure he'd paid extra for that squeak just to impress us with their newness — insisted that she live at the factory. The normal working day for her was supposed to be eleven and a half hours, but the factory had received government permission to work fourteen, even fifteen, hours each weekday and ten on Saturday. There was to be only one day off — Sunday, of course. And that's why Mister Foreman wanted Shura to spend the night at the factory — to be more efficient. He said she would make more money too because she was paid by the piece and the rate was very low, so he said that if she slept on a plank bed by her workbench she would be able to work more and make more, too. And at first Shura agreed to that. After all, she was a good girl from the countryside, devoted to Tsar and Motherland, submissive, and without a political thought in her dear, sweet head. *Da, da, da,* she wanted to obey her manager, but I said no.

"You are my wife!" I said to her. "I will not be separated from you! I will not agree to meet you just one day a week!"

And I won, and so we became "corner" dwellers. We found a place way out in the Narva District in the cellar of a building that cost us 4 rubles each a month, which seemed like a lot, particularly since all we got was a bed in one part of the cellar, a corner that was partitioned off by a dirty curtain. Three other families lived down there, all of whom, like us, had just arrived from the countryside. Children in makeshift cradles hung everywhere from beams, and it was all so uncomfortable and smelly, but that was all we could afford. Rents were very high . . . why, an apartment with its own bedroom in a sensible neighborhood cost

25 rubles a month, which of course was more than Shura would make in a month. So there we were in that dark cellar, packed like herring in a barrel. There were armies of cockroaches running this way and that, and the plaster was peeling from the ceiling in great scabs. And it was so cold, so incredibly cold. We shared the kitchen with seven other families, and the toilet, too, which was so dangerous that children weren't allowed to go there by themselves. Frankly, the stench of the toilet was so thick you could cut it with an axe.

It took me several weeks to find a job.

Every morning I went to the gates of the great Putilov Works, which was one of the largest metalworking plants in the entire world, making locomotives, tractors, railcars, artilleries, and employing some 13,000 hands. It was located in the southwest part of the Narva District, not too far from that nasty place where we were living, and each day I stood at the big gates and called out for a job, and finally one of the foremen came over and examined my hands, tops and bottoms. When he saw that my fingers were thick and calloused from the farm, he knew I was a good worker and so he took me as a smith, placing me at the very lowest rung and giving me 21 rubles a month.

Even though the conditions of the factory were a kind of living hell, I was thankful for the start. Our incomes were just enough for food and rent each month and we were together, my Shura and I. And even though each night we were nearly dead from exhaustion, even though we had no privacy in our little corner of that cellar, somehow it happened.

My Shurochka became with child, much to our joy.

Yes, before long she even began to show, perhaps, I suppose, because she was no longer a plump country girl but had become so thin from working so hard.

CHAPTER 5
ELLA

For the Christmas holiday we had been staying at the Neskuchnoye Palace, which belonged to the Crown and was nestled in the suburbs along the Moscow River. But one night our good rest was broken in the late, late hours by heavy pounding on our bedroom door.

"Your Imperial Highness!" came a gruff voice.

Before I knew what to make of this, Sergei was up and out of bed, slipping on his silk dressing gown.

"What is it . . . what's happening, Sergei?" I mumbled.

"Remain in bed — let me handle this!" he snapped as he made his way to the door.

He stepped into the hallway, shutting the door behind him. Sitting up in bed, I listened, for just outside I could hear two or three heavy voices, none of which sounded calm. Something serious had happened, of course, for Sergei was awakened only in dire emergency. So what was it now, had the strikers seized an official building? Had another minister been killed by the subversives? Or, dear Lord, had something happened to Nicky or Alix or, God forbid, to the children?

Suddenly Sergei started yelling, and I wanted to rush out there but didn't dare. Of such things, I was allowed to know next to nothing. It was true, my husband showered me with jewels and gowns, but I understood this was my job to him, an adornment.

The door was flung wide, and my husband, his stern face flushed red, boldly strode across our bedroom. The fury burned on his face as brightly as a lamp.

"Sergei, what —"

"Get dressed, my dear!"

I looked at him — what did he just say? — and said, "But —"

"Don't argue with me! Put on some clothes! We're leaving!"

This made no sense, and yet I had never disobeyed, let alone rarely questioned, my husband. I rose from our bed and made for my dressing room. Immediately my thoughts turned to Maria and Dmitri, our young niece and nephew, whom God had seen fit to send to us and watch over as guardian parents.

"What about the children?" I asked.

"They're being wakened and dressed by Mademoiselle Elena," he said, referring to their governess. "They'll join us in the hall downstairs."

Sensing the gravity of the situation, I asked, "But where are we going?"

"The Kremlin. Now just do as I say, get dressed at once! And take nothing, our belongings will be brought later!"

One of my maids came in, and as she quickly dressed me my mind leaped at all the possibilities. It took no imagination. The Neskuchnoye was nestled not just in a beautiful park but near the factories and the neighborhoods of the poorest workers. Had the general uprising, which we had so feared, finally broken out? Was a band of revolutionaries ready to attack us here? For a few days now extra cavalry had been camped in the Palace yards, but I took small comfort in them, for I feared even their loyalty.

Dressed in plain walk-about clothing, I was downstairs within minutes, where Sergei and the children were already waiting. A fur cloak was thrown over my shoulders, and without word to us or farewell to our staff Sergei rushed us outside and into the cold. His big closed carriage stood out front with our ever-faithful Coachman Rudinkin perched atop the coachbox in a heavy blue coat. Four large black horses had already been harnessed, and Sergei hustled the children and me into the pale-gray silk interior. We were off at once, traveling full speed, the curtains drawn, the lamps mounted on the front of the carriage oddly darkened. Ahead and behind us I could hear the many horses of our escort charging along.

I of course knew the way to the Kremlin, and I soon realized that we were traveling by any but a direct route. Instead, still at racing speed, we were passing down small streets, through quiet neighborhoods, and across unknown bridges. None of us spoke, but glancing at the handsome, wide-eyed children, I saw that they were not afraid, just curious, even excited. Heavens, did they not sense what a crossroads Russia had come to?

Our coach slowed only when we finally reached the security of the Kremlin and passed through one of its gates. Driving through the quiet territories of the bastion, we soon arrived at the Nikolaevski Palace, where we were met by just two servants who helped us disembark and saw us up to the reception room on the first floor. Within a short time we were given tea, for the poor children were shivering — the long unused Palace was so very cold — and we four sat up for a good while, waiting first for my lady-in-waiting, the children's governess, and my husband's aide-de-camp, and then for our servants who in time brought us just enough of our things to pass the night.

And even though the rumored attack upon our country residence did not materialize that night or any other, we never returned to Neskuchnoye. Such were the times that Sergei deemed it safer behind the thick fortress walls of the mighty Kremlin.

CHAPTER 6
PAVEL

After months of working, working, working, we came to realize one day that our prospects were not so very bright after all. And that is precisely why we decided to go to one of Father Gapon's tearooms, which was called the Society of Russian Factory Hands. It was open to all, including Finns, Poles, and even *Zhidki,* the Yids. Simply, we wanted a better life. I had a child coming, and I didn't want the little one to grow up in the filth of that cellar. I didn't want to work every waking moment of my life, breathing the foul air from the smelter, only to die not as a human being but some kind of rat. And I didn't want the little one getting ill with no medical help at hand. So we went to one of these tearooms organized by the Father Gapon, where only tea and mineral waters were served — absolutely no vodka — and where each meeting was opened and closed with prayer. And there, in the Assembly Hall, we heard about the condition of the worker and the need for betterment of his life and so on. It seemed very promising and very good at first. Father Gapon himself spoke with such power, and the portrait of *Otets Rodnoi, Batushka* — Our Own Dear Father, the Tsar — hung on the wall, and really there was no dark talk whatsoever. None. In fact, many praised our system — that we had an autocrat who stood above all classes and nobles and bureaucrats, a God-given leader who, when he learned of our sufferings, would make things right with a single *ukaz.*

But then the great strikes of January, 1905, broke out. It all started at the very place where I was employed, the Putilov Works, when three or four men were unjustly fired. I can't even remember why they were sacked, but the manager, Smirnoff, who could easily have fixed the problem, only succeeded in making it worse by doing nothing, absolutely nothing. And so the list of demands from the workers grew and grew — including better ventilation for us smiths, which pleased me greatly — but when there was no agreement, all 13,000 of us walked out. Almost immediately the Schau Cotton Mills in the Vyborg Quarter stopped work, even work at the Semyannikov Shipyard and the Franco-Russo Shipyard ground to a halt, too. Why, by the end of the first week of January it all became a general strike — nearly 150,000 workers refusing to do anything! — and it scared the government a great deal because we were at war with the *Yaposki,* the Japs, in Manchuria and the production of ships and cannons and uniforms had completely stopped. I tell you, it was all amazing. Shocking even, especially for Shura and me. We were not but a few months in the capital — mere minnows! — and the world around us was being swept away by a great wave. It was all so very different from life in our quiet village.

It must have been that Friday that someone gave us a hectograph copy of an amazing idea — that we were all to go to the Tsar! Of course Shura, as the daughter of a priest, could read very nicely, and with a strong voice she recited:

Workers, Wives, Children!

We will gather together and all go to Batushka, the Dear Father Tsar, and bow before Him and tell Him how we, His children, hurt. We will tell Him how we toil and suffer and live in starvation. We will tell Him how the master foremen and bureaucrats at the factories fleece us. True, it is true, Batushka does not know how we need His help. But once He does our lives will become easier. For the sake of Mother Russia, let us gather! Let us march to Batushka and bow and kneel before Him so that He can bathe us with His love!

This was how we learned of the great demonstration, and the instant we learned about it, why, Shura and I were seized with excitement. Immediately we set off for Father Gapon's Assembly Hall where we had drunk tea and which, by the time we got there, was already packed, so packed that people were fainting from lack of oxygen. When the kerosene lights even started going out because of the bad air, why, that was when I grabbed a copy of the petition and rushed my pregnant Shura from the hall. But it was a beautiful idea, so beautiful in its simplicity: We would all march peacefully to the Winter Palace, where Father Gapon would hand our Tsar-Batushka a petition telling him of our needs. It was even promised that the Sovereign himself would be there to receive us and hear of our sufferings.

"Oh, Pavel, we must go!" exclaimed my Shura, her face radiant with a smile, her breath steaming in the winter air.

"You just want to see the Tsar!" I laughed knowingly.

"Yes, you're right. I want to see him because once he sees all of us kneeling before him, once he sees our love for him, he will understand how much we suffer. And then he will make everything right, our Tsar-Batushka will ease our pain and make our lives good. Just listen to the words on this paper." And with a trembling hand she lifted up this paper, this plea to our Tsar, and read: " 'Sovereign! We, workers and inhabitants of the city of Sankt Peterburg, members of various classes, our wives, children, and poor old parents, call upon Thee, Sovereign, to seek justice and protection. We are poor and downtrodden, buried beneath work, and insulted. We are treated not like humans but slaves . . .' "

Shurochka read on and on, and I must tell you, it thrilled both of us, these words, calling for such unheard-of things as freedom of speech, equality for all before the law, compulsory and free education, and even an eight-hour workday. These things delighted me because in them I saw not just simple hope but a real future for my young family. Yes, with promises like these we could stay in the city, we could build a real life.

We could even prosper.

CHAPTER 7
ELLA

Like all women of my time, I was carefully taught in the arts of needlework, piano, and painting. It was the latter of these that I found most appealing. Often in the mornings I could be found at my desk, if not writing a letter, then drawing a design — a flower or forest scene — on an envelope or on the edge of a piece of blank stationery, which I would later write on and send.

One day soon after New Year's as we were slowly but surely settling into our apartments in the Nikolaevski Palace of the Kremlin, I was doing just that, painting an envelope there in my cabinet. Hearing a quiet knock at my open doorway, I raised my head and saw standing there not only one of my footmen dressed in his fine white uniform but also my dear little dog, Petasha. Immediately I smiled, for in my eager companion's mouth was a piece of paper.

"Come, my little postman!" I called.

With that, Petasha, a fox terrier of great personality, burst forward. The entire Palace, from servant to prince, took great joy in this pup and the way she delighted in bringing me my mail, and I lifted an envelope from her mouth as carefully as if I were taking a letter from a silver platter.

"Thank you, *dorogaya maya.*" My dear.

Good Petasha was gone as quickly as she had come, leaving me with a smile upon my face and a letter in hand. My good humor quickly vanished, however, when I recognized the handwriting of my sister, Alicky. Oh, dear. These days I had nothing but worry for her and Nicky.

Quickly opening the letter, I read:

My Own Darling,
Surely you have heard what worrisome times we are passing through here in the capital, and yet I write to tell you we are holding up well. Reports come daily that the strikes in the city have been terrible, and we hear of a socialist priest who is at the head of some dark movement. Apparently he plans to lead a great march upon the Winter Palace, hoping to deliver some paper — saying what we do not know — to Nicky. It's all very concerning, of course, but we are told

51

everything is under control and my dear, dear Nicky seems not too concerned.

Yes, it's difficult these days, and I am generally very tired. The children, though, are well, and Baby is a continual bright spot in these . . .

My eyes flew over the last sentences, and then I clutched the letter and let my hands fall to my lap. Dear Lord, what was happening? What troubles lay ahead? I worried so for Alicky and Nicky, and I worried so for my new country and how it seemed to be coming apart. Nicky, I feared, was not being tough enough, for he was far too sweet to wield a strong hand like his father. Where were the ministers he needed? Where was the proper advice? I supposed it was a good thing that Alicky and he had their main residence outside the capital in Tsarskoye Selo — the countryside and the air were so good there — but I feared our royal couple was becoming too distant not simply from society but from events in general.

Oh, poor, poor Alicky, I thought, glancing out the window at the snowy courtyards of the Kremlin. For ages the entire Empire had been waiting and praying for a miracle, which was finally delivered upon us this past year: Alicky had given birth to a beautiful boy, Aleksei.

And yet . . .

I shook my head with grief. Yes, Russia had her heir to the 300-year-old House of Romanov, and, yes, the treasured boy was a wonderful, handsome child. But I knew the horrible truth, I knew what only a small handful did, that the dear, sweet baby was a bleeder. Only three or four of us in the immediate family knew this sad story, while to the rest of the Ruling House, the Empire, and the entire world, this fact was guarded as nothing less than a state secret. And so my poor sister suffered alone and in silence, forever fearful that her precious baby, her Alyosha, would befall the same fate as our own brother Frittie: he would simply bump himself and bleed to death. In the past year poor Alicky had aged ten.

Hopeful that my husband might know more, I wiped my eyes and rose from my desk. Stopping in front of a mirror, I checked myself, for Sergei expected nothing less than perfection from me. I primped at my fair hair, pinched at my cheeks, and made sure that the pale-pink satin dress I wore — which was decorated with a delicate pattern of acacia and was of my own design — was flattering. Although I had a weakness for jewels, Sergei was even more fond

53

of them, and he was forever showering me with precious gifts. He often informed me which jewels he wanted to see on a specific day, and today he had told me to wear the large freshwater pearl earrings and long pearl necklace, all so perfectly matched in color and size. Yes, they were beautiful, I thought, straightening them. Then, as confidently as I could, I headed out, making my way toward the large front staircase and down to Sergei's office on the ground level.

My husband was loath to be interrupted during his workday, but nevertheless the large, uniformed guard opened the double door for me. Entering Sergei's cabinet, I found him in undress uniform at his large walnut desk, which was covered with photographs in Fabergé frames, jeweled mementos, and other bric-a-brac. After a moment or two of my standing there, he raised his head.

"What is it, my child?" he said in his slow Sankt Peterburg drawl.

Sergei was tall and thin, with both his light beard and hair cropped short, and while he was pleasing in appearance, he was forever hesitant to smile. Though he had received much criticism for his stern rule of Moscow, I could honestly say none worked harder, which was why he was clearly annoyed by my presence during his working hours.

"I've just received a letter from Alix," I said. "Apparently there's a group that plans to march upon the Winter Palace."

"Yes, I'm aware of this. I've been receiving steady reports for the last week."

"Oh . . ." I replied, surprised, though I shouldn't have been that Sergei had not mentioned it. "Well . . . is there danger? Is there anything to worry about?"

Sergei reached for a pen and bottle of ink. "I've been informed this morning that this band of dissolutes means the Emperor harm."

"Dear Lord . . ."

It had been over 20 years since Sergei's father — and Nicky's grandfather — was assassinated by revolutionaries, who'd thrown a bomb at the royal carriage and blown off the Emperor's legs. Ever since the entire Ruling House had been living in the shadow of that nightmare, forever fearful that it would happen again. For this reason, Sergei had practically dedicated his life to ridding the Empire of ungratefuls, which was why, sadly, his tenure as Governor-General had begun with the expulsion of the Jews from Moscow. Though I hadn't been privy to great information at the time,

I'd since heard that altogether some 20,000 souls had been herded out of Moscow, some to Siberia, most off to the Pale, women and children alike, and all in the freezing cold of winter, no less. While Sergei had always felt this had been wisely done for security, I had seen in it nothing but shame, and could not believe that for this we would not be judged in some way in the future.

Had that time now come? Were the dark days now falling upon the Empire merely a kind of retribution for the sad events of fourteen years past?

"Does this mean Nicky won't be there, that he won't meet them at the Palace?" I asked, tightly clasping my hands.

"The Director of Security has insisted that Nicky refrain from greeting these marchers. In fact, for the Emperor's own safety they are requesting that he and Alicky not travel to the city for the next week but remain at their residence in Tsarskoye."

With that, Sergei picked up a document, which he began to read, and I retreated from his office, overcome with worry. So my sister and her husband would be safe . . . for now. But the shame of it all, Russia's Emperor all but imprisoned behind the gilded fence of his own Palace.

Oh, and what a tragedy that march turned

out to be . . . how sinful, how painful. I still weep at the lost opportunity.

CHAPTER 8
PAVEL

For weeks it had been dark and snowy in Peterburg, of course. And cold, so incredibly cold. But that morning of the march the sun came out in all its glory. True, it was still awfully chilly and there was snow on the ground — after all, it was January — but rarely do you see so bright a day in the middle of a Russian winter, the sun so low but so sharp, cutting across the roofs and into our faces. Just gorgeous.

And because of this beauty you could see it everywhere, hope on everyone's faces, for we all took the sunshine as a golden omen. Some even claimed that the Tsar himself had ordered such a fine day. After all, we were not asking for a new government. We were not asking for the Tsar to abandon his mighty, God-given throne. Why, no, we just wanted our beloved Tsar-Batushka to come to our aid, to reach over the conniving courtiers and bureaucrats who divided us, his devoted children, from Him, our fatherly Tsar. He would stretch out his illustrious hand and help us up — yes, we were confident he would. The massive march to our Sovereign, we were told, was to be like one great *krestnii xhod* — religious procession — leading right to the home of our Sovereign so that we could sob our griefs on the chest of our Little Father. And so we wore our Sunday best clothes, that was how we were instructed. All of us were told, "Put on your nicest clothes, take your wives and your children, carry no weapons, not even a pocket knife!" Likewise we were instructed not to carry anything red, not even a red shawl or scarf, for the color red was of course the sign of the revolutionaries, which we absolutely were not. After all, just as it was impossible to go before the Almighty God bearing arms, so was it unclean to go before the Tsar with devious thoughts.

Because of the huge numbers wanting to see the Tsar, because the procession was to be so enormous — well over a hundred thousand were expected — we gathered in different parts of the city. I think there was one group that met on Vasilevski Island, another along Kameniiostrovski Prospekt, somewhere else, too, and we were all to march to the Palace and congregate there on Palace Square. Shura and I joined the crowd at the square in front of Father Gapon's Assembly Hall in the Narva District, and naturally ours was the largest group.

A great "Hurrah!" went up when Father Gapon himself appeared on the steps of the hall.

"Look, Pavel!" said my Shura, clutching my arm. "Look at Father Gapon and how handsome he is!"

I turned and in the cold saw a handsome man, his hair long and dark, his beard thick. But honestly he seemed pale. Nervous, too. Did he know, did he fear, what lay ahead? Perhaps . . . but just then no one gave a thought or a worry, for the air was too crisp, the golden domes of the nearby church too bright, our hopes too high. And, as Father Gapon moved toward the head of the crowd, we parted. Wearing not simply his long black robes but a chasuble — a sleeveless outer garment that I had never seen a priest wear anytime but at Mass — he passed right before us, and I watched several old women reach out and kiss the hem of his cloth.

"Bless you, Father!" one of them called.

"Thank you for helping!" sobbed another. Suddenly Shura was grabbing my hand

and pulling me along, urgently saying in a hushed voice, "Come on, Pavel, let's go to the front of the crowd! Hurry! I want to be right in the lead so as to better see the Tsar!"

And, laughing, I let her pull me along after Father Gapon. The mass of people closed behind us, and soon we were up there near the head of the vast crowd, which numbered, they were saying, somewhere near 20,000 folk. And yet everyone was peaceful, not a word of dissent was heard anywhere, so united were we. Just to make certain that our good and religious intentions were perfectly clear, a great call went out for icons and other items of the church. Within minutes we were surrounded not just by men and women workers of every age, from young to old, but by large crosses held high, tall banners from a nearby church, huge icons, and glorious portraits of our Tsar Nikolai II, too.

In fact, a man in felt boots hurried by, calling, "Who wishes to carry an image of *Otets Rodnoi, Batushka!*"

"I do, I do!" shouted Shura.

And such it was that Shura was given a framed portrait of the Tsar, pulled right from the wall of Father Gapon's Assembly Hall, to hold high and carry forth. And such it was, too, that shortly after eleven in the morning on Sunday, the 9th of January, 1905, we slowly started forward, this great mass of suffering humanity that was so full of love and hope for Tsar and Motherland.

We had not gone five steps when one man pulled his fur *shapka* from his head and began singing our great national anthem, "God Save the Tsar!" Immediately we all fell into dutiful song, and when we came to the line blessing our Tsar, we sang, "God Save Nikolai Aleksandrovich." Along with our solemn voices came the pealing of church bells, and though I should have been, I wasn't at all nervous, not even when I saw a large banner held aloft that read, "Soldiers, Do Not Fire Upon Your Brothers!" No, I wasn't nervous, because I saw several policemen pull their hats from their own heads and cross themselves as we passed. And when we proceeded to sing "Save Thy People, O Lord, and Bless Thy Inheritance" these policemen began to sing, too. No, I was quite sure of it, there was nothing to fear. We were in God's hands and, as if to prove it, yet another group of officers ran up the side of the procession and began to clear the way for us. They even turned away a few carriages that attempted to cross our path.

Oh, if only the Tsar had been waiting for us . . .

It wasn't long at all before we reached the great Petergofskoye Highway and turned north. By this time Father Gapon himself was no longer in the front rank but just behind, surrounded by a handful of what appeared to be bodyguards, big men who kept close and tight rank around him. Shura and I were not but three or four people away from this group, and it wasn't long before the Narva Triumphal Arch, built to welcome home the troops from their victory over Napoleon, came into view. But what caught my attention wasn't the glorious copper arch or the copper chariot with six ponies atop. No, what seized my heart was the sight of kneeling troops, rifles at the ready, blocking our passage over the small bridge spanning the Tarakanovka River in front of the arch.

"Shura," I muttered, "there are *soldati* ahead."

Still holding the Tsar's portrait aloft, my dear wife, along with the crowd, was now singing "Our Father" and seemed barely concerned. In fact, she and everyone else only began to sing louder. But it scared me, I confess, and a shiver went through my body when I saw behind the troops a line of cavalry — men mounted on horseback, their faces stern, their fur hats tall. Oh, dear Mother of God, I thought. All we had wished for was that our meager voices be heard by our rightful ruler, not that the Cossacks be brought in.

"Shura," I said, taking my young pregnant wife by the arm, "perhaps we shouldn't be here, perhaps we —"

"Don't worry, Pavel!" she said, holding the portrait higher.

"But —"

"It's all right. Trust me, no one would dare fire at a picture of the Tsar!"

Instinctively I started to slow, for like all peasants of Russia — serfs that we had so recently been — there was nothing I feared more than my master's whip. But these stout men atop their horses did not bear whips. No, it was far worse, for at their sides were swords. But whatever the danger, there was no stopping our mighty procession now. Even though I tried to slow my pace, I could not. Indeed, the great mass of humanity seethed with excitement, pushing me forward faster and faster.

When we were but 300 paces away, the line of kneeling troops suddenly parted and the Cossacks came roaring out on their small, strong horses.

"Gik! Gik!" they cried as they spurred on their horses.

Thanks be to God, though, their swords were still not drawn, and yet a great shout arose from all of us, and our procession parted down the middle. It was through this empty alley that the Cossacks charged, their horses bellowing steam like dragons as they thundered across the trampled snow. Yes, we parted for the Cossacks, but we did not disband, we did not scatter down side streets, as I am sure was the desire of the soldiers.

Father Gapon, his voice shaking, bellowed, "Be brave, Brothers! Freedom or death!"

All of us stood in shock as we watched the Cossacks pass through the entire crowd and then, like a great eagle, circle back. Because we had not fled, an order was given. In one lightning move, the Cossacks drew their *shashki* — their famous swords — and came charging back faster than before.

"Gik! Gik!" they shouted.

It was a dazzling sight, these brutes on horseback, the silvery metal of their *shashki* glinting in the golden winter sun. We pulled back even more, and again there was no incident as they surged past, their voices whooping and their swords raised high.

They charged back across the small bridge and disappeared behind the line of soldiers.

Immediately, almost instinctively, the great mass of us, so many thousands, rushed back into the street like floodwaters whooshing into a void. My heart was pounding like a locomotive, and though I knew I should be carrying my young pregnant wife out of the way, I couldn't stop myself. We were great, we were mighty, we workers so desperate for a good life, and all of a sudden we were locking arms, one to the next, united in our desperation. The singing erupted from us all — what song I can't even remember, something religious, to be sure — and faster than ever we poured forward, those behind pushing us in the front. When we were less than 200 paces from the line of kneeling soldiers, I heard it, the bugler giving the call to fire. But nothing happened. It came again, the sound trumpeting into the thin winter air. Then a third time, all to no avail, for we were all brothers and sisters, workers and soldiers alike. Finally, I heard the scream of an officer ordering his young men to shoot upon us. And fire they did, the dry snap of their bullets shattering the air. But the rifles that had been aimed directly at us were by then raised to the heavens, firing high overhead. That was the first volley.

Then came another order, and the second volley likewise went into the air. And somehow we were running by then, all of us gathering power and courage, our icons and religious banners and certainly the image of the Tsar held high. And I remember looking at the kneeling soldiers, seeing the fear on their young faces. Boys, they were, brought in from some provincial town, Pskov perhaps. Terrified boys who, faced with this mob, lowered their guns and, this time following their orders, took near-point-blank aim.

Again, that dry snap, over and over.

An unbelievable wail rose from our procession, unified at first, then shattering into one scream here, another there. A man not ten paces in front of me suddenly fell to the ground, his religious banner tumbling and ripping to shreds underfoot. I tried to stop but could not, so great was the force of the masses behind us. Glancing over at Father Gapon, I saw the horror in his eyes, then saw two of his bodyguards, the ones right in front of him, stumble and fall. And right above my Shura something exploded into a million pieces and she screamed . . . she screamed as the portrait of Tsar-Batushka was riddled with bullets.

"Shura!" I cried to the heavens.

There came another volley and yet another as the soldiers fired straight at us, and we all fell to the ground nearly as one, man atop woman, atop grandfather, atop child. Knocked down, I dug into the snowy street as the shots were fired over and over until their clips were completely spent.

At long last the guns were quiet. For the briefest of moments there was nothing. Then came something awful, wailing and sobbing that bubbled up all around me. Lifting my head, I looked around and saw a carpet of bodies. A young girl screamed to the heavens as she reached for her trampled mother. An old man tried to get up, stumbled, and fell again. Turning and looking back, I saw many people now fleeing, cutting into the side streets and running for their lives.

But my dear wife was just lying there, facedown and within reach, and I touched her, calling, "Shura! Shura! Come, we must run away! Get up!"

I scrambled to my feet as best I could and reached out, pulling at her arm. But why was she making no movement, why was she making no effort to get away? Why was she not rising?

"Shura!" I yelled. "Shura, get up!"

It was then that I saw that the snow in

which my dear wife was lying was no longer white. No, it was a hot, steaming crimson, and she lay there in it, a rapidly growing sea of red snow, and I realized that I, too, was standing in it, a deep puddle of her blood.

And behind me a man cried like a child, muttering, "God has abandoned us and so . . . so has the Tsar!"

CHAPTER 9
ELLA

Sobbing, one of my ladies came in and told me the horrid news, and as soon as I heard it I rushed from my boudoir. Wasting not a moment, I scurried down the grand staircase, my dress dragging behind me, and burst through the doors of Sergei's cabinet. Hurrying in, I found him not at his desk but gazing out a window at the Kremlin grounds, his hands clasped behind his back. Standing a few steps away was the military governor of the city, our very distinguished Count Shuvalov.

"Oh, Sergei!" I exclaimed. "Salvos were fired upon the marchers — I'm told many were killed!"

"Yes," he muttered slowly. "Count Shuvalov himself has just brought me the news. I'm told nearly a thousand have died."

"Oh, Lord!" I gasped, crossing myself. "Were they just workers, or —"

"Women and children, too."

"No . . . !" I said, bursting into tears.

Sergei turned around then, his face paler than I had ever seen, his eyes red, for we both sensed what this meant for the country and what darkness it would bring.

He said, "Come, child, we must pray for the dead."

We did just that. Leaving the Count, we headed directly to the attached church, where we were on our knees the rest of the afternoon and well into the night, offering blessings for the newly departed.

Sadly, only later was it proven that the vague rumors were actually true, that the workers had meant the Emperor no harm, that they had merely intended to gather at the Palace and present him with a petition requesting his help. Just think if it had been so . . . if the Tsar had met directly with his lowest, neediest subjects! Just think what wonderful things we could have done for our beloved country!

Instead, all went from bad to worse, and the strikes spread like a terrible fire, leaping from factory to factory.

CHAPTER 10
PAVEL

That was how my path started, right then and there on that Bloody Sunday as I reached for my beautiful Shura and found her lifeless. That was the day my sweet wife and unborn child died and that was the day the Tsar died, too. From then on I dedicated my life to revenge . . . and swore my life and soul to the Revolution. Day and night my cry was: Workers of the World, Unite! Down with the Autocracy! All Power to the People! So many innocents were killed that day, which proved to be the dress rehearsal for the Great October Revolution twelve years later. Yes, for decades if not a century Russia had been a boiling cauldron just waiting to explode, and explode it did with vicious power.

It was true, in a matter of moments all that I lived for was cruelly taken away, and there was no bottom to the depth of my pain. I do remember collapsing in the red snow and sobbing as I never had, I do remember a Cossack coming by and beating me with the flat of his sword, but . . . but suffice to say that, I don't know, three or four days later I found myself hiding in an attic with a group of revolutionaries, for my transition to hatred was just that quick.

Of course, Father Gapon survived as well. But his bodyguards did not. Those men who had volunteered to protect the priest did just that, acting as a human shield and taking the bullets and falling for the Revolution. If only I'd thought to do likewise, to stand before my wife and protect her. But I didn't, and to this day I still don't understand how those bullets could have missed me, how I was not even grazed, and how my Shura, standing right next to me, could have been killed so quickly and cleanly. But that was what happened and that was how I lost my faith, for if there had been a God he would have spared her and our unborn baby and taken me instead. Or, perhaps best, taken all three of us together.

As for Gapon . . . within moments after the shooting had stopped a group of his ardent supporters rushed over and whisked him away. I vaguely remember seeing this, somehow remember watching as they hustled him down a lane, shaved his familiar beard, pulled his priestly garments from his body, then dressed him as an ordinary worker and sent him scurrying into hiding. I didn't see him again or cross his path for almost two years until that one day when he was murdered in a dacha outside the capital. Hung from a hook, he was. No, it wasn't the Tsar's secret agents who did that. It was our people, revolutionaries who were so displeased with him for his betrayals, for it turned out that all along he'd had secret contacts with the police. I actually helped kill him, and I was glad to do so: four of us hung him from a hook on the wall, and when the hook proved not high enough from the floor, me and another comrade pulled on Gapon's shoulders until he was strangled. The police didn't find his body for a whole month.

With the murder of my own wife, I turned freely to hatred and seized the opportunity to murder any Romanov I could. We were determined to get rid of our oppressors and their capitalist dogs, we were determined to turn a page in history and make sure there was no going back. And that was how and why of course we decided to go after the Grand Duke Sergei, that bastard who had ruled Moscow with an iron fist for, what, some fourteen years. There was no question, he was the worst Governor-General that Moscow had ever seen. After all, it was he who ran the *Zhidki* out of town, and he who made those few *Zhid* boys who stayed in the city to register as stable boys and the few *Zhidka* girls as prostitutes.

That was how, too, I ended up in Moscow a few weeks later. I traveled there to participate in the incredibly glorious plans to murder the Grand Duke Sergei. Within days of Bloody Sunday it was decided in the highest echelons of the revolutionary committee that, first off, the most reactionary and hated of the Romanovs should be executed. A kind of trial was held, and it was determined by all that the Grand Duke Sergei should meet his death. I think, actually, that after the events of Bloody Sunday not just me but the masses as a whole were crying out for revenge. On top of Russia sat the disgustingly rich Tsar, beneath him came those 1000 or so conniving titled families, then the merchants and little bourgeoisie people. Finally at the bottom came us, hungry peasants and weary workers who made up the biggest part of Russia, some said as many as 80%. We meant to change all that, we did, by whatever means necessary. We meant to turn society completely upside down and completely reverse the table of ranks so that we were on top and Nikolai the Bloody and his greedy family and all the others were smashed down there at the bottom beneath us. I volunteered to join these terrorists, and so some three weeks after the murder of my wife and unborn child, I traveled to Moscow and joined this secret group, which was determined to kill the Grand Duke Sergei Aleksandrovich.

And if in the process of killing that despicable oppressor we also killed his beautiful bride, well, so be it. What did I care? Nothing, that was what.

My heart had turned to cinder.

CHAPTER 11
ELLA

As I stood in front of my tall, triple mirror in my dressing room, I was not especially pleased with what I saw. Was the yellow silk dress, which I myself had designed, just the right one for tonight? Were the sleeves tailored snugly enough? Was the collar, which was decorated with seed pearls and petite diamonds, too extravagant in detail? Or was it the color, was it somehow all wrong?

Turning to my dressing maids, I asked, "What do you think, girls?"

"Lovely, Your Highness," replied Luba, a trim gray-haired woman who had served me since my marriage some twenty years past.

The other, Varya, a plain short girl in my service for only a few months, practically whispered, "Beautiful, Your Highness."

As the two maids began to tighten my whalebone corset and fasten the long row of buttons up the back of my dress, I continued to examine myself with great criticism. So many had told me how pleasing I was to the eye — the kind proportions of my face, my fairish hair, and soft gray-blue eyes — but I could never find that beauty in myself. Yes, I made quite a ceremony of dressing for the evening, but the truth was that I spent all those hours looking for problems, for I was all too aware how much my husband hated imperfections, from the curl of my hair to the cut of my dress. If there was so much as a crease or an uncomely fold in my gown, the wrong necklace or uncalled-for earrings, my husband would demand that I change.

Yes, Sergei was a difficult one, and though I loved him and remained ever dedicated to him, I could not deny that over the course of time we had pulled apart, in large part, of course, due to his sternness and demands. Too, the painful truth was that I had fully expected and hoped to bear a number of children, yet for his own reasons Sergei had made this not possible — though we shared a bed, I was forever denied more than a brusque kiss. Thus, in truth, a kind of tense fondness had come to exist between the two of us. From the bedroom to the stable, every decision, every choice, made within our household was his, with the strictest belief that we were all to obey and all was to run punctually and with great order. Even the smallest decisions, the petticoat type, were not mine to make, and in no way was I expected to busy myself with intellectual burdens. Almost as if I were his decoration, Sergei planned my life to be filled with painting and piano, social occasions, and, at most, participation in charitable activities. Yet such a carefree life was not entirely pleasurable, for among other things I could not deny that I was pained by the absence of little feet running about the Palace. And so it was that in my great disappointment and loneliness I longed to do more good for the people, the suffering ones, just as my own dear mother had taught me.

Heavens, as I readied myself for our public appearance at the opera that evening I couldn't help wonder what gossip would make the rounds of tomorrow's tea tables. On the subject of my married life, the most horrid things had been told and retold about my husband's predilections, and over and over it came as a great astonishment that people could talk of such things. And while these stories hurt me, all I knew was that if one were guided by gossip scant good would get done in this world. Such was my life and my fate, however. I just had to keep in mind that my only duty was to obey the vows of marriage, which were sacred before God and could not be altered. As a member of the reigning family, it was up to us to set the best example for the nation . . . and yet as of late there had been a rash of unequal marriages, even a few divorces. Shameful, it was, not to mention simply immoral, all these morganatic unions. Even Sergei's younger brother, the dear, dear Pavel, had broken this firm family law by taking a bride not from another ruling house but from a lower station — and not even a princess at that but a commoner — for which the Emperor had banished him from the Empire.

I had long held it dear to my heart that to live in amplitude one must have an ideal. Ever since my childhood in Germany mine had been to become *eine vollkommene Frau zu werden.* A perfect woman. And most definitely that was difficult because first one had to learn how to forgive everything, and to do so with full understanding. And could I do that? Could I achieve my ideal? I was always striving, but feared it would forever escape my grasp.

I loved Sergei, I truly did, but what I had never revealed to anyone was that the first person I had to forgive — and which was proving so very difficult for me — was none other than him, my husband, from whom I so craved kind word and soft touch.

CHAPTER 12
PAVEL

My secret group had been tracking the Grand Duke for weeks, and it was true, we were so confused by the way he darted from the Neskuchnoye Palace on the banks of the Moscow River to the Governor-General's Palace on the Tsverskaya, next to the small Nikolaevski Palace within the Kremlin. We had no idea why he was moving around like a scared mouse, darting here and there. Some of us proudly convinced ourselves that he was dashing around because he was afraid of us and thus trying to lay no regular path, others had heard rumors that there was to be a shake-up in the government, still others claimed that all the stories were true, that the Grand Duke was no lover of women and was simply darting from boy to boy. And while I had no reason to doubt these tales — I had heard tell that there were a handful of other grand dukes inclined to stable and ballet boys alike — I really didn't care where or with whom His Imperial Highness dabbled after dark. All I was certain of was that he was not so high and mighty, or so pure and noble, as he pretended. On account of his irregular movement, however, it was nearly impossible for us to pinpoint a time and place for our attack. It was so frustrating for us who were so ready to kill for the sake of our toiling workers and Mother Russia's hungry peasants.

When, however, we saw in the *Moskovskaya Vyedomosti,* that major newspaper, that the royal couple would be attending the opera at the Imperial Bolshoi Theater on the night of February 2, well, we developed our plan almost instantly and quite easily, too. It was not far at all from the Kremlin to the Bolshoi, and there really was only one route for them to follow from that ancient, massive fortress — through the Nikolsky Gate, to the left across the end of Red Square, past the Aleksandrovski Gardens, and then onto Voskressenski Square and from there to the Bolshoi. So we decided that we would be waiting along the way, hiding in the shadows.

Of course, we all wanted to do the deed, none perhaps more than me. I had been admitted to this select group of revolution-

aries because I had recently passed a test —
I had slit the throat of a pathetic government fellow in Novgorod and stolen a big
sum of money too. And because of this success I was allowed the honor of helping to
kill the Grand Duke Sergei.

Heading our group was Ivan Kalyayev —
"Our Poet," we called him because he wrote
beautiful words and always carried around
worn books of poetry. He was an educated
fellow, most definitely, and everyone knew
he was eager to kill for the Revolution, and
eager to hang for it too. But you'd never
know his dark intentions by looking at him,
for he had a girlish kind of face, so soft and
tender, with a big forehead and dark hair
and intense blue eyes that would sometimes
fall with great sadness. He was the comrade
chiefly in charge of our group, and because
of his seniority, even though he was young,
maybe twenty-five or -six, he was given the
honor of throwing the bomb. This made
sense, naturally. My only hope was that I
would be caught along with Kalyayev and
be allowed to hang with him too. *Da, da, da,*
that was my secret wish, to avenge my wife's
death and then dangle, spinning in the
wind, from the gallows.

Also in our group was Dora Brilliant, a
smart Jewess, and a pretty one at that, who

had abandoned her good home and easy life and become very dedicated to the Revolution. She was a trained chemist and she made good bombs, very effective, the kind packed in a tin container with kieselguhr. This Dora made the bomb, and my first duty was to pick it up.

It was promising to snow the day we planned to kill the Grand Duke, the sky a dark flinty gray, the wind strong and determined. Finally, the snow started sometime after six, just as I wound my way across Red Square and past the Upper Trading Row, a vast building of shops constructed in the old Russian Style with big arches and heavy windows. Heading into the small lanes of Kitai Gorod, I passed row after row of shops, each one given over to a specialty, this one selling lace, the next canvas, then honey, lanterns, furs, and dyes. Turning onto the Ilynka, I watched the snow blow this way and that up the street, and I thought how good it was. In fact, knowing what we were about to do, I was happy for the first time since my dear Shura had been gunned down by the Tsar's command.

By this hour the many banks and trading and lending houses lining the Ilynka had long since closed, so there really weren't that many people about, just a few lowly clerks and such scurrying through the cold, their heads bent. At the appointed time — seven o'clock — I reached the designated corner and glanced around as gently as I could, seeing no one. I was, it seemed, in front of some kind of money house, and I drew back into the deep, arched doorway, my collar pulled up, more to hide my face than to block the cold. Not two minutes later, I heard the dull clatter of hooves on the snowy street and peered out. A small sleigh was making my way, its driver huddled against the snow. As if I were greeting an old friend, I stepped out, smiling and waving to him. This was our Savinkov, who, I think, was born in Warsaw and who had long been dedicated to ridding his homeland of the tsars. He had a keen, intelligent face, and when he saw me he smiled, his teeth so white in the night. Really, no one ever took him for a terrorist. He looked much more like a minor aristocrat from Poland, with that medium-brown hair, that sharp face, his tall forehead.

The bomb that Dora Brilliant had so carefully made for us was wrapped in a handkerchief, and I accepted it from Savinkov as if it were nothing more than a pot of warm *pelmeni*. We exchanged a few stupid words, and then I trundled off toward the Kremlin.

Glancing back only once, I not only saw Savinkov and his sleigh disappear into the dark — he had one more bomb to deliver to another of our conspirators — but could detect no one following me.

Yes, this was going to be easy, very easy. All we had to do was lob this bomb through the carriage window, and that, without a doubt, would be the end of a Romanov or two.

CHAPTER 13
ELLA

Half to myself, half to my maids, I said, "I'm just not sure about the color of this dress. Perhaps that's what's bothering me. It may be too bright. Perhaps something more muted would be more appropriate for tonight. After all, we are at war and there is great suffering." I turned to my maid. "Varya, fetch me my green velvet dress, you know, the one Madame Auguste finished recently. I know this is a gala event to benefit my Charity Fund, but I think that one might be more suitable for the times."

Varya bowed her head and replied, "I'm sorry, Your Highness, but that one has yet to be brought over from the Governor-General's Palace."

"Oh, I see . . ."

What a pity, I thought, my thin lips coming together in a distinct frown. Ever since the workers in Peterburg had stirred things up and organized the march upon the

Winter Palace, there had been nothing but confusion, confusion, confusion. Yes, it seemed that over the past month nearly every worker had gone on strike, and prices were soaring. Why, even as protected as I was, I knew that Moscow itself had nearly shut down, and in my dealings at the workrooms I'd even heard talk from the street of assassination and revolution. Turmoil everywhere, that much was painfully obvious. And that was how scared we were, that we had to hide behind the thick walls of the Kremlin fortress, that we couldn't travel about without worry. What had the world come to?

"Well, then," I said, smoothing the fabric around my waist, "I suppose this dress will have to do. But, honestly, Varya, will you see to it that all of my personal belongings are gathered here at the Nikolaevski as soon as possible?"

"Of course, Your Highness."

Sergei's work here in Moscow would soon draw to a close; after so many years of service there remained only a few more weeks. Because of this and the fact that we were constantly moving from one residence to the next, none of the people of my Personal Household — not my mistress of the wardrobe, parlor maids, linen maids, stewards, footmen, dressmaker, and so on, let alone either of these two lady's maids or any of my official ladies, for that matter — was sure what was to be sent where, whether here to the Nikolaevski, to our Palace in Peterburg, or to Ilyinskoye, our country residence. And it was no wonder such confusion reigned, for when we officially moved from one residence to another — even just for the summer — it was as if we were moving an entire village, for no fewer than 300 souls were attached to our household.

"Once all of my things have been gathered here," I continued, "a decision will be made on what is to be sent where."

"Yes, Your Highness."

As my maid turned to a velvet-lined case and lifted a stunning diamond diadem topped by five exceedingly large aquamarines, I stood silent, still carefully examining myself in the mirror. If I were not mistaken, the skin cream, which I myself concocted from fresh sour cream and cucumber, did appear to be doing its work. My complexion, even for a woman over forty, seemed fresh and supple. Of course, a proper woman of good station never painted her face, merely applied a touch of rice powder or rouge from time to time, but even this I always refused.

For the performance th... had informed me that I s... parure, consisting of this aquamarine diadem, match... and bracelet all done in garlan... had no idea of the value of such a price in gold rubles was never p... ...ny of my gems, and I was forbidden ...o ask. Actually, both Sergei and I valued such treasures by their real worth — design and color — and this suite was extraordinary, one of Fabergé's most original. And yet as my maids settled upon my head the exquisite headpiece and fashioned upon me all the rest — the necklace, stomacher, bracelet, and rings — I felt a distinct sense of unease. This blaze of fine stone simply seemed too brilliant, too jubilant, for this evening, particularly surrounded by the shimmering collar of my dress. In fact, I could almost hear my grandmother, Queen Victoria of England, hissing with disapproval.

"It's not safe there in Russia, I tell you!" Grandmama had sternly warned upon hearing of my marriage proposal more than twenty years earlier. "There is such excess there, so much vulgar show. Really, my dear, the government does so little to improve the well-being of the common people — it's shameful! Truly, I will be sick with worry ear child."

et I could not tread against the formidable will of my husband, so I had no choice but to wear such riches that evening. I only hoped that tonight's gala event, a benefit for my charities, would be a success.

As I gazed into the triple mirror and admired and adjusted the veritable cascade of diamonds and such, I heard the sound of quick footsteps, and knew immediately who it was, my young niece, the Grand Duchess Maria Pavlovna, herself all of fifteen years. Against my own will, my spine tightened.

"Why, Auntie, you look beautiful this evening," said Maria, rushing up and kissing me on the hand.

It was true, the child was a spoilt one, just as it was true she'd had more than enough trouble in her short life, for her dear mother had died giving birth to her brother. And that was how the two young ones came to us, for after Maria's mother had passed so sadly from this world and her father banished for his morganatic marriage, the Emperor had placed the two children under our guardianship. Sergei, who insisted that he was their father now, adored them both, but I was not at ease with them, particularly the girl, for, to be brutally forthright, they were painful reminders of my own failures in marriage.

At this child's kiss, I couldn't help but stiffen and even physically retract, pulling away quickly from the girl. Wondering what she'd done wrong, Maria looked up at me, her new mother, in confusion. As a granddaughter of the Tsar-Liberator Aleksander II, this child had her own jewels, her own furs, her own servants, and of course a most substantial income, yet what she did not have — the soft touch of a warm mother — was what she needed most.

I turned to my maid, and even I was surprised by the words that came out of my mouth as I said, "Varya, please inform my young niece that it's rude to make such personal remarks in front of a servant."

Maria couldn't hide her shock, and tears welled up in her eyes, but I pretended not to notice. Yes, I thought, I mustn't be touched like that. Sergei didn't, and neither must the children.

Less than an hour later, looking every bit a Grand Duchess of The House of Romanov, I descended one side of the double grand staircase of the Nikolaevski Palace. I wore long kid gloves that came up over my elbows — it had taken both maids to put them on — and a long sable cloak that trailed the floor. Behind me, a puffy frown on her face, traipsed Maria, who had been dressed in finery appropriate her age, complete with a mink coat, and her younger brother, the forever sad but forever sweet Dmitri. He was wearing a mock uniform of sorts. And behind the two children came my gowned *Starshiye Freilini,* the ladies-in-waiting of my own court who would attend me that eve.

No sooner had I set foot on the ground floor than a uniformed guard opened a large side door, through which my husband and his aide-de-camp promptly stepped. With the exception of the Emperor, who took after his petite Danish mother in stature, Romanovs tended to be either as tall as a tree or as big as a bear, on occasion both. Sergei was among the former. His posture was always impeccable, if not unnaturally stiff, and he was toying then, as he so often did, with a jeweled ring on his little finger. And that night as he studied me with his small, intense eyes, he wore a brilliant blue uniform jacket with gold-thread epaulets and numerous diamond-studded medals.

I stopped before him for inspection, and stood as beautifully as I could. How could he possibly find fault with me?

"Open your cloak, my child," he commanded as he screwed up his eyes and studied me with great intensity.

I did just that, pulling aside the sable and exposing my pale-yellow dress and sparkling diamonds.

Finally, he all but grumbled, "Fine."

The Grand Duke then turned to the children and suddenly smiled, stretching out his arms. His obvious joy at seeing them did nothing but hurt my heart.

"Why, my children, don't you look ever so beautiful tonight!" exclaimed Sergei. "Come here, come into my arms and give your new Papa — yes, I'm your Papa now! — a great big kiss!"

I just stood there, my face stern, my anguish hidden, reluctantly watching as my husband scooped these children up into his eager arms. Yes, I had always wanted children of my own — I had wanted them almost as much as I still wanted the intimate affection of this man whom I had once so tenderly loved and looked up to.

Suddenly a footman rushed forward, placing a fur cape over the Grand Duke's shoulders, and we were off. With great pomp, two uniformed guards threw open the Palace doors, and we four royals stepped into the cold, snowy night, followed immediately by my *Starshiye Freilini* and my husband's aide-de-camp. As we approached the large, old-fashioned carriage — a re-markably heavy brougham, its carbide lamps now blazing brightly — the Grand Duke's driver, Coachman Rudinkin, silently bowed his head and tipped his stubby top hat. A footman hurried ahead of us all, opened the carriage door, and the Grand Duke and I and our young charges climbed in, settling on the silk cushions. Once our attendants were settled in a lesser carriage behind us, the whips began to crack and we went dashing across the inner territories of the mighty Kremlin, soon to pass through its gates.

CHAPTER 14
PAVEL

By the time I reached the end of the Upper Trading Row, the snow, which had promised to be heavy, had faded to a handful of flakes. Crossing onto the vast Red Square I could see no carriages or sleighs, merely a handful of peasants wandering this way and that, as they did round the clock. I imagined that I looked just like them, a lonely man, his purpose unknown and certainly not of interest, merely in a rush to cross the rather desolate space.

As I passed the corner of the tall redbrick History Museum, I eyed someone emerging from the shadows. They said half of the city's street janitors were spies for the police, and at first I couldn't tell who this person was. I pressed on, pretending not to have noticed him, thinking only that we were so close, so very close, to seeing our dreams fulfilled. All I had to do was deliver this bomb, which I cradled as dearly as if it were my unborn child. And then, of course, my next duty would be my greatest.

Suddenly the man behind me, the one who had blossomed out of the shadows, hurried alongside me. When he was right by my side, I glanced over and saw the familiar face of Kalyayev, our poet. I smiled, he grinned back, and in a single gentle movement I passed the bomb from my arms to his. It only took a second. No one could have noticed. And, with the goods delivered, I crossed the cobbles and melted into the white shadows of the snowy Aleksandrovski Gardens. Meanwhile, Kalyayev pressed farther on, disappearing into the gardens as well.

I felt such elation. Such happiness. We were assured success now, weren't we? All I had to do was spy the carriage, cross onto the street, and if I saw the Grand Duke himself inside the coach I was to drop the black rag. Yes, it was black, the color of death and night, specifically chosen so that Kalyayev could see the signal on the snowy street, and then he would dart out and heave the bomb through the window of the carriage. The Grand Duke would be killed immediately and everything would change, right?

I felt no cold. No chill. And certainly no

dread. Only excitement. The Grand Duke and probably his wife would come, I thought, staring up the slight hill toward the towering Nikolsky Gate. They would emerge from the Kremlin via that gate, turn left, and pass us by. And they would do so within minutes, perhaps even seconds, for the opera was due to start shortly.

I waited, my eyes trained on that very spot, and I don't think I blinked until it appeared like a mirage in the night, not a sleigh but a carriage exiting the Kremlin. It was like some kind of fantasy, yet when it turned and crossed the corner of Red Square and started down the low hill it became real, for I saw the carriage and its two bright lights. That had to be the Grand Duke on his way to the Bolshoi. He had to be inside. How wonderful!

Stepping out of the shadows, I followed our plan exactly. The carriage was making its way toward me, I was making my way toward it. And all I had to do as it passed was glance inside. If by chance it wasn't the Grand Duke's carriage, I was to do nothing. If the Grand Duchess was inside and alone, I was to do nothing. But if he was in there, with or without his wife, I was to pull the black rag from my pocket and drop it on the cobbles. That would be the signal.

Kalyayev would rush from the shadows of the gardens and hurl the bomb through the glass window and onto his lap.

The lights of the carriage became still brighter and larger as it neared, and within a few steps I saw the white harnesses on the beautiful dark horses. And I saw, too, that the driver was wearing a fine coat bundled over his livery. There was no doubt about it, I thought as I reached into my right pocket and clutched the dark rag, this was the vehicle of a highborn gentleman. And, yes, when the carriage was but twenty paces away, there it was on the door itself, the Grand Duke's royal crest.

Now the only question was who exactly was inside . . .

I felt the eyes of the coachman upon me, for he was most certainly protective of his master. I knew he was studying me, wondering if I posed some kind of danger, and so to look a simple, harmless fool I pulled both hands from my pockets and rubbed them together as if to beat away the cold. Satisfied that I carried no gun or bomb, the coachman drove on at his normal pace.

And then like any Russian fool upon suddenly seeing his master, I stopped, took off my hat with my left hand, and bowed as the carriage passed. With my right, I reached into my pocket and clutched the black rag, eager to drop it onto the street. A lamp burned inside the large old carriage as well, and in its soft light I saw him, the royal bastard, our Grand Duke, bearded and caped and looking remarkably smug. Sitting right next to him, of course, was his bride, and it's true, I was stunned by her beauty. Never had I seen a more pleasing creature, the gentle shape of her face, the softness of her lips. This was the first time I had ever laid eyes on the Grand Duchess Elisavyeta Fyodorovna, of course, and her skin glowed and diamonds sparkled all around her. Nevertheless, I retained my sense of duty and pulled the black rag from my pocket and was all set to drop it when Her Highness saw me standing out there in the cold. Looking directly at me, she caught my eyes with hers, lured me like a golden icon of the Mother of God, and smiled softly, even gently, as if she understood my misery and even felt a kind of compassion for me and my life.

Surprised — no, shocked — I hesitated.

I should have dropped the black rag right then and there. Had I done so, Kalyayev would already have been darting from the shadows of the Aleksandrovski Gardens. Instead, I waited a moment too long, and in that moment I saw not just the Grand Duke and Grand Duchess Sergei but two others sitting right opposite them. And not two other adults . . . but children! *Bozhe moi,* my God, it was their young charges, the girl and the boy! Nothing could have stunned me more. We had rejoiced at the idea of blowing up the Grand Duke Sergei. We had all agreed, if need be, to kill his wife, the Madonna of Romanov princesses, as well. But young ones? Could I throw the black rag to the cobbles and thereby condemn these children to a bloody and violent death?

Without even thinking, I turned away, my body shivering madly. Killing a man known and hated for his iron rule was one thing. Even murdering his wife as well was somehow acceptable. But blowing to pieces these young ones, royal or not, was not right. I couldn't do it! We hadn't talked of this possibility, that the young Grand Duchess Maria and Grand Duke Dmitri might be accompanying their foster parents to the opera, but there they were, sitting opposite their guardians!

I turned and hurried off without dropping the black rag, proving beyond a doubt that despite the murder of my own wife and unborn child there was still something human left alive in my dark heart.

CHAPTER 15
ELLA

"Why do you always do that?" asked my husband.

"Do what?" I replied as we drove toward the Bolshoi.

"Greet people like you just did with that man back there. He charged up to our carriage and you met his curiosity with a pleasant nod of your head."

"Well . . . well . . ." I said, rather flustered. "I suppose I was simply trying to do my duty."

"In the future you shouldn't be so open. People are always staring upon us, and if you acknowledge them in any way it only encourages them. Is that what you want, people looking upon us as if we were monkeys?"

My face burning, I muttered, "Of course not."

I folded my hands in my lap and glanced out the window, not venturing another word and not daring to gaze upon the children, either, for I knew they were studying me, perhaps taking delight in my humiliation. But . . . but wasn't that my duty, to reach out to our people, to inspire the best in them? Of course it was. And yet I couldn't counter my husband, not in front of the young ones.

I wanted to cry. I wanted to lash out. Instead I reached out and rested my trembling hand upon my husband's arm. Sergei's inner soul, I knew, was so conflicted, so tortured, and I had to remind myself that my greatest duty was to him, and my greatest task then was to soothe the poor man, who, it was true, had become embittered not just by his own appetites but by the murder of his father as well. Yes, it was Sergei's own father, Aleksander II, who had freed the serfs in 1861, saying "Let us liberate the serfs from above or they will liberate themselves from below." It was Aleksander II, as well, who had planned to end autocratic rule in Russia by introducing a European-style constitution. This would have long come to pass were it not for the revolutionaries, for just days before the constitution was to be released they had blown the Tsar apart.

And with what result?

The revolutionaries had believed this death would spark a great revolution, but in fact it created not a single demonstration, only widespread mourning. And the new Tsar, Aleksander III, what did he and the Grand Dukes think, including my dear Sergei? Well, they came to hate any kind of revolutionary or progressive thought, for it was the revolutionaries who had killed their father. Worse, they fully believed the murder of Aleksander II was God's punishment for the Tsar's folly with liberalism. My husband, shocked by the savage murder of his father, especially felt this, just as he believed that the only way to deal with unrest was by force. And so the great constitution, Russia's first, was promptly withdrawn.

Oh, I knew revolutionaries wanted to go from Tuesday to Friday in one giant leap, but were it not for them Russia would long ago have had a constitution. One had only to look upon the murder of Aleksander II to realize that that horrific act took our dear land not forward but back to Sunday, if not further.

And just look at what was now happening, I thought, peering out at a broken street lamp and windows that had been smashed during the recent riots. Just how far were we retreating into chaos? Oh, the simple people of our Russia didn't know what they were doing in these dark days. They were like sick children whom one loved a hundred times more in their illness than when they were well and happy. One longed to ease their sufferings, to teach them patience. This, I knew, was what I felt more every day.

And then the opera . . .

Suddenly the grand building with its great columns and electric illumination came into view. Suffice to say that it was a command performance, that our beloved talent, Boris Shalyapin, sang his most famous role, Boris Godunov, which, Sergei remarked, the poor man probably had to sing as often as a teakettle whistles. And all society, dressed in their finest uniforms and gowns, were greatly pleased to see Sergei and me in attendance, so I did collect much money for my Charity Fund, and the evening was a grand success.

CHAPTER 16
PAVEL

Having failed in my task, I retreated into the night shadows of the Aleksandrovski Gardens, shaking and sweating despite the frost. What had I done? Had I ruined the plan altogether? But how else could I have acted, what choice was there?

Little Kalyayev, his sweet face tense with anxiety and cradling the bomb, came dashing toward me, and demanded, "What is it? What happened? Was the Grand Duke not in the carriage?"

"He was there — I saw him!"

"Then what — ?"

Shaking and nearly in tears, I pleaded, "I couldn't kill children!"

"What do you mean, what children?"

"Tell me I did the right thing!"

"You fool, what are you talking about?"

Savinkov, the Polish fellow on the sleigh, the one from whom I had got the bomb, suddenly appeared out of nowhere. Together the two of them pulled and pushed me into a hidden area, where they pinned me against a tree.

Pressing a knife against my throat, Savinkov hissed, "The Grand Duke's carriage passed right by me as it drove around the corner — he was in there! I saw him with my own eyes! And he'd already be dead if it weren't for you! You failed and now you've put the entire operation in danger!"

"But children . . . I saw them in there, that young Grand Duchess and Duke, and . . . and . . . !"

"What children? I saw none!"

"They were in there, the young ones, sitting just opposite the Grand Duke Sergei!"

All but screaming in my ear, Kalyayev demanded, "Are you a traitor to our cause? Have you betrayed us to the police?"

"No, I swear!" I pleaded. "The Grand Duchess Elisavyeta was in there, too, and I would have given the signal . . . but the children, the two little ones! I saw the Grand Duke and Grand Duchess and the two children — I saw them all! But . . . but we never talked about this, what we should do if there were children present! Forgive me, I just couldn't do it!"

Kalyayev turned away, slammed his fist against his own forehead, and said, "If all four of them were really in the carriage, then our friend here is correct, we couldn't kill them, not the little ones."

"What the devil are you talking about?" demanded Savinkov.

"We want the Grand Duke's death to unleash revolution and . . . and . . ." Kalyayev fell into desperate thought. "And that wouldn't happen if we started killing children. That would turn the workers and mothers against us, not for us."

"But I saw no children!" snapped Savinkov. "He's lying — I say we kill this one here and now!"

"Go ahead," I said, only too eager to pass from this world. "But I swear all four of them were in the carriage!"

A long minute of argument followed, but Savinkov and Kalyayev decided to spare my life, at least for the moment, at least until they could figure out if I was telling the truth. And so they led me from the park and delivered both me and the bomb to several other conspirators, who were dressed as peasants and who in turn led me to a small apartment with only one window. There I was shoved onto a chair and my arms were tied behind my back. The bomb was placed on a table, and Dora Brilliant herself appeared before too long. It was her job to disarm the explosive, which she proceeded to do right before my eyes.

"Did I do the right thing?" I pleaded, my brow beading with perspiration. "Or did I ruin it all? What have I done?"

As she coolly went about her business, she shrugged, and muttered, "You did what you needed to do."

"Yes, but —"

"Sh," she said, carefully pulling some small piece from the bomb. "The others will discover for themselves that you are telling the truth — and I'm sure you are, for I can see it in your eyes — and then we will decide upon another time and place to put an end to the Grand Duke."

Of course I was telling the truth. But of course I didn't care if they killed me. And yet I couldn't stop trembling, which perplexed me a great deal and only caused me to tremble more. I had thought everything dead within me, every morsel of compassion, of feeling, long gone. Or was it not? I realized that that was what scared me more than anything else — that I carried a weakness, a softness, which could and would dampen my thirst for blood. I'd felt not a moment of hesitation or remorse when I slit the throat of that unimportant bureaucrat in Novgorod, and yet the sight of those two royal children had caused me to fall apart. What did this mean, the end of my revolutionary path? Was I not destined to avenge the deaths of my wife and child and fellow workers who had fallen on Bloody Sunday?

No, I thought, just picture Shura lying there in that crimson snow, just remember her bright death in that blinding sunshine . . .

Her delicate work completed, Dora Brilliant disappeared behind a curtain and into the next room. Alone and tied to the chair, I drifted in and out of self-pity for what seemed like hours, one moment lashing myself for my failure to hasten the end of the Grand Duke, the next silently sobbing at the loss of my wife and unborn. I wanted to die. I thought of breaking loose and finding poison, of hanging myself, of taking a gun and blowing my brains out, of leaping across the room and grabbing the disarmed bomb and somehow making it explode . . .

Hours later the door opened. The two of them, Kalyayev and Savinkov, came stomping in. At the sound of them, Dora Brilliant and some other comrade reappeared. But one glance at Kalyayev and I knew my fate. From the satisfied smirk written all across his brow, I knew, unfortunately, that I was to live.

Throwing his fur hat on the table next to the disarmed bomb, Kalyayev said, "I waited outside the Bolshoi in the cold. Handfuls of drivers were huddled around fires, and I moved from one to the next, gleaning what information I could, asking: 'Did the Grand Duke come to the theater tonight? Which carriage did he come in? Was his wife in attendance also? Was there anyone else with them?' "

"Meanwhile I went inside," confessed Savinkov, who, owing to his aristocratic looks, I was sure, had had no trouble entering the Imperial Bolshoi. "And I asked and inquired, and everywhere I heard exactly what they were saying out on the street, that the Grand Duke had arrived with his wife as well as his two young wards."

"Not only that," added Kalyayev, "but I waited outside until the end of the performance and I saw the four of them for myself. All bundled up, they hurried through the cold and climbed back in the Grand Duke's carriage, returning directly to the Kremlin."

"So our little new revolutionary, our Pavel here, did quite the correct thing," began Dora Brilliant, running a hand through her dark hair. "Not only would it have been morally wrong to kill the children but we would have lost many supporters and sympathizers. In fact, it would have set us back years."

Realizing that I had told the truth as well as, by some fluke, acted in the best interests of the Revolution, they freed me, cutting loose the cords that bound me. I slumped forward, my face falling into my hands. More than anything I was overwhelmed with self-doubt, for the truth was that I had made no heroic decision, nor had I even briefly thought what might be best for the cause. Simply, I had been defeated by the sight of the two youths.

Or had I?

Rising to my feet, I crossed the dismal room to the window and peered through the small pane of glass. And what I saw on the other side was not the depths of the Moscow night but her, a white mirage of her, the Grand Duchess, staring back at me.

Despite my failure that evening, all of us were determined to continue with our plan until either we succeeded or every last one of us was killed trying. And that was how we ventured out well after midnight that same night, eventually arriving at The Alpine Rose, a restaurant on Sofiyka. The restaurant was long closed, of course, but

Savinkov bribed the porter and in we went, warming ourselves around a stove and formulating a new plan. We decided — or I should say, they decided, because I spoke not a single word — that the Grand Duke should not live to see another week. And then it was agreed upon that we should all separate for a few days of rest and rejoin on the fourth of February. With any luck, our next attempt at blowing up the bastard would take place on the fifth. Kalyayev pleaded to act alone, stating that if he were dependent on no one and nothing but his own resolve he could easily succeed. To this we all consented.

"Excellent, the glory will be all mine," said Kalyayev with a smile as we stepped out of The Alpine Rose. "I doubt that I shall survive to see the Revolution, I doubt I shall live to see the masses rise up. However, I delight in the thought of killing the Grand Duke, which means I shall almost single-handedly cause the fall of the dynasty, for his death will certainly cause the masses to act. I shall act alone, and if I die in the blast as well, then so be it. Of course, it would be far better if I lived through the explosion and were caught and put on trial and hung before a great crowd, but there's no guarantee of that. Nevertheless, I can dream, can I not? I really would love nothing more than a public execution, which would certainly stir the masses to action."

Staring into his sweet face as we stood outside in the cold, I didn't know what to think. I envied him everything, though — his enthusiasm, his passion, and especially his righteousness. All I knew, meanwhile, was a kind of exhaustion such as I had never felt before, a kind of overwhelming desperation as if I were bleeding and the life were dripping out of me drop by drop.

My allegiance to the Revolution still under suspicion, I was escorted to some small, pathetic hotel, where I slept for an entire day, and Savinkov himself stayed in the room next door just to make sure that I didn't slip off to the authorities. As for Kalyayev, he took a train to a nearby village, while our bombmaker, Dora Brilliant, retired to a room at one of Moscow's nice hotels, the Slavyanski Bazar.

And thus we passed the time, resting and waiting until that fateful day.

CHAPTER 17
ELLA

A cloud of dread had been hanging over me those months, a cloud that by early February, 1905, seemed only to thicken and darken.

I worried about the unrest that had seized the entire country, about the safety of Alicky and Nicky and the children. I was saddened as well at the prospect of leaving my beloved Moscow, where I felt so at home, and I worried endlessly about my husband and the death threats against him. For the past several days he hadn't been varying his routine — why wouldn't he? The commander of security had just this morning suggested doing so, commenting that the Grand Duke's afternoon visits to the Governor-General's residence were becoming too regular and hence too well known. The eyes of the revolutionaries were everywhere, he added, and there was nothing they loved more than a predictable path.

"Sergei," I gently pleaded after the last dish had been cleared from our noonday meal, "perhaps you should take a different route today, or perhaps you should be traveling with an escort or —"

"Matters of security are not your concern," he replied in his autocratic manner as he rose from the massive walnut table.

"Then allow me to accompany you."

"Children," said Sergei, ignoring me and turning to our young wards, "you may kiss me goodbye and return immediately to your lessons."

"But . . . but what about my mandolin," muttered the young Grand Duchess Maria. "I . . . I wanted to talk to you about —"

"We will talk later this evening, my child. Your tutors are waiting. Please return to your studies at once."

Knowing perfectly well that they had no choice but to do as their new papa commanded, the children dutifully approached the Grand Duke, who leaned down and pecked each of them on the cheek. Appearing out of nowhere and exactly on cue, the children's governess, Mademoiselle Elena, escorted them off, Grand Duchess Maria to her mathematics lesson with an old gentleman, the young Grand Duke Dmitri to his lessons with his tutor, General Laiming.

Once the children were gone, I rose from the table and gently pressed the issue, saying, "What of it, Sergei, may I accompany you?"

"Absolutely not. And you are not to speak of such serious matters before the children ever again, am I clear?"

"Yes, of course."

"They must not be raised to question the loyalty of their people."

"My apologies."

Standing there, I watched as my husband silently turned and strode out of the room. For months now Sergei had all but forbidden me to travel publicly with him — the other night to the opera had been one of the few exceptions — and I knew that while he was not concerned for his own safety, he did worry about mine. What troubled me, however, was that my husband was as determined as he was punctual, and I now steeled myself as I heard Sergei head down the great marble steps to his awaiting carriage. I knew, of course, that he was departing at exactly the same time he had the day before, and the day before that as well. If only he'd take his aide-de-camp with him, I thought, or better, allow an escort to lead his carriage. After all, his own father had been killed following a regular route in the capital.

As if to banish my worries, I quickly turned to a valet, and said, "Have my sleigh brought round front."

The uniformed man silently bowed and disappeared.

There was so much war-work to be done this afternoon, I thought. However, before going to my workrooms here at the Kremlin or checking on my ambulance train, which was set to leave this evening on the Trans-Siberian tracks, I had one personal call to make. My chamberlain's wife, Countess Mengden, was recovering from an operation, and of course it was my duty to pay her a visit, the least I could do for someone who had been so loyal to me.

Minutes later I had changed into the plain gray-blue walking-about dress I wore every day to the workrooms, for I went there not simply to supervise and oversee hundreds of women of every age but to work alongside simple seamstresses and common daughters of carriage drivers. In fact, later this afternoon I was expected in the bandage store. Truth be told, I enjoyed all this, for it not only presented the opportunity to be of use and to help those in need but gave me a function and employed a part of me theretofore unchallenged. And in this my sister, the Empress, was quite correct, that members of proper Russian society and rank were far too active not in helpful matters but rather in merriments and late-night get-abouts. Why, of course it was our Christian duty to take positions of responsibility, to do something constructive for our people below. And yet for this — her so-called prudish nature — my sister had been ostracized in the highest court circles, including her own mother-in-law's. Perhaps the two of us, Alix in particular, were too Protestant or too English in our sense and view of duty, but the seeds of dissent in our adopted homeland were not sown by Alix's withdrawn social nature, not by any means. All that was sown as a result of her lack of frivolity was ugly, ugly gossip, resentful and spiteful, which sprouted with great gusto even in the best circles.

And yet as I finished dressing all seemed so peaceful, the snow, the serene winter sky, the soft noises of the city going about its business. With a simple turn of my head, I peered outside. The sun would fade early, of course, as it always did in these dark winter months. Usually there were many balls at this time of year, including several wonderful *bals roses* for young marrieds, but this year so much had been curtailed because of the disturbances. Perhaps by springtime things would be different — surely the mood of the people would improve with the fine weather.

Then suddenly the quiet day was ripped in two by an enormous explosion.

Reflexively, I gasped and grabbed for a side table. It was as if one of the great bells had fallen from the Kremlin's Assumption Cathedral. No, I thought in panic, for I still felt the reverberations in my chest. It was as if not one of the bells but the Ivan the Great Bell Tower itself had collapsed under the weight of the winter snow. Virtually every windowpane shook frightfully, and I, trembling, looked up and saw even the chandelier swing side to side. A moment or two later brought absolute quiet, a kind of total stillness that was even more frightening, as if everything and everyone were frozen in fright. Or death.

And in that moment of terrified silence I guessed exactly what had happened — a bomb! — and I clasped a hand to my mouth and cried aloud, "Sergei!"

I ran out of my chamber and to a small hallway window. Peering out, however, all I saw was a great flock of black crows wheeling around the golden church domes. Looking into the square below, I saw nothing, no one, only stillness . . . and then suddenly a great number of people running toward the Nikolsky Gate. At that moment, I knew. I knew by the direction in which the people ran that the worst was true, that my darkest fears had come to pass, for Sergei would have been heading toward those very gates. Gathering up the folds of my dress, I made as fast as I could down the corridor and toward the great staircase. Practically flying down the marble steps, I prayed, muttered, "Oh, dear God, please, no!" Had Russia's great dark demon — those bloodthirsty revolutionaries — swept down upon us again? Had those shameful barbarians, so determined to bring Mother Russia to her knees, attacked again, this time taking my dear Sergei?

Panic seized me, exploded within me like another bomb. As I ran across the vast entry a servant flew at me, rushing forward and throwing a sable pelisse over my shoulders, while behind I heard another set of quick steps. Glancing back, I saw the children's governess racing after me.

"Your Highness!" called Mademoiselle Elena as she desperately tried to catch up to me, her mistress.

As pale as the moon, I stared at her with terror, clasping a hand over my mouth, but, alas, I could say nothing. I had to get there, I had to be there. Sergei needed me, of that I was sure!

Yet another servant rushed forward with a man's fur coat, which Mademoiselle Elena pulled awkwardly over her shoulders, and the two of us rushed out into the cold, barely covered and absolutely hatless. Directly in front of the Palace stood my awaiting sleigh, which had pulled up only moments earlier, and I clambered into it, followed immediately by the governess. With one bold snap of the whip and a sudden jolt, my driver set off, flying toward the gates. As we raced the brief distance, I felt my own heart beating with a fright and terror such as I had never before experienced. But no tears came to my eyes, nor did I mumble anything or even reach out and clasp Mademoiselle Elena's hand for comfort. No, I had to be strong . . . strong . . . strong.

Of course I had seen many badly wounded soldiers, either on my own ambulance trains or in one of the hospitals I sponsored, men who had lost eyes and arms and legs in the fight against the Japanese, men who had been horrifically burned or riddled by bullets or who were slowly dying of gangrene. But by the time I saw these soldiers they had long been attended to, cleaned up, operated on, and bandaged. Never had I seen these men in action and under attack, bleeding in the field or pulled screaming from the waters, their bodies blown wide and their insides spilling forth. Never until this moment had I seen any such reality.

Within seconds the sleigh reached a massive crowd gathering just before the gate and the driver was forced to slow. When he could go no farther through the dense mass of people, I alighted from the still moving sleigh and charged ahead. I had gone but a few paces, however, when two peasant women, kerchiefs tied tightly around their puckered faces, charged right at me, waving their hands frantically.

"*Nyet, nyet,* Your Highness!" cried one babushka, falling at my feet and clutching and kissing the hem of my dress. "You must turn back, you mustn't see!"

"Turn away, Your Highness!" sobbed the other. "Turn away!"

But I would not be deterred. I couldn't say why, and I certainly didn't know what took over, but something hardened right then and there within me, and my face turned cold and blank and practical. I pressed forward. Suddenly, recognizing me as the wife of this dreaded Romanov, the throng of people bowed and parted. And what opened up before me was a battlefield of carnage and destruction such as I had never dared imagine.

Not only was my husband dead, but of the man himself and his fine carriage there was little that remained.

I gasped, nearly fell to my knees, and yet not a single tear came as my eyes swept the scene and tried to comprehend what had taken place. I saw a bent wheel, searched for a recognizable bit of my husband, but . . . but . . .

The remains of Sergei's once substantial carriage barely rose above my knee. Of my once mighty and indomitable husband, the severely proud Grand Duke Sergei Aleksandrovich, all that I could see was, here, a chunk of his torso from which hung, somehow, his right arm, and, there, a leg with a foot torn away, and, glancing downward, a severed hand lying in the reddened snow. As if the bomb had landed directly upon my husband's lap and he had stared down upon it in horror, nothing remained of his head, face, or neck. The rest of my beloved Sergei was scattered everywhere, bloody pieces of muscle and organ and bone blown wide across the snow.

The shock seized me cold and hard. Ever

tearless, I started trembling as I tried to comprehend what had happened, what this meant, where my husband had got, what I must do.

Up ahead I saw some men grabbing the terrified horses, which were dragging behind them a single wheel and some shattered planks, that was all. Off to the side I noticed someone struggling, heard someone shouting. There was a man there whom the police were seizing upon and holding. This man, rather young, was actually doing nothing to resist, and I saw that his clothes were torn and singed and that his face, seared by the heat of the explosion and pierced by hundreds of slivers of wood, was streaming with rivulets of blood.

It was the revolutionary, the very one, I understood, who had thrown the bomb, and who now shouted, "Down with the Tsar! Long live freedom! Long live the Social Revolutionary Party!"

Above the mayhem someone else was calling that a cab be fetched at the moment. Within seconds one pulled up, and two policemen stuffed the man into the sleigh and sped off.

Off to my left I noticed more commotion, and I saw a handful of people struggling to support someone else, a man not fully conscious and dreadfully hurt, his body shot full of nails and splinters. Dear Lord, it was our dear Rudinkin, the coachman who had so dutifully served the Grand Duke for so many years.

Finding a strength and resolve that I had never before possessed, I commanded, "Get him to the hospital at once!"

A stretcher, already fetched from the Kremlin hospital, was put down with great haste, and my husband's man carefully laid upon it. Wasting not a precious moment, two soldiers quickly carried off the mortally wounded servant.

Stepping forward, I saw a precious glint of something golden in the snow and I reached down. It was the chain of medals Sergei had always worn about his neck, and I grabbed it up, clutching it tightly in my hand. Quite nearby I saw something brilliantly red, and I snatched it up, too. A finger. And there, I realized, dropping to my knees and picking up something else as well: his boot with the foot still in it. Next a mound of flesh and then a bone of some sort. And, yes, some clothing, part of his jacket, the blue one he had put on just before lunch.

Kneeling there, I pawed through the snow for more and more remnants of my husband, all of which I desperately gathered up into the folds of my dress. Only then did I look up and only then did I take notice of the crowd of people, larger than ever, pressing forward not simply to get a look at the carnage but to stare upon me, Her Imperial Highness Grand Duchess Elisavyeta Fyodorovna, wife of their feared Governor-General of Moscow. Carefully holding the bits of my husband in the folds of my bloodied dress, I rose to my feet, shocked by the incredible affront: everyone staring upon me still wore their hats, which no one had ever dared in the presence of a Romanov, let alone in a situation such as this.

"You, all of you!" I shouted as forcefully as a tsaritsa of olden Moscow. "You shouldn't be here, you shouldn't be standing around staring like this! At least you can take off your hats! At least you can do that — show some respect for the dead! Go on, off with them!"

Behind me, I heard a weak and quavering voice, that of Mademoiselle Elena, whose own face was streaked with a massive quantity of tears, and who now struggled to say, "Do . . . do as Her Highness commands . . . take off your hats! Do it!"

While no one was shamed into leaving, virtually all of them reached for their hats and pulled them off. Crossing themselves, some over and over, all continued to gawk at me, more so than ever, actually, for I was smeared with the blood of my murdered husband.

And assuming control of a situation in a way I never had, I called, "Get me a stretcher and bring it here — *now!*"

Within moments a pair of soldiers broke through the crowd and set a stretcher in the snow alongside the demolished carriage. I went directly to the litter, knelt down, and gently placed the remains of my husband there in a pile. I then turned to gather more, and the soldiers did likewise, picking up the hunk of the torso, the other boot, part of his hat, and everything else that they could find, scrap by bloody scrap, placing it in the small heap. Hysterically and silently determined, I continued searching under shattered carriage seats and pawing through snow, finding still more and more splintered bones and pieces of flesh and shreds of clothing. Yet still not a single tear fell to my icy cheeks, this despite the blood dripping from my own clothing and caught up, as well, under my finely manicured fingernails.

Clutching my husband's gold medals more tightly than ever, I searched on and on, desperate to find every last scrap of him, and all the while thinking, "Hurry, hurry — Sergei so hates mess and blood!"

CHAPTER 18
PAVEL

We killed the Grand Duke — *hurrah!* Word raced across town, the Grand Duke was dead, his body blown to smithereens — *hurrah!* All Moscow was rushing to the Kremlin to see the blood — *hurrah!*

Oh, we had such a celebration, and we rejoiced at every single story, that someone saw the Grand Duke's heart on the roof of a neighboring building, that a finger with a gold ring was found on the other side of the square, that the snow on the cobbles was sure to remain red until the first thaw melted it through the cracks and into the soil. We took delight in it all! The Grand Duke was dead!

Our magnificent bombmaker, Dora Brilliant, nearly fainted with joy, muttering, "I did it, I killed the Grand Duke!"

Everyone else seemed to take credit, too. Our Savinkov, who'd been so active in the planning. Kalyayev, our little poet, who had actually tossed the bomb. And others, like Azev, that notorious inciting double agent, who was always in the background of every revolutionary act. And even me to a degree. There were dozens who'd had a hand in the murder, and we felt so very proud. I guessed, too, that there were those who hadn't played a part at all but who perhaps felt guilty, maybe an aide-de-camp or a colonel, those close to that wretched man whose minds might have echoed with all the things they could have done, should have done, would have done, to avoid calamity.

But, no, none of that was correct, for none of us was actually due the glory or, for that matter, the blame. Only one person was responsible for the murder of the Grand Duke Sergei Aleksandrovich, and that was the Grand Duke himself. He was so arrogant, so pompous, so reactionary, and so convinced of the holiness of himself and the Tsar. Just think how different things would have been if he'd even been able to tolerate talk of a constitution, let alone admit that we, his downtrodden subjects, were not animals, after all, but human beings.

And over and over we shouted, *"Da zdravstvuet revolutsiya!"* Long live the Revolution! The Grand Duke is dead!

CHAPTER 19
ELLA

Within minutes after the bombing some priest had got himself back to the Kremlin's Chudov Monastery, where he started ringing a lone bell against the steely winter sky. In turn that single bell, a beautiful but, oh, so sad sound, sparked many others, and within a few short minutes all of Moscow's forty-on-forty — yes, all 1600 of her churches — had a bell ringing. This was how my poor Sergei was carried to the heavens, to the toll of bells and on the wings of my very own prayers.

It was only when I had scoured the bloody site again and again and felt certain I had gathered all the scattered pieces of my husband that I rose to my feet. A handful of soldiers hurriedly rushed about, roping off the murder site, and at my command the remains of my husband, nothing more really than a small pile, were covered with a soldier's greatcoat.

"To the monastery," I ordered.

Two soldiers stepped forward and took the stretcher by either end and silently started off, and I, clutching the chain of my husband's medals, followed. Once I began to move, the dense crowd, which was still silent and hatless, erupted into piercing cries and deep wails of grief. But I, as if carved from stone with my lips pinched tight and my eyes still dry, belied neither the shock nor pain I felt. All that I was focused on were the drops of my husband's blood falling from the stretcher as it was carried along, drops which fell one after another and which formed a bright albeit haphazard trail through the Kremlin's territory.

To the side I noticed our Mademoiselle Elena, whose face was red and twisted and soaked with tears, and I ordered, "Hurry ahead . . . don't let the children onto the square . . . and keep them away from the windows . . . they mustn't see."

Mademoiselle Elena, trembling and hysterical and blue with fright, managed to nod. She then turned and hurriedly stumbled along through the snow, desperate to reach the Nikolaevski Palace before this parade of horror passed on its way to the Chudov Monastery.

Out of the corner of my eye, I noticed a figure rush toward me. I turned, saw an old man with a big tangled beard, a long dirty coat of uncured skin, and tall felt boots. He doffed his rough fur hat, tucked it under his arm, and then started bowing to me quickly and repeatedly, one deep bow after the other, the way the old peasants — particularly the ones who'd been serfs — did at our country estate.

"Forgive me, forgive me," he muttered through broken teeth as he held something in his outstretched hands.

I looked at his gnarled, worn hands and in them saw something wrapped in a white handkerchief that was blooming a brighter and brighter red right before my eyes. I immediately understood that he had found something I had missed, a part of my husband, a piece none too large for it was a small package, hastily wrapped as well. A finger, perhaps.

"*Spacibo.*" Thank you, I said, motioning toward the stretcher with a sweep of my hand.

The peasant man hurried forward and carefully tucked the royal remains under the greatcoat. He then backed away, crossing himself — three fingers to the forehead, stomach, right shoulder, left — and bowed once deeply at the waist and froze thus, bent over in humble respect.

"Oi, *gospodi!*" Oh, for the sake of God, sobbed a woman, a kerchief tied around her apple-fat, tear-streaked face, as she likewise rushed forward, a torn piece of material clutched in her hands.

I silently watched as this woman, without seeking permission, tenderly reached for the greatcoat, lifted it, and laid the torn material there among the ghoulish remains. It was then that I recognized the brass buttons, for it was a singed part of Sergei's own coat, part of the collar from the very uniform he'd been wearing.

"Spacibo," I repeated.

The woman, with tears enough to fill a dry salty marsh, scurried toward me, fell to her knees, and grabbed the hem of my coat, which she clutched and kissed. Soon she was bowing all the way down, pressing her forehead firmly against the frigid cobbles.

I moved on, uttering not a sob, dispersing not a tear. Overcome with shock, my breathing was quick but shallow, my thoughts intent but scattered. I could not faint, I would not allow it, but where was I? What must I do? Oh, yes, the stretcher. I must follow the stretcher and that, those drops, the trail of blood. And this I did, one foot after the other, unaware of the wailing crowd following behind, or for that matter the multitude of wet eyes focused upon me. As if in a trance, I trailed the soldiers step by step, traipsing along as they made their way to the Chudov Monastery and into the main chapel, which was attached by covered walkway to our own Nikolaevski Palace.

Entering the chapel, I was embraced by something, a soothing darkness that felt like the warm hands of the Lord upon my aching soul. Breathing in, I inhaled the sweet perfume of incense and familiar mustiness of centuries past and, too, I felt lifted upward as if into a cloud. In the flickering candlelight I watched as the soldiers gently, carefully placed the remains of my husband upon the ambo, that raised area directly before the iconostasis. I dropped to my knees and fell into prayer, unaware of the low murmurs and shuffling feet of the panicked priests circling about. Hearing the steady drip of something, I opened my eyes and glanced at the stretcher. That single boot with the foot was poking out, cockeyed, from beneath the greatcoat, and from it fell one drop of blood after another, splattering with strange regularity upon the stone floor. My eyes traveled farther down the stretcher and caught a glimpse of that scrap of uniform, the very one the merchant woman had tucked into the litter.

Dear Lord, I realized with a violent start when I recognized it! Sergei had been wearing a coat of the Kiev Regiment! Now what was I to do? I knew all too well — I could remember the exact time and place when he'd told me — that my husband desired nothing more than to be buried in the uniform of his favorite regiment, the Preobrajensky! But how in the world could I dress him as he wished when there was no body left to clothe?

Washing away my senseless earthly thoughts came a rich, melodic voice, which flowed over my soul like a great wave. Briefly glancing up, I saw a bearded, golden-robed priest, who with but trembling voice intoned the service for the newly departed servant of God, my Sergei. Chanting, the priest called out to God the Almighty, and the crowd, swelling by the moment, surged forward and in turn sang their reply, their mournful voices as raw and discordant as my pain. Another priest in golden robe stepped out and swung an incense burner over the remains of my husband, and the next moment I was engulfed by a cloud of sweet-smoky frankincense. I crossed myself and bowed my head to the floor, begging

God for forgiveness and praying for mercy upon my dead husband's soul.

I had no idea how long I knelt prostrate, my soul and body inextricably bound in grief and prayer. Only once the service had been completed did I sense someone by my side. Looking up, I saw the highborn Count Shuvalov, which came as no surprise since he was in fact the military governor for the city of Moscow and had worked so hard for my husband.

"May I assist you, Your Highness?" said the uniformed count gently, offering his arm.

Without a word I reached for him and rose to my feet, my bloodied dress glistening in the candlelight. Only then, turning, did I see that the chapel was thronged with loyal subjects, virtually all of whom were kneeling upon the stones, many crying, many clutching candles. Looking farther, I saw General Laiming, my husband's aide-de-camp, standing by a column and weeping. And there, toward the rear, by the small corridor that led from our Palace, was Mademoiselle Elena. Her face contorted and blue, she was holding the hands of the dears, our adopted children, Maria and Dmitri.

I muttered, "Please, I must see them . . ."

With the service concluded and the congregation now rising, Count Shuvalov led me directly to the young ones. I could see the fright clearly pocked on their innocent faces — what had happened, who killed, what next? Their eyes darted all about me, for I certainly looked a horror, my blue dress stained red, my face twisted in pain, my skin pale and so very cold. Although still not a tear came to my eye, I was flooded with emotion and nearly rushed the last steps, and when I held out my hands to the children they ran to me and I took them into my arms, embracing them as I never had before.

Pressing their beautiful heads into me, I murmured over and over, "He loved you so, he loved you."

And I would never have moved again had the dear young sweets not gently and by slow degrees led me away from the curious eyes there in the church and to my rooms deep within the Palace.

Chapter 20
Pavel

Back in the small apartment with one window, we poured cheap vodka from a bottle with a red label and drank toast after toast, the brew burning my throat each time I tossed down a shot. *Da, da,* the Grand Duke was dead!

After her fourth or fifth glass, Dora Brilliant, her eyes glistening with joyful tears and her speech slurred, turned to me, clasped my hand, and said, "Pavel, history has told us that the luxurious tree of freedom needs blood to quicken its roots!"

I looked into her dark eyes, and replied, "What beautiful words."

"Yes, but it also needs money."

And that was how, right then and there in the middle of our celebration, we started planning our next murder, that of Fat Yuri the Sugar Baron, whose factories produced most of the sugar in the Empire. He was known, too, for hoarding his gold rubles in his huge mansion in the Arbat District. So that day we made a drunken plan and I, my poor head spinning from the vodka, took another shot of brew and a chomp on a freshly salted gherkin, and swore I could accomplish this one on my own. That was how eager I was to prove my loyalty to the Revolution. And accomplish it I did, within days as a matter of fact. Deep in the night, I climbed over the iron railing of Yuri Mikhailovich's mansion, broke through a window, and traipsed right through the huge front room with its rotunda ceiling. Then I crept up to the bedroom and shot both Yuri and his fat wife in the head, but not before getting him to hand over a sack full of nearly 10,000 gold rubles!

Inspired by our glorious success, we worked harder than ever in the weeks and months ahead, spreading strikes like wildfire, cutting phone lines and looting stores. And we did it again and again: Murder! Assassination! Governors! Factory bosses! Landowners! Sure, we killed as many as we could, for as our poet Kalyayev himself decreed from prison:

"You have declared war on the people, and we have accepted the challenge!"

CHAPTER 21
ELLA

Without a doubt, all went from bad to worse in the months ahead, the mess was all around. Our post and electricity were stopped over and over, and one could not make oneself any illusions of better times for months to come. We were in the Revolution. What turn all would take, nobody knew, as the government was so weak, or sooner to say — did not seem to exist. Nonetheless, I felt physically very well and had good nerves. Of course if the nightmare came about, I knew I could always have the children safely sent off, but nothing would have made me leave that place, as I was determined to live or die there. Somehow I seemed to have grown into Russia, and did not fear whatever might come my way. And in the months soon after Sergei's passing I became quite calm and happy — yes, happy to know that my darling was at peace near God, and, too, that he was spared that awful time. In the depths of my suffering it became all so beautifully clear to me: we must at any time be ready — as far as our weak souls can be — to go to our real home.

So there I was, stunned by the path that that violent explosion had opened before me . . .

Upon my return to my boudoir, I sank into a chair, from which I did not move for a great length of time. I cannot recall what was in my head or what lay before my eyes, but I sat there so cold, my hands white except for one thing, the blackish red blood dried now beneath my fine nails. My servants and my ladies of my court nervously shuffled in and out of my room and all about the Palace, none of them knowing what must be done, nor, for that matter, to whom to turn for direction, for it was from Sergei that we had all received command. Suddenly it occurred to me that I was quite alone now, and alone actually for the first time in my entire life, and it was up to me and me alone to act, for with the flash of a bomb I had become complete mistress of both my own life and this house and all the people therein. Yes, it became perfectly clear that I had gone from beneath the protective roof of my father directly to the heavy, sheltering wing of my husband — my husband who for more than twenty years had not only issued every household order but also directed nearly my every movement and thought. And now he was quite gone from this world. As if awakening from all those years and from the day's tragedy, I rose to my feet, flooded with a frenzy of energy such as I had never before experienced.

Calling to Varya, my young lady's maid, I ordered in a loud voice that no one had ever heard of me, "Fetch me my black mourning frock! And someone tell me, does our Coachman Rudinkin still live? Someone go find this out — at once!"

My maids changed me, gladly so, from my bloodied blue dress into a frock of black, and immediately I entered my cabinet. There I sat down at my desk and, by my own hand, began the task of drafting telegrams. At first I took quill and inkpot, but then pushed them aside, for to write with these tools was too tedious and slow. Instead, taking a pencil, I began the first, which was of course to the Emperor, and in French I quickly wrote:

Son Majesté Imperial, l'Imperator
Nicholas Alexandrovich, Zarskoe Zelo

Oh, I thought, momentarily buckling beneath my grief, I wanted Nicky here, and I wanted my sister, my Alix, by my side, so that I could sob on her shoulder and find solace in the family of my youth. Yes, absolutely. But I couldn't fall apart, and, no, they mustn't and they couldn't come. For Nicky the trip was too dangerous; who knew what else the revolutionaries had planned. For Alix it was too arduous; she had the young Heir Tsarevich to nurse. And so I composed a telegram, informing them of the horrible events that had befallen, that I was unharmed and could see to myself, and that they must not under any circumstance come the distance to Moscow to attend the funeral. Wasting not a moment, I drafted the next and the next, for I had telegrams aplenty to draft to my relatives abroad — to my sister, Princess Victoria of Battenberg, to Sergei's sister, the Duchess of Edinburgh, and to my own dear sweet brother, Grand Duke Ernest of Hesse und bei Rhein. After these I rose to my feet and nervously paced about, momentarily overwhelmed by all that needed to be done, and then I sat down once again and composed many more wires.

As the wintry Moscow sky turned grayer to black, word came back to me that our faithful Coachman Rudinkin lay terribly wounded and on the edge of death. I knew what must be done.

Calling to a footman who cowered in the hallway, I brusquely ordered, "Bring my sleigh round front at once — I must go to the hospital immediately!" And spinning the other way to the maid Varya, I demanded, "Help me off with this frock! If Coachman Rudinkin sees me dressed in black, he'll know the worst. I must change back into my blue dress." When she screwed up her eyes, I said loudly, "The doctors will not want my visit to distress him — so I don't care how soiled it is, just fetch me my dress!"

The girl made a frantic curtsey and darted off for the dress that was streaked with Sergei's dried blood. I was changed and out of the Palace within minutes.

Oh, our poor, poor Rudinkin — so jolly, so full of life and devotion. Never had there been a more dear servant of man or God. What harm had he ever done another soul? Why could he not have been spared?

I arrived at the hospital toward six and found him drifting in and out of consciousness. The poor fellow, quite a substantial man with big beard and big stomach, too, had been ripped wide, not to mention pierced by countless splinters of wood. As I approached his bed, the sister of mercy quietly told me he had suffered more than a hundred wounds to his back and that gangrene had set in.

Bending over him and gently taking his weak hand in mine, I quietly said, "Oh, my dear man."

Opening his eyes, he stared up at me in vague recognition, clutched my fingers, and with no great ease, asked, "How is . . . how . . . how is my master, the Grand Duke Sergei Aleksandrovich?"

It would have been far too easy to finally unleash a torrent of tears. It would have been far too simple both to confess Sergei's death and to express at last my piteous grief. But what good would that kind of answer have done him? How would that have helped his soul, let alone his damaged body, in these, his final hours?

"All is well with him," I said with the gentlest of smiles. "Why, it is he who sent me to see you."

Relieved of worry, the man ever so slightly smiled through his pain, and said, *"Slava bogu."* Thank God.

His eyes closed again, and I remained there for quite some time, holding his hand. And it was good, for I sensed it, his soul

148

focusing on what was soon to come: his earthly end. Yes, dear Rudinkin died later that night. In short, in the days to come I walked behind his coffin as well, and from my own purse I of course saw to his funeral and made accommodation for his widow and also arrangements that his eldest son, Aleksandr, should attend the Imperial Trade School.

Returning that eve to the Nikolaevski, I found that the Palace continued to run like clockwork, as if nothing at all had happened, for my personnel, like all servants, feared the variation of routine. Quite on regular time, dinner had been announced and served, and the only thing that was remarkable was that the children were eating alone. Still wearing the blue dress, I entered the dining room and took my seat, but I could neither face food nor make conversation. The children stared upon me but spoke not and ate little, as if ashamed.

Soon thereafter I once again donned black, and afterward I knelt down in prayer with the children. I saw young Dmitri to bed, but as for returning alone to my own apartments I could not, so I accompanied Maria to her room.

"May I, child, sleep up here?" I humbly asked.

Although Maria could not hide her surprise at my pathetic need for the very tenderness that I myself had denied her, she acquiesced. We laid down side by side, and, with my eyes fixed on the ceiling, I began to speak of my darling, of how much he loved Maria and her brother, and, too, I confessed to Maria how I had suffered at Sergei's so total devotion to her and her brother, and begged forgiveness for my brusqueness. The girl listened and held my hand, and I talked on and on. Completely forgetting the physical attention that Sergei had so crudely denied me, I felt immeasurable sadness for the tormented life he had been forced to live. And then I rambled on of everything that was truly sweet between us — of our happy days at Ilyinskoye, of the books Sergei loved to read to me, of the music he loved to hear, of our walks, the dinners, the balls, the operas. And somewhere in the midst of all this, something broke within me and one tear finally came and then all the rest, and I wept well into the hours until I thought I, too, would die.

Chapter 22
Pavel

When I first heard the story, I couldn't believe it, it was too incredible. They said she wished it kept secret, that no one was supposed to learn of her hush-hush trip. Russians feasted on gossip, though, and it wasn't long before word of her bizarre actions spread to every corner of the Empire. The guards were perhaps the ones who leaked it, maybe first to their wives, then over tea or beer at the corner *traktir.* None of which was a surprise, because stories of the tongue were the way those who couldn't read have always passed news from hut to hut and village to village. I'd even heard some of our educated masters say, "Who can trust the papers and their censors, anyway?" Right, what better way was there to get information than gossip?

But the trouble was, which story was true?

One fat droshky driver told me that one of the guards personally told him she was allowed all the way into his cell, but when Kalyayev recognized her he went crazy and leaped at her and nearly ripped out her throat — and she would have been killed on the spot had not two loyal guards pulled her away. Another, a charwoman at the prison, swore that with her own eyes she saw Kalyayev fall to his knees upon seeing her, that they talked of God and mercy, and that in the end he kissed her hands and feet and begged for mercy. Yet someone else, a herring man at the market, said he'd heard that she had arranged for Kalyayev to be transferred to a monastery lost in the farthest parts of Siberia, where he was to be walled into a cave with just a window for food, buried alive like a forgotten hermit. Still another story claimed that she begged the Emperor for clemency, but that one I didn't believe at all. She couldn't be that crazy, could she?

So why did she do it? Why did the Grand Duchess take it upon herself to visit Kalyayev, the man who'd murdered her husband, the very next day? It made not a bit of sense to me.

CHAPTER 23
ELLA

There were countless matters of importance, but first came the children, to whom I tried to amend my ways and see after as I never had. I worried about them constantly in the days and weeks to come, and I prayed to God for his guidance, that I might bring up Maria and Dmitri as well as Sergei had begun. I promised my very best and knowing his ideas and principles, only needed to try and follow what had always been before my eyes and warm up those tender little hearts as true Christians and real Russians, founding all on faith and duty.

With good speed Sergei's remains were placed in a coffin beneath a silver canopy there in the Church of St. Aleksei. The coffin had to rest open, naturally, for such were the standards of Orthodoxy, but of course this presented quite a situation, for so much damage had been done to him, so much blown away, even, God forbid, lost. And so it was that I ordered and the next day found my husband in the open box, his destroyed face and hands — what was left of them, anyway — completely veiled, and his lower body draped in brocade edged with gold braid. In front, placed on a brass stand, stood the icon Savior Not Made by Hands, which I know would have pleased Sergei, while stacked all around were nearly 300 wreaths and floral decorations. Services were held all that day long, and while the children came only for morning and evening prayers, I remained on my knees before the bier nearly the entire time. Indeed, I attended services each and every one of the following six days, and after the funeral I was at all prayers for the following forty days.

I, who had never so much as commissioned a new dress without Sergei's express approval and permission, was suddenly issuing constant instruction with surprising confidence. By my command — and expressly against the advice of my security — the gates of the Kremlin remained unlocked and open to all, and access to the church itself was completely at will to Muscovites of every rank and walk of life, who were allowed inside one hundred at a time. Most touching to me was that as they passed by so many, if not all, dropped coins into Sergei's coffin, wanting that the whole of the Orthodox people pay for continued masses for this "True Believer." So moved was I by this and countless other kindnesses that on the day of the funeral I ordered that Moscow's poor receive, at the expense of my private purse, a free meal in memory of the newly departed.

To my horror, sad word had got round that the revolutionaries were intent on exterminating the entire Ruling House, so travel to Moscow was not simply deemed too risky for any member of the Imperial Family, it was forbidden by strict order of the Emperor himself. A gathering of royals, it was feared, might stir the revolutionaries to more violent action, or at the very least prompt more strikes in the factories and shops. Indeed, it was reported to me that it had been discovered that another of us, the Grand Duke Aleksei, was being hunted like a wolf. For this and other reasons it was deemed too dangerous for Their Majesties to leave Tsarskoye, and by official letter all Grand Dukes were even forbidden to attend requiem services at either the Kazanski or Isakovski Cathedral in Peterburg. This was all quite shocking and what a disgrace, and I knew how inconsolable were the two

Empresses — both Alicky and Minnie — that they could not pay their last respects to the dead, and how particularly pained was my sister that I was alone, but it made no matter, not really. In the end, lovely Grand Duke Konstantin managed to get permission to come and, too, Pavel — the children's father, who had been banished from the Empire but had received special permission to return to Russia and Moscow. From abroad also came my brother and sister and a small handful of others, so that in the end there was not a complete absence of relations at the funeral, and this was intense comfort. In any case, I had any number of things that needed my immediate attention, and though my ladies and my doctors predicted my collapse, I could not and would not and did not.

The day after the explosion, as I knelt in prayer before my Sergei's coffin, I understood more profoundly than ever the differences between the faith of my birth, the Lutheran Church, and the faith to which I had converted, Russian Orthodoxy. Western faiths adhered strictly to a belief in purgatory, of course, whereas in my new land we turned away from such absolute condemnation. Instead, we believed that there was not a sin that could not be redeemed by complete spiritual cleansing and impulse. Simply, we Orthodox held firmly that in an attempt to get closer to God all souls passed from stage to stage, suffering agony for past sins, as we all awaited judgment. Where my Sergei's soul now lay on that path to God and just how much he was suffering, I did not know, but I feared for his past sins, I feared that he had far to go. And for this I doubled my prayers for him, hoping that my earnest requests to the Lord would pull Sergei further along, moving him a touch closer unto the feet of God.

And then as I knelt there, a remarkable thing came to my attention: I heard a voice, quite mystical but entirely clear in both voice and intent. As if my dearest were whispering intimately into my ear, I was told that I must not concern myself with earthly justice, specifically that I was to think of Kalyayev's soul and not his body. Taking this entirely to heart, I commanded a carriage, and that afternoon a black brougham draped with black crape was brought to the Palace. And so off I set for the Piatnitsky police station, for my husband's murderer was being kept there. Too, by my most forceful order, word of my visit was to be kept with the utmost secrecy, but of course little success came of that. Oh, people,

people! As my sister once said to me, "Without character, without love for their Motherland, for God, people of any rank can be such petty dishrags . . ." And on that subject I did agree a wee bit with my Alix.

Needless to say, beginning with my household and right to the police station, my visit did throw officials into quite a muddle, for I daresay that a princess of any rank, let alone royal, had rarely, if ever, set foot in such an institution. However, the request of a Grand Duchess could not be denied by any excepting husband or Emperor. So toward evening I was taken to the Piatnitsky District, and the director-chief himself led me to a small office where the young Ivan Kalyayev was already waiting for me. I had strongly insisted as well that no one else should be in attendance — not even a guard — and so it was that we were left alone.

What shocked me immediately upon entering the small room was how young he was, how kind and pleasant-looking, this despite the numerous small wounds the blast had left on his face. As the door shut behind me, it struck me how proud he looked, of this I was quite sure, for there appeared not an inkling of regret or remorse. And this nearly knocked me over: how could a civilized person, someone certainly literate, take it upon himself as duty to kill another human being, let alone my husband, a Grand Duke?

I couldn't stop staring at him, for this young man was not the monster I had imagined, and I slowly crossed the small room, my black dress dragging the floor, my eyes unexpectedly blooming with slow tears.

"Have you come to identify me?" he asked without rising from his chair.

"No."

"Then why are you here?" Obviously not recognizing me, he pressed, "Who are you?"

"I am his wife."

A sharp look of surprise crossed his face, yet he did not rise, nor for that matter did he bow. I didn't care in the least for matters of etiquette, however. I slumped into the chair next to him and quite against my will the tears came aplenty.

Gently, he said, "Princess, don't cry. It had to be so." And then, as if thinking aloud, he snapped, "Why do they talk to me only after I have committed a murder?"

I found my eyes staring upon his small hands, the very ones that had hurled the bomb, and to banish that path of thought from my mind I reached out and clasped one of his soft hands, and quietly said, "You must have suffered a great deal to take this decision."

Clearly, he felt somehow belittled or otherwise offended by my comment, which was of total innocence, and he pulled away and leaped to his feet, blurting out, "What difference does it matter whether I have suffered or not? But, it's true, I have suffered throughout my life, and I join my suffering to millions of others. Too much blood is being spilt around us, yet we have no other form of protest against a cruel government and a terrible war." He slammed a clenched fist into his leg, again repeating, *"Radi boga,"* for the sake of God, "why do they talk to me only after I have committed murder?"

I felt this man's pain, his torture. Surely there was something good within him, surely there was reason to appeal for mercy for the fallen. He was, after all, as a second godly creature after God.

And, quietly, I said, "It's a pity that you did not come to see us, that we did not know you earlier."

"What? You must know what they did to the workers on January ninth, when the people went to see the Tsar, yes? Did you really think that this could go unpunished? There's a war of hatred being waged against the people. I would give my life a thousand times again, not just once. Russia must be free!"

"But honor, the honor of our country —"

"Honor?" he barked, interrupting me. "What honor?"

"Do you really imagine that we don't suffer?" I pleaded, for my heart was breaking not simply for my husband but for my country. "Do you honestly believe that we do not wish for the good of the people?"

"Well . . . you are suffering *now* . . ."

We both fell into silence, and he, somewhat calmer, sat down again next to me.

I softly said, "The Grand Duke was a good man, but he had been expecting death, which was the great reason he was preparing to leave the post of Governor-General."

"Let's not talk about the Grand Duke. I don't want to discuss him with you. I'll tell everything at the trial. You know that I carried this out completely consciously. The Grand Duke assumed a specific political role. He knew what he wanted."

"Yes, but . . ." I shook my head. "I'm sorry, I can't enter into political discussions with you. I only wanted you to know . . ." I took a deep breath. "I only wanted you to know that the Grand Duke forgives you, and that I will pray for you."

He looked upon me with soft eyes, then

turned away, and confessed, "People have been spared. By will of the Organization, by my will as well, people — and by this I mean you and the children — have avoided bloodshed."

"What — ? You mean — ?"

He nodded, and replied, "We could have acted sooner, and nearly did, but we decided to wait until the Grand Duke was alone."

It was too incredible a thought: the children nearly killed as well? Dear Lord! I gasped, didn't know how to reply. I felt only a duty to weep with the weeping.

Entering the curious air between us, Kalyayev said, "Between the act of killing your husband and my scaffold lies, I confess, a whole eternity. Which is to say, I can't wait — I should like to die immediately. You see, Princess, to commit the deed and later die on the scaffold — it is like sacrificing one's life twice. It's wonderful."

His words took my breath away. There was hardly anything to say or do, so great was the abyss between us. And from my handbag I took an icon.

"I beg you to accept this icon in memory of me," I said. "I will pray for you."

He tenderly accepted the icon and in fact kissed my hand, and I departed the room. That eve, perhaps as he sat in his dark cell, he wrote a poem, which in due time was shown me:

A woman like a shadow, a ghost with
  no life
Sat next to me clasping my hand
She looked, and she whispered to me: "I'm
  his wife"
And wept and shed tears with no end.

Her frock was so black and it smelled of
  the grave,
But her tears . . . They simply told
  everything
So I didn't reject her, I spared woman-
  slave
From the camp of the Enemy King.

Then she nervously murmured: "I'm
  praying for you . . ."

Without a doubt, I was touched by Kalyayev's writing, for he was quite a capable wordsmith, but most importantly he was reaching for a kind of understanding.

And I did do exactly that: I prayed on my knees for that man's soul.

CHAPTER 24
PAVEL

With the money we killed for and stole, we created so many spies. If the Tsar thought he had many secret agents watching us, why, within months we had more than him, an entire secret army watching him and his. People were sick of the way the Romanovs had treated us, sitting upon us and trading us like we were cords of wood. But no more, we had stepped forward and we would fight back! Yes, and so we had spies spying on people, and people spying on spies, and so on and so forth. Frankly, there was only one problem: I never knew which comrade to trust.

Our Poet was soon taken to the Boutyrsk Prison, where with a few bitter words about capitalism and a fistful of rubles we managed to convert some of the guards to our side. We wanted — we needed — to know how Kalyayev was getting along, not just because we cared for him but more importantly because we needed to know if he'd cracked and revealed anything about us, which, as we learned, he hadn't. That he continued to be the perfect revolutionary and remained loyal to the Organization came not as a surprise, just more of a relief, and his unbroken dedication to the over-throw of the Tsar inspired us more than ever.

There was only one thing that caused us distress, news of which came directly from Kalyayev in a smuggled letter. He was incredibly angry. Tormented. And in the smallest handwriting on a scrap of paper, he told why, that it was because of her, that Romanov woman, the Grand Duchess who should have died with her evil husband. What filled him with bitter regret was that news of his meeting with her was passed up and down the street, and appeared in every newspaper, each version more strange and different than the last.

"Comrades," he wrote to us, "please forgive me my foolish deed, please don't think ill of me! I should not have met with her . . . it makes me feel a traitor to the Organization!"

So upset was he that in short time he even wrote her a letter, a copy of which he made sure our spies got to us, for he wanted us, his comrades, to know what really happened.

Princess —
I did not know you, you came to me of your own accord: therefore the responsibility for the consequences of our meeting lies solely with you.

Our meeting took place, to all outward appearances, in circumstances of intimacy. What passed between us was not meant for publication but concerned us alone. We met on neutral ground, at your own direction, tête-à-tête, and were thus entitled to the same right of incognito. How otherwise to explain your selfless Christian feeling?

I trusted your nobility, supposing that your exalted official position and your personal merit would provide sufficient guarantee against the kind of malicious intrigue in which even you, to some extent, have been implicated. But you were not afraid to be seen involved: my trust in you has not been justified.

There is malicious intrigue and tendentious versions of our private meeting. The question arises: could either have happened without your participation, albeit passive, in the form of non-

166

resistance, when your honor dictated the opposite course of action? The answer is contained in the question itself, and I protest vigorously against a political interpretation of my decent feelings of sympathy for you and your grief. My convictions and my attitude to the Imperial House remain unchanged.

I fully recognize my own mistake: I should have reacted to you impassively and not entered into any conversation. But I was gentle with you, and during our meeting I suppressed that feeling of hatred, which in reality I feel for you. You know now what motive guided me. But you have proved unworthy of my magnanimity. Because for me there is no doubt that you are the source of all the stories about me, for who would have dared to reveal the substance of our conversation without first asking your permission (the newspaper version is distorted: I never admitted to being a Believer, I never expressed the slightest repentance).

The fact you remained alive is also my victory, and one that made me rejoice doubly when the Grand Duke had been killed.

— Kalyayev

Ha! Talk about a real man, talk about honesty!

Actually, though, that last part was not quite right. His victory? Not really, more like my little mistake. And back then I was quite sure she never, ever realized it — that that Romanov woman never knew that the reason she lived past her husband was not because of some God or Kalyayev, but because of me, a cowardly revolutionary who was afraid to act as she traveled to the opera. Oh, and when I read that letter I came up with a fat wish, that one day our paths should cross and I could . . . could . . .

Yes, my revolution burned with the hot embers of revenge.

A few months later, that May, actually, Kalyayev was secretly transferred to the capital and from Peterburg to the Shlisselburg Fortress way out on that small island, where they planned to take his life. I saw it all, too, for I killed someone else, a stupid merchant. Sure, I cut that guy's fat neck, stole all his money, and then used those rubles to bribe one of the guards to get my way into the fortress just so I could watch them kill my great hero.

The execution of Our Poet was supposed to be secret, because they wanted no one of the people to know, because the bigwigs were afraid that riots would break out. And so at two o'clock in the morning, just as the first of the northern morning light was beginning to color the sky, they brought Kalyayev out. In the yard there were only a handful of officials, some guards, some prison people, and me, too, standing way at the back in the uniform of a yard worker. I wanted to wave, to call out, to say, "Don't worry, I will witness your end and spread word far and wide of your bravery!" But I kept quiet. To my eyes he looked thinner, otherwise normal. And he mounted the scaffold without hesitation or assistance. Yes, true to his word, he was eager to die for the cause.

At the top of the steps he was met by a gray-bearded priest robed in black, who asked, "Would you like to address a last prayer to God, my son?"

Kalyayev shook his head, turned to the few of us there, and shouted, "I am happy to die for the cause of the Revolution! I am happy to have retained my composure right until the end!"

His words made me smile with pride, and I've always cherished the thought that maybe he recognized me out there, for I saw something — a grin of recognition, perhaps even a wink — when he looked my way. The next moment he was led up onto the block, and the beasty executioner, wearing a white shroud and red bonnet, smiled as wide as an opera singer. Having done this hundreds of times if not more, the executioner threw a rope over Kalyayev's neck — and then in the blink of a second he knocked away the very block on which my hero was perched.

But the rope was too long!

Oh, dear Lord, it was so cruel the way Kalyayev fell, dropping through the air until his feet hit the ground. He cried out as he choked and struggled and half tumbled over, yet the rope kept him kind of upright. It was disgusting to see the way that young man twisted this way and that like a fish hanging from a pole and slapping the ground! Even the officials cried out in shock! Even I shut my eyes, so painful was it to see Our Poet stretched between life and death! It was only when the idiot executioner in his red bonnet and two others hoisted desperately on the rope, yanking Kalyayev completely up into the air, that they finished the job, either breaking his neck or choking him, I couldn't tell which. *Radi boga,* even I had never been so mean, even I had always done a better job of killing someone.

And though our beloved Kalyayev met an

early end, our young Revolution, its roots fed by his blood, was bursting with violent life! And I'll shout it again and again, *"Da zdravstvuet revolutsiya!"*

CHAPTER 25
ELLA

Yes, the revolution took great hold that year of 1905 and caused such turmoil that I thought we would all be washed away. On top of this, the war in Manchuria continued so poorly, and while I could not busy myself with the doings of the Empire, I did have my beloved Moscow and countless wounded and abandoned who were in need of my attention. In essence, I had begun my withdrawal from the magnificent world where fate had cast me, and it was sometime during these months that my great scheme took birth and grew, it seemed, by the day if not the moment.

I accomplished many things, and one of the first things I did was to gather as many of Sergei's diaries and letters and papers as I could. I myself read only a handful or two of pages, but it was more than I could bear, and so that history would never know the beasts that tore at the poor man's soul, I took the papers I had gathered and tossed them in the tiled stove in my chamber, burning Sergei's confessions completely and absolutely. With that accomplished, I turned away from the pain of the past and looked forward to the future.

Too, I prayed for many months for poor Kalyayev's soul, and in my heart I found forgiveness for his deed, just as I prayed he found forgiveness for any of my sins upon him. I never visited him a second time, but if I had I would have said to him that I told virtually no one of our conversation. My visit to him was reported everywhere, but the thought that I could have betrayed his spiritual confidence was and still is repugnant to me. The only thing I can imagine is that we were secretly listened upon, for someone quite apart from me spread our conversation.

The day my husband was killed was the day I turned away from animal meats and began to wear black garment and avoid festivities of any sort. It was a completely natural step, one that I took without even thinking. From then on, as if the decision had been made for me, I did not even partake of a glass of champagne at a christening and rarely appeared in public, and for these offenses society widely criticized me. But it made no matter what the tongues said, just more petty dishrags. Fortunately, Nicky gave me delicate kindness by permitting me to remain in the Nikolaevski Palace, and that I could live in that house was an intense comfort, and I found great strength and peace being near St. Aleksei's relics and, of course, near my husband who had been laid to rest in a peaceful chapel of the Chudov. I made a request to Nicky, which was granted, to have the historical furniture taken out of my rooms and stored away with the catalogue kept in the Kremlin, so that after my death all would be put back as it was. With the luxurious appointments removed, I had my chambers painted white and the walls hung with icons, and there were those who with dismiss said my rooms quite resembled a nun's cell. But I found it full of tranquillity. In addition, I gathered together some tattered pieces of Sergei's clothing that he had worn on his last day, and I tucked them inside a large hollow cross, which I placed in a corner of my room. This, too, brought me great comfort.

The first step into my scheme was a small one, but that step led to a larger one and to yet another larger after that. That autumn I took a house beyond the walls of the Kremlin, and it was there that I organized a hospital for fifteen wounded soldiers. It was incredibly exciting, I must admit, for this was the first time I had ever been able to do such a thing, organize something beyond my official role without Red Cross or government participation, let alone Sergei's heavy oversight. Virtually every decision was of my own, and I oversaw each and every detail, not as a Grand Duchess but both as an administrator and nurse. I spent nearly every day there, for it was among the suffering of these simple men that I was able to forget my own grief and, too, learn a new path. I so enjoyed reading to them and writing their letters for them and helping with their meals. They were my big babies.

However, that year was the most disgraceful of times, with many wondering why we were being reprimanded so by God — was it for the banishment of the Jews, for which I had long feared our punishment? Whatever the cause, in summer the war with Japan finally came to an end, albeit disastrously, and to add to our woes our shameful peace sparked such things as the mutiny on the battleship *Potemkin*. Just a nightmare for our poor Russia, there were so many assassinations, including that of Count Shuvalov, the military governor of the city, who had reached out to me that very day of Sergei's death — the revolutionaries likewise extinguished him in a most bloody manner. Too, all across the countryside the peasants burned manor house after manor house and killed any number of landlord. It was all a great sin, perpetuated by the revolutionaries who told them that the Emperor himself had granted permission to do such, that is, take the land back from their greedy masters. What was happening to Russia? What disorganization, what disintegration, just like a piece of clothing that was beginning to rip and tear along the seams and fall completely open. Yes, it was the pure revolution.

The busier I kept the more at peace I felt, and yet late that September things took a particularly bad turn in Moscow. It seemed the entire city went out on strike, and the post, telegraph, telephone, and railroad, too, were all shut down. All the trams came to a halt and the bakeries as well, and also to my shock the ballet companies refused to work. Indeed, stranded as we were in the Nikolaevski Palace, the children and I were entirely cut off and abandoned from the outside world, guarded by those whose loyalty was at best dubious. Even the electrical workers walked away, so the entire city was left in dark, only in the distance could one see the glow of buildings that had been set afire. And while the Kremlin had its own power station, we feared turning on lights, so we too sat by oil lamp in the eve, the lamps themselves hidden from the windows — and to this several of my maids said it was all for the best, particularly for the children, as they had heard from someone of authority that reading by unnatural illumination was most poor for the eyes, damaging even. Then late one day came reports that the Kremlin was about to be assaulted and the children taken as hostages, and it was only then that I acquiesced and gave my permission for all the Kremlin gates to be shut and locked. Admittance was by special pass only. Another report claimed that the revolutionaries' plan was to catch the new Governor-General of Moscow and kill him, then kill countless other authorities throughout the city and seize the Kremlin along with the Arsenal and, in the hope that the troops would join, hold Moscow, a month later go to Tsarskoye and, of course, the horrible end was only too clear.

One beautiful afternoon toward the end of October we heard a particularly violent ruckus beyond the fortress walls. Street fighting, I could tell from the din, had broken out all over, for one could discern from every direction shouting and cries, any number of horses' hooves, and the crack after crack of the Cossack whip. Gunfire as well. But I could not and would not be stuck here in the Kremlin, for I had duty, I had made promise.

Glancing out my window, I said, "I am needed at my hospital — there is to be an operation, an amputation, and I must be there to assist."

"But, Your Highness, it's far too dangerous," gasped Countess Olsuvieva, my *Grande Maîtresse,* "Your carriage would be attacked the moment you were out the gate!"

"Then I'll go on foot."

"You mustn't, Your Highness. Please, I beg you! There's chaos everywhere. Even if you were to take a guard, your safety could not be guaranteed."

"No, I won't take a single person — that also would attract too much attention. I'll change into something simple and go alone."

"But it will be night soon!"

I had to admit that since the death of my dear one my reasoning had not been entirely logical, and yet here I knew a different kind of truth, certainly a more important one, and I said, "The soldier who needs my help doesn't care in the least whether it's day or night, dangerous or not, and neither do I. All that matters is that his leg is removed soonest so that the gangrene doesn't spread further."

My countess could not hide her disapproval, and she obeyed me only with the greatest hesitation, reluctantly helping me rid myself of all my jewelry, right down to and including my rings. Once I had put on an insignificant dress, I summoned our General Laiming.

To my husband's aide-de-camp I said, "Sir, I am entrusting the children to you while I am away. If there are any disturbances of a profoundly serious nature, I ask you to hide them away or flee if need be."

"But, Your Highness, where in the name of God are you — ?"

"Please do not worry, for I have an important task at hand, and God will watch over me."

I waved him away and made my way down, careful to keep my plans secret from the children. Exiting the Palace I made toward the Nikolsky Gate, passing the very spot where Sergei had met his end and where, according to my wishes, a large cross had been placed with the inscription, "Father, forgive them, for they know not what they do." I stopped, crossed myself, and continued, leaving the vast complex of the Kremlin via a small portal.

Emerging on the other side of the thick Kremlin walls, I entered a world of chaos such as I had never seen and which in truth broke my heart. The great square before me, always such a source of beauty and national pride, had forever been known as *Krasnaya Ploshchad,* which in old Russia had meant "the Beautiful Square." In more modern times, *krasnaya* also meant a particular color, and I could see that our country had indeed crossed a distinct line and sensed that this place would now forever be perceived by that very color: red.

Yes, I could see the blood of workers and peasants and students splashed across the cobbles.

A gust of wind blew a sheet of paper against my dress. Grabbing at the paper, I saw that it was a printed leaflet, of which, I was sure, thousands had been distributed, and which read: "Brothers! Sisters! Take up arms! Long live the uprising of the exhausted people!"

Tears welled in my eyes as I pressed the leaflet to my heart, and I glanced across the vast space toward the beautiful onion domes of St. Basil's Cathedral and saw so much more: ripped and torn clothing, a dead horse here and there, rubbish lying about in great quantity, and a number of smoldering carriages. It was through this very square that Nicky and Alix had entered the Kremlin for their coronation, and at that time this place had been a sea of exuberant exultation, thousands upon thousands of joyous subjects casting flowers and hurrahs at their new Emperor and Empress. Today, however, I had heard cries of quite a different nature, those of rage and desperation, and with my own eyes I could see that what had been cast were not flowers but pitchforks and, too, cobblestones dug up from the pavements.

God save and protect Russia . . .

I was one of but two or three souls about, and I wiped at my eyes and crossed the square. Making haste, I passed by one end of the Upper Trading Row and descended into the narrow, twisting streets of Kitai Gorod. All seemed relatively quiet, in fact eerily peaceful, but this calm was soon shattered by a sudden breaking of glass and any number of shouts and coarse words. Of course I should have just continued on my way to my hospital, but I couldn't, for so much more than my curiosity had been aroused, specifically my need to understand.

Turning a corner, I headed toward the sound of rage and destruction, which grew more pronounced each and every second. I heard a scream, and yet another — good Lord, was someone being beaten to death?

And then from behind me came the clamorous noise of charging horses, their hooves thundering on the cobbles. I froze, glanced back, saw dragoons, their swords and whips drawn, coming round a corner and charging down the street right toward me. Making haste, I ducked into a small side alley, and within moments these men, some fifteen or so Cossacks on horseback, stormed past. No sooner had they disappeared around the next corner than a roar of panic and desperation emerged. A shot was fired, then another and another. I heard the clear sound of sword clanking upon metal, and of whips cracking here and there with rapidity. Above everything came the sudden wailing of a man or woman, just which I couldn't tell, so shrill was the pitch.

I was only several blocks from my hospital, and for a moment I wondered if I should abandon my venture altogether and return with haste to the safety of the Kremlin and the beauty of my Palace. In truth, however, this was not a real consideration. Perhaps I had simply been taught well by my mother, for I did feel an intense need to go out amongst the people to better understand their plight, and so gathering up my dress, I stepped out of the alleyway and hurried directly toward the mayhem. A half block down I turned and came upon a small opening, a square of sorts, and I froze in place, horrified by what I saw. A war was taking place here, with shop windows shattered, and barrels of sauerkraut and herrings and salted gherkins smashed all about the ground, and any number of bodies lying about bleeding too. The Cossacks had been called in to suppress whatever had been happening here, and they were going about their task with aggressive devotion. Across the way I saw two mounted soldiers whipping a man, who tumbled to the ground, and, there, not fifty paces from me another Cossack was beating a boy with the flat of his sword.

I covered my mouth in horror and stepped forward, standing as still as a statue.

It was then that a Cossack spotted me and started charging toward me, his whip raised high, for of course he was completely unaware that I was part of the Imperial Family, not the rose thereof but her sister nonetheless. Yet I would not be intimidated, not because of my lofty rank but because my soul commanded me strength. As this bearded man with high hat raced at me, I raised my right hand. Still he came, with greater and greater speed, but I stood calmly, not so much as flinching. With three fingers I slowly pecked at my forehead, my lower stomach, my right shoulder, my left. Still he did not stop, and as the horse charged right at me, it seemed if nothing else that I would be run down by the beast. At the last moment, though, the Cossack, nimble horseman as were they all, veered to the side, and man and horse swooped past only a few hands from my left side, leaving me standing and my garment flapping wildly about in the vacuum.

And then with a whoop the Cossacks were gone, hurrying off in pursuit of a handful of young men who were fleeing down a side street.

All fell quickly and disturbingly quiet, the silence broken here and there only by desperate sobs, for there were a handful of people lying about in pain. The time-honored and hallowed manner of dealing with dissent or disturbance in Russia had always been the iron fist and, of course, the whip. Like all the Grand Dukes, my husband had been a great proponent of such, for amongst society it was widely believed that our uneducated masses understood nothing but force and could be controlled by nothing but a master's power from above.

And yet . . . these were not animals . . .

Neither were they peasants or workers. No, it all came into my mind quite quickly, for judging by the clothing of those who had fled and of those who were left lying about — clothing that was neither fine nor ragged — these people, all seemingly young, were quite different. What were they, then, who were they?

Overwhelmed by the conflict, I rushed forward. First I came to a young man with the soft face of a boy, the silken blond hair of a child, and a bloody whip mark across his cheek. Reaching out, I helped him to his feet.

"What happened here?" I begged.

"There was a demonstration not far from here . . . we . . . we tried to force our way into the city council."

"We? Who is this 'we'?"

"A group of us from the University."

"And this, the shops? Did you do all of this, break these windows and ravage these places?"

"The city is on strike!" said this boyish man in a surprisingly deep voice. "And these shopkeepers defied us. They stayed

185

open during the strike, and so they got their punishment!"

"But —"

We both heard it then, another whoop, more clattering of hooves. Were the Cossacks coming back, or were they merely charging down a nearby street?

"Madame, you must get out of here before they return!" the young man said, turning and hobbling off. "Go, get out of here! Run! They show no mercy!"

He scurried off, as did a few others, terrified of what might come next. But I couldn't move, so overwhelmed was I by the destruction. Were the people really so desperate? Was this really their only recourse?

Off to the side I saw a woman struggling to rise, and I hurried to her. She was a pretty, young thing, reddish hair, long blue skirt, her fair face now smeared with grime and a curl of blood.

"Please," I said, reaching toward her with outstretched hands.

She accepted my aid and I pulled her to her feet. For a moment it seemed she might faint, and I clutched her.

"Oi, *bozhe moi!*" Oh, dear God, she cried, holding her side. "One of . . . one of them came alongside me and kicked me with his stirrup. But Misha . . ." she moaned, tears welling in her eyes as she searched the small square. "Where's my Misha?"

"This Misha, he's your —"

"My husband . . ." she said, starting to cry. "Misha! Mishenka, where are you?"

"I'm sure he's fine, I'm sure you'll find him. But please, child, let me help you. I know of a small hospital not too far away," I said, nodding in the direction of my very own place.

I ripped away part of my sleeve, and with this scrap blotted at the blood seeping from her mouth. I prayed that she'd merely broken a rib, that there was nothing more serious damaged within her.

"I can't leave!" she said almost in panic. "What if he's lying somewhere? What if he's hurt and he needs me?"

"Let's just get you taken care of first. Let me get you to the hospital and I'll come back and look for your Misha."

Her eyes welled with a torrent of tears. "But —"

"Come along, the hospital's just down several streets, just this way."

"Wait, you can't mean the hospital run by one of them, do you?"

"Them?" I hesitantly asked, fearful of the answer.

"Yes, *them,* the Romanovs, I've heard it's

run by one of their stupid cow princesses."

"Why . . . yes . . . of course . . ." I managed to mutter.

"No," she pleaded. "No, I won't go there. Haven't you heard, don't you know? It's the talk of the neighborhood."

I felt a greater pain than any whip or sword could inflict as I inquired, "Know what, my child? What are you talking about?"

"That hospital is for officers and aristocrats only. They say they won't help any of us!"

"No," I gasped as if the wind had been knocked from me. "No, I'm quite sure that's not true."

"Yes, it is! I heard it from one of the strike organizers. He told us all about it, all about a babushka who went there for help. She was so sick, and all they gave her was dirty water!"

"No!"

"Yes, this striker told me he'd seen it all with his own eyes, that the Romanovs gave this old babushka dirty water with poison and she died the very next day, writhing in pain!" exclaimed the girl. "I won't go there!"

And with that the girl, painfully clutching her side, hobbled off. Within moments she had disappeared, leaving me paralyzed with grief and with only one shocking thought:

Dear Lord, when and how had we come to be so widely hated?

CHAPTER 26
PAVEL

There were all these papers and leaflets and booklets and pamphlets being passed around by all the different parties, the Social Revolutionaries, the Social Democrats, the Liberals, the Marxists, the Mensheviks, the Bolsheviks, and so on, this one preaching for a democratic bourgeois republic, another for a constitutional monarchy, still another for a complete socialist revolution. As for me, in the months after we killed the Grand Duke, well, I realized I was a complete Nihilist, the old-fashioned kind. I wanted everything gone, tsar and prince, merchant and factory owner. Death to them all. And all power to the people. That sort of thing.

It was none other than Dora Brilliant, our beautiful bombmaker with those deep, dark eyes, who helped make everything so clear to me. We met that fall near Konny Rynok, where horses were traded, and ducked into one of the many *traktiri,* the cheap cafés scattered about. Each one of the places in the area was fancied by different pet lovers, one by horse traders, the next by dog owners, and so on. The one we slipped into was full of bird sellers, and so as not to seem suspicious Dora and I made a pretend of turning to the icon and its red lamp by the door and crossing ourselves. Several small yellow Russian canaries twittered in a cage up front, and tables of canary lovers huddled about, drinking tea and arguing about the best grains to feed their treasures, ways to teach song, and so on and so forth.

Dora and I moved directly to the rear of the place, and I ordered a glass of hot tea loaded with four sugars, while she got a tea with two sugars and a slice of lemon, plus a nice white serviette for her lap. Dora, always so sad-looking, so forlorn, took a sip of her tea, and then pulled a piece of paper from her worn leather purse and nearly smiled.

"Here, Pashenka, this is for you," she said, using the cozy form of my name.

"What, a present?"

"It's a catechism — you must repeat it daily."

I looked at her, sure that this was some kind of joke, and repeated exactly what I had learned at one of our recent meetings, loudly whispering, "Christianity is the religion of slaves."

"Yes, but this catechism *is* you," she insisted as she pushed the paper across the table to me.

"What are you talking about? Don't you know how dangerous it is to tease a bear? Is this some kind of test?"

"Please, just read it to me, Pashenka. It's *The Catechism of a Revolutionary,* by Bakunin and Nechayev."

And though words were not my specialty, and though it took me time to pronounce many of these fancy terms, tears nearly came to my eyes as I began to read and understand what was written.

Keeping my voice hushed so no others could hear, I said, " 'The Revolutionist is a doomed man. He has no private interests, no affairs, sentiments, ties, property nor even a name of his own. His entire being is devoured by one purpose, one thought, one passion — the revolution.' "

Dora said, "Do you see what I mean? Is this not you?"

A cool tingling feeling crawled up my spine, and I nodded quickly. Nothing had ever described me so . . . so completely. I felt these words not just in my ears but deep inside me.

192

"Only one thing," I commented. "I still have my name: Pavel."

"Well, from now on you have no family name, you are simply that: Pavel, a man of the people."

"Right," I said, liking the sound of that. "My family, my wife, my village — they are all gone."

"Your entire past is over — nothing, no more."

I nodded strongly, and continued: " 'Heart and soul, not merely by word but by deed, the Revolutionist has severed every link with the social order of the civilized world — with the laws, good manners, conventions, and morality of that world. He is its merciless enemy and continues to inhabit it with only one purpose — to destroy. He despises public opinion. He hates and despises the social morality of his time, its motives and manifestations.' " I took a deep breath and asked her, "What does this 'manifestation' mean?"

"Ah . . . it's like showing something, like bowing to the Tsar, like bowing to him is a manifestation of your respect for him."

"Ach, the Tsar — *k chyortoo!*" To the devil, I exclaimed, and then read on. " 'Everything which promotes the success of the Revolution is moral, everything which hinders it is immoral. The nature of the true Revolutionist excludes all romanticism, all tenderness, all ecstasy, all love.' "

I put the paper down and looked away. I looked through the months and I looked through my memory to that past January. Everything that was sweet, anything that was tender, and all that I could ever have felt for another person died with my wife and unknown child there on the pure white snow. And what was reborn in this shell of my body was dark and black and hateful.

Dora poked at me, asking, "So what do you think?"

I nodded. "Yes, these words . . . they are me, one hundred percent me."

"Then will you do it?"

"Do what?"

"We are succeeding," began Dora, carefully choosing her words. "We are being energized. It's no longer we Revolutionaries leading the movement but the common working men and women of the factories and the simple field peasants, all wanting more than just a few crumbs and more than a disgusting hovel to live in. Everywhere — everywhere! — they are striking and marching, tens and even hundreds of thousands of them. The Revolution is growing with each day, but . . ."

"But?" I asked.

"We are in great danger of failure, Pavel. We are too many groups, too many ideas, too many voices. Our great wave of dissatisfaction is about to break into a million drops on the rocks rather than crash as one onto the beach and wash away everything we hate. And the Romanovs know this and are using this against us. As Caesar said, 'Divide and Conquer.' "

"Divide and what? Who is this . . . this Caesar?" I asked.

"A tsar from another country who lived many, many years ago. And what that means for us is that if we are separated into small groups and not united, the Tsar and the capitalists can walk all over us and smash us like beetles, and everything we have worked so hard for will be ruined forever."

I didn't understand all of her educated words and ideas, but the peasant in me did understand one thing: Dora had a plan, and that plan involved me.

"So what is it you want me to do?"

Staring at me as seriously as a gravedigger, she quietly said, "This Christmas — in two months' time — we want you to dress in disguise as a chorister."

I laughed. "But, Dora, me? A chorister? Dear sister, I could never go in disguise as someone like that. Why, I have the ear of a toad!"

"Don't worry, you won't even get to the singing part. To make sure our great revolution is not broken apart but washes everything away, we want you to dress as a chorister . . . and send you with a group right into the heart of the beast, the Aleksander Palace."

"You mean —"

"Yes, directly into the Tsar's own home. We want you to carry a bomb beneath your robes, and when the Tsar himself comes into the room to hear the beautiful voices we want you to throw that bomb right between his feet. What do you think?"

This idea — right away it made me feel good. I glanced across the room and saw several bird traders — or were they police spies? — come in. After a moment, I took a sip from my glass, but more than just the tea warmed my insides.

"I think this is right," I said calmly. "I think I will be happy to do this."

"But, Pavel, it will most certainly mean the death of women and children, which you didn't want to do before, remember?"

"That was, well . . . it was different before. Somehow it was different."

"Yes, now we have awakened the masses

and we are at war. Almost the entire country is on strike and the Tsar and his princes and capitalist warmongers are afraid, so they have sent his troops after us." She took a long sip of the hot tea, wiped her mouth with her special serviette, and added, "Pavel, before you give a final answer you must think seriously about this. You must think long and hard, because if you throw the bomb it will most certainly mean your own death as well, either from the bomb or from hanging."

Looking directly into her nightlike eyes, I said, "Don't forget, I was the only one to see Kalyayev dangling there from the gallows, and I want that too. I want to face death with such bravery, just like him. Yes, I can tell you without hesitation: I would be happy to die for the Revolution, the sooner the better. And if this means killing others so that things get better for the collective, then why not?"

"Exactly," replied Dora, reaching out and clutching my hand. "Our duty is to make sure things keep going forward, and by eliminating the Tsar we will make sure of one thing for certain: that there is no going back."

Just then one of the tiny yellow canaries up front began whistling. But rather than chirping beauty and delight, it began singing "God Save the Tsar."

"Ach," I moaned. "What do you think, Dora, shall I go up and strangle that bird right this minute?"

"No, Pavel, just be patient. I've heard it said that it takes about a year and a half to train those things." Smiling for the second time that afternoon, she said, "And I would wager you a gold ruble that within two years' time all the birds around here will be singing the 'Internationale.' "

CHAPTER 27
ELLA

I quite remember how my sister first lost the affection of the people, and she did so innocently and against all the force of her strong will too. Contrary to her great determination and prayers, she gave birth to Olga. And while Nicky and Alicky soothed their disappointments by telling each other that because their firstborn was a girl they wouldn't have to give her up to the people, good society and the rest of the Empire were not entirely pleased with Alicky, not really. Nicky's youngest sister had been born to a seated and anointed Emperor, of course, but an heir to the throne — which had to be male according to the Semi-Salic laws initiated by Emperor Paul — had not been born in the purple for, heavens, longer than anyone could remember, and we were all awaiting this glorious event as a heavenly sign of Russia's future prosperity. But after Olga came beautiful Tatyana, and after

Tatyana came Maria, and after Maria came Anastasiya. By that time of course Alicky had become so unpopular, not just in the highest court circles but among the common people as well, with many certain that she was a traitor to our nation for not producing a boy. Then finally and at long last came our dear, sweet Aleksei, and with the birth of the Heir Tsetsarevich, well, Alicky was in some ways redeemed, for the dynasty could go on.

I thought of this sad lesson often in the days after my venture beyond the Kremlin walls. I thought of it often due to the great disharmony I had seen on the streets and the fear that that poor wounded girl had expressed toward us members of the Ruling House. Alicky had only barely repaired her image and reputation, but I sensed Nicky's present situation to be poor at best, and his future prospects dim.

Hoping to prove myself wrong, I forced the issue with the wounded officers at my hospital, begging them to overlook my high rank and speak truly, and I gathered word of the street from others as well, and as far as I could tell these things were passed to me without corruption. In short time it was perfectly clear that Nicky had lost completely the affection of his people, and this broke my heart. And while Alicky had in some ways improved her situation with the birth of the Heir Tsarevich, I knew only too well that love for an emperor once lost — worse yet, betrayed and shattered — was almost impossible to reclaim. And yet the power of Nicky's Throne was based upon this, upon love of God and Tsar, and without this what would happen, what fate awaited us all? Without a tsar to keep this vast nation glued together, then what?

Among other things, whatever the future had in store for the Dynasty I sadly had to accept that Nicky and Alicky would never again be safe in the midst of their people. There would henceforth be a far greater fear of assassin's bullet or bomb, and ultimately, one had to admit, there would likely be a bloody deed once again, for I knew only too well that our simple people could be sweet and kind one moment but so very cruel and violent the next. I had heard tell that there had been no fewer than ten attempts upon Nicky's grandfather, Aleksander II, before that hideous success, and God only knew how many attempts had been made against my beloved Sergei before he too was taken.

Oh, I cried and I prayed as much for my dear sister and her huzzy as I did — no, I prayed even more — for my beloved adopted homeland. What path had we gone down? Were we forever lost? God help and guide us — that was my prayer morning, noon, and night. How had this hateful current sweeping across the country been awakened? Could prayer and love actually soothe its tempest, or were we doomed? No, I told myself over and over, God would not forsake this wonderful land.

Throughout all these dark days I heard regularly from my sister, who wrote me at length several times each and every day. Nicky and she dared not leave Tsarskoye, she told me, and so in essence they continued to be trapped there behind the great gates of the Palace. Simply unimaginable and what a disgrace! Alas, because of the disruptions I received her letters only with difficulty; they were brought to me not by post, which had ceased to function, but by one of my countesses, who somehow managed to travel back and forth between our two great cities, this despite the railway strikes and the many dangers en route.

From Alicky I learned that through all of those trying days, Nicky met constantly with Count Witte, whose past policies had encouraged the industrialization of Russia and brought such explosive economic growth.

Too, Witte, a large, gruff man, had just been sent to America to negotiate the peace with Japan, and he had done such an admirable job that he made our defeat nearly tolerable. Because of these successes, Nicky had him fetched to the Palace each and every day to discuss and, God willing, find a solution to the quagmire in which Russia was now stuck. They met not in Nicky's New Study, decorated in the Style Moderne, but in the Working Study just next door. Nicky, I knew since years, preferred meeting his ministers and councillors in this smaller room, with its dark-wood paneling and Nicky's L-shaped desk, covered with family photos, appointment diaries, and folders. And Alicky, trying to comprehend what was happening to our world, recounted me at length of their meetings.

"Sire, it seems that there are only two ways open," said Witte, who was seated not on the nearby large divan but on the wooden chair in front of the desk. "The first would be to find a soldier with an iron fist who could and would crush the rebellion with sheer force. If this is the course you choose, perhaps your uncle, Grand Duke Nikolai Nikolaevich, would be the right person. He has always enjoyed great respect amongst the soldiery."

Nicky clearly understood all that this meant, and replied, "By this you mean essentially establishing a dictatorship?"

"Yes, Your Majesty, I'm afraid so."

"That would entail rivers of blood, and in the end we would be where we had started." Nicky sighed and glanced over to the wall at a portrait of his father, Aleksander III. "If Papa were still alive, that is of course the path that he would follow. And there are many members of my family who would encourage me to do so as well, to hang each and every revolutionary."

With a sad shrug, Witte replied, "Unfortunately, the unrest is so widespread that to hang them all would require many lampposts — more, I would venture, than would be tolerable. Perhaps even more than exist in the whole of both Sankt Peterburg and Moscow."

"Yes, I'm afraid you are correct on that. Of course, the other way out would be to give to the people their civil rights — the freedom of speech and press and so on. This is what is being asked of me . . . and, as you know, some are demanding such things even for the Jews."

"This I understand all too well. And virtually every faction is demanding that all new laws be conformed by the new State Duma, which Your Majesty has promised to convene."

Just that past August, of course, Nicky had issued an Imperial *ukaz* declaring that a State Duma, a kind of parliament, be organized. And while that had been well received amongst many, many others agitated that it wasn't enough. In short, Nicky's manifesto hadn't been sufficient to quell the unrest. The people wanted more. They wanted this Duma to have real power, real oversight, which, of course, would mean the complete finality of autocracy in Russia.

"In essence," said Nicky, "we are talking about a constitution."

Witte bowed his head. "Most definitely. And this is a path I defend most energetically. As I have said, if this is agreed to and my actions are not interfered with, then, Sire, I will be pleased to accept the Presidency of the Council of Ministers."

But of course a constitution was quite intolerable to both Nicky and Alicky. It was not simply a matter of the giving up of power, for I knew for a fact that Nicky would have been only too glad to walk away from this business of ruling. A farm or an estate in a distant province, that was his sincerest wish. But God had laid upon Nicky's shoulders the heavy burden of

Throne, and a constitution would mean the abandonment of the pledge he had sworn to the Almighty. And if the Tsar abandoned God, would not God abandon him? And what, then, of the Heir Tsarevich, who was so in need of a miracle? Even worse, would God next not abandon Russia as well? Most of all, Nicky and Alicky feared what would happen to their subjects if he turned his back on God, for Nicky had solemnly sworn to protect and lord over his people and lead them to prosperity. That was his oath, sworn to before God and man at his coronation. So many criticized Nicky this way and that, but I knew firsthand what others might not, that there was no one more dedicated to the Motherland.

In all her letters, Alicky was so concerned, so worried for the future of her country, so distraught at the thought of handing over a weakened Empire to her son, this boy who was the hope of the Dynasty yet who himself was not of strong health. And yet she wrote me that there were only two who tried to convince Nicky to hold steadfast the Throne and not bow to pressure — and these two were Count Ignatiev and Court Minister Fredericks, the dear old sweet. All the others whom Nicky consulted were of the same opinion, that there was no other course.

Within the family I even heard it said that Nikolasha — Grand Duke Nikolai Nikolaevich — threatened to blow his brains out with a revolver if Nicky did not sign. For days on end Nicky and Witte discussed every option at great length, and in the end, invoking God's help, Nicky signed. It was, I knew in my depths, a difficult decision for Nicky, one that he nevertheless took quite consciously.

"In the end," he later told me, "I had no other way out but to cross myself and give what everyone was asking for."

Yes, quite. And with a single signature the autocracy, which Holy Mother Russia had known for time on end, had capitulated.

But Nicky's *ukaz,* granting liberties of speech and gathering and press, not to mention rights to the Duma itself, seemed to satisfy no one. In short time a handful of Grand Dukes and nobles started grumbling, saying they continued to believe in the autocratic principle, and claiming over and over that the peasant masses needed a master to rule over them, that Russia was far too backward and uneducated for such drastic reforms. Sadly, most everyone else felt the Tsar hadn't gone far enough, some spouting for a republic, others saying we needed a constitutional monarchy modeled on that of England. To everyone's surprise, the workers were like greedy children, the more they got, the more they wanted. Indeed, these new freedoms seemed to do nothing but make matters worse, for the common people, so naive and ready to believe anything, began clustering here and there at will, listening to the revolutionaries, who were speaking any number of provocative and disgraceful things. As if this weren't enough, telegrams began arriving from across the Empire about attacks upon the Jews. Just appalling, and it was no wonder that word came around, too, that many of them were taking their few possessions and fleeing to America.

May God bless Russia and send her peace, that was the prayer we uttered with every breath. It was anyone's guess what the future would bring. One could only hope that the Lord had not and would not abandon us. I was only happy that my Sergei was at peace near God and had been spared this awful time.

Towards December, when the revolutionaries grew particularly violent and began setting up barricade after barricade, it became perfectly obvious that Nicky's government was teetering on the verge of total collapse. Finally, our troops began appearing in the streets, and though at first we all feared that they would cross over to the other side, they were somehow rallied and fought back with great force, even using machine guns and artillery. Still, the outcome was anything but certain. As the days fell one darker than the last, as the sounds of bullets shattered the moments and our nerves, it seemed that nothing could forestall the gathering storm, and the revolutionaries abandoned any pretense and began calling openly for total revolt. The cry for blood could be heard everywhere.

Only those who were there know the horrors through which we lived. How the Empire managed to survive was anyone's guess.

And yet for me there was one bright spot that burned brighter and brighter with divine clarity. This idea of mine, which had, I supposed, been brewing for quite some time, years even, burst forth with great intensity soon after the death of Sergei and became completely clear by the end of that year. Yes, I had longed to do good for people, but it was true I had long been constrained as much by my husband as by my high position. The tragedy of the past year, however, had torn my reality to shreds, freed me for a truer calling, and in this way my duty and my future were more easily seen than ever before. My plans occupied my every waking moment.

One day I beckoned Varya, who had become my most devoted lady's maid, requesting simply, "Please see to it that virtually every one of my jewels is brought into my boudoir."

Varya, a kind soul, not tall of stature and of plain face, hesitated, and then asked, "Your Highness, what . . . ? I mean, is there a particular piece that Your Highness is searching for? Perhaps your Mistress of the Robes could be more helpful in this matter than I. I could fetch her, if you like."

I smiled gently. Those closest to me had expressed such kind concern these past months, worried by the sad look in my eyes, the way I seemed detached and uninterested in my customary doings. I could see on their faces their misgivings for me, and I was aware to a degree how my people had been watching out for me and trying to cushion me from the difficult events beyond the Kremlin walls. It was true, my thinking had not been entirely logical since the death of my husband. However, in the decision I was about to make I was entirely certain, and in a most odd way there were but few whom I trusted more than this maid, whose modest soul, I knew, was of complete purity and honesty. Indeed, she was one of a handful I gladly kept on, for in recent months I had greatly reduced my quantity of servants and the size of my court, kindly pleading to most of my ladies that their services were no longer required.

I repeated, "I would like all of my jewelry brought from the glass-topped cabinets of my dressing room. Please bring these things into my boudoir and open the cases and the velvet bags in which they lie. And please do not be alarmed, Varya, this is all of good intention."

"*Da-s,* Your Highness," she said with a polite curtsey.

It was no secret in proper society — let alone amongst the petty dish rags — that with the death of Sergei, I was now the richest Grand Duchess in the Empire, for I had been Sergei's sole legatee. Of course, I still had use of the 100 million gold rubles that upon my marriage Alexander III had placed on deposit for my use, but now I had inherited so much more — when presented with the figures, even I found them staggering. But in truth I did not see myself as owner of so many grand palaces, or these vast estates with their villages and thousands of peasants, or the priceless works of art and so on. No, I viewed myself a steward. And now I was a steward with a calling. It was odd. Once I had cared for nothing more than fine gowns and jewels, fancy balls and extravagant entertainments, not to mention the admiring eyes that followed me — more than once it came to my ears that the two most beautiful women in Europe were the two Elisabeths, myself and Sisi, the Empress Elisabeth of Austria-Hungary. However, costume and dress and dance, for which I had been so well known in the best society all across the Continent, were gone from me now, things virtually not of interest, not anymore. Where once I had found joy in merriments that lasted until dawn, now at sunrest I found complete and utter peace there on my knees and at prayer before an icon. Yes, at the end of my day I longed for nothing more than to pop into the chapel to bid Sergei good night.

In an hour's time my devoted Varya informed me that all had been done as requested, and it was with a rush of excitement that I made for my boudoir. Over time I had come to understand what my Grandmama had not, that the jewels of Russian women were not prideful decoration alone but also a symbol, an emblem, of the power and riches of our great Empire. In short word, nowhere on earth was there a more lavish display of gem than here. Of course Alicky had a collection befitting the Empress of Russia, and the jewels of Minnie, the Widow Empress, were equally blinding. My collection followed soon thereafter, perhaps just after Grand Duchess Maria Pavlovna, the senior, who herself ranked third of ladies in the Empire. In any case, Sergei had built my collection quite admirably, taking as much pride in their beauty as he did in knowing that my jewels were famous beyond our borders.

And while I had always loved my accessories, opening my chamber doors now and seeing the sheer quantity of jewels laid out before me, I was filled with a kind of joy I had never experienced. My bed, my bureaus, the chairs and divan were covered with sparkling and glistening goods, more than I realized or could have imagined, and certainly enough to fill the entire inventory of the finest London jewelry store. Upon the bed sat a handful of tiaras, one of white gold set with 250 diamonds of the first water, another of platinum from Cartier set with perfectly matched freshwater pearls and 15 diamonds each of 15-carats, another with seven large emerald cabochons, and on and on, a blaze of wealth that even I found astounding. In one glance to the left I saw a stunning necklace of magnificent sapphires and cut diamonds, a diamond choker and earrings in the fashion of rose petals, a complete parure of aquamarines and diamonds, a stunning ruby brooch of 110-carats surrounded by white diamonds, and ropes of pearls measuring several arms in length. Turning the other way, I saw diamond clasps, pearl buttons, a number of stunning brooches by that Swedish jeweler Bolin, one a 60-carat emerald brooch surrounded by rose-cut brilliants, another a butterfly of rubies and diamonds and sapphires. Pearl-drop pendants in white gold, bowknot brooches, diamond-studded posy holders, stomachers, chokers, hairpins — they were all spread out before me, a simply dazzling and near-priceless array of the very finest jewels.

My eyes lit up and my physical self surged with a kind of energy that I had not felt in month upon month. For the first time ever I saw these treasures not in terms of their beauty and show, but in value of gold rubles and pound sterling — a veritable fortune! — and never had I appreciated them more. Oh, what plans I had!

"Varya," I said, "also fetch my Fabergé pieces — the frames with diamonds, the golden egg with sapphires, and anything else of significance. Search everywhere, high and low, at once."

"Yes, Your Highness, but —"

"At once!"

I had been named after one of my ancestresses, Saint Elisabeth of Turingen and Hungary, known for her humility, her piousness, and her dedication to the poor. Upon the death of her husband, she had been cruelly forced from her royal home, whereupon she led the life of a wanderer yet remained ever true to her charitable intentions. And it was from my mother as well as this namesake that I had always taken good intention. Now from the both of them I drew not simply strength and determination but great conviction. Further, I had to admit that somewhere inside I also felt a keen desire to make right, if possible, some of my Sergei's transgressions — his impatience not only with me but others, his intolerance of those not pure Russian, and his inability to reach down to those in need.

Oh, I thought then and there with this great fortune of jewels glittering before me, it was hard to believe that I alone, without any outer influence, had decided these steps, which I was sure many would think an unbearable cross. Perhaps one day I would either regret this, throw over, or break down under, but I would try and I knew that He would forgive me my mistakes. In my life I had had so much joy — and in my sorrows such boundless comfort that I longed to give a little of that to others. Oh, this was not a new feeling, this was an old one which had always been with me. Simply, *I longed to thank Him.*

To this pile of jewels Varya brought in tray after tray of Fabergé bric-a-brac, bejeweled knitting needles, guilloche pens, gold frames, and the such, all glorious and precious items. As she did this, I surveyed everything. Yes, I knew from whence came each and every gem — that large sapphire and diamond brooch from Sasha and Minnie upon my engagement, that stunning diamond and emerald tiara for our wedding. Yes, and that Siberian amethyst brooch from Sergei for our anniversary, and those gorgeous emerald-and-diamond earrings had belonged to Sergei's mother, and that lovely 50-carat ruby brooch was a present from dear Kostya, and . . . and . . . and . . .

Sometime later I looked up and saw dear Varya still staring upon me, awaiting further command.

It was true, I was almost in a state of delirium, or so it felt, and to Varya, who was by chance the first person I was to tell, I confessed, "I will keep Ilyinskoye for my purposes of rest and replenishment, but all of my other palaces and properties I will give to Dmitri, just as Sergei would have wished. As for Maria, I will build an appropriate dowry — I will see to it that she will have no concerns for the rest of her life. As for all of these jewels before me now, I mean to divide them into three unequal parts. Those things that were presents from the Imperial Family will be returned to them and, where appropriate, to the State Treasury. A second lot, a much smaller one, shall be collected for gifts to my dearest ones — perhaps the emeralds to my brother and sisters abroad. And the third part, the largest, I shall sell."

"Oh, my!" gasped Varya, clapping a hand to her mouth. "But, Your Highness, all . . . all of it?"

"Yes," I said, with a surge of joy that filled my heart. "Absolutely all of it!"

But there was one more piece of fine jewelry not laid out. Looking down at my own slender hand, I saw that in the months since Sergei's death my skin, neglected, had grown drier, and my nails were no longer those of a fashionable lady. And yet glistening on that hand was something quite gorgeous of platinum and *brillianti,* the thing that had bound me in holy pledge to my husband: my wedding ring.

Oh, it was time, and I was eager to leave those dazzling days behind, for my new calling was ever so much more important . . .

I hesitated not a moment, for I knew that the value of this single item alone could accomplish much. In a rapturous moment, I pulled from my finger the ring I had worn for more than twenty years, setting it firmly on my bed.

And with the joy of both liberation and anticipation, I proclaimed, "Yes, I will sell everything that I possess, for I have the absolute conviction to follow Christ's Commandment: 'Sell that thou hast, and give to the poor.' Further, I have decided that I will pension off my servants and close entirely my court. You must help me sort these things, Varya, for I intend to dispose of every last one of these jewels, and with the proceeds to realize my great dream. On the other side of the Moscow River, down along Bolshaya Ordinka, I have found an impressive piece of property. It is upon these premises that I intend to build an *obitel* — that's right, a cloister, a women's monastery — dedicated to prayer, labor, and charity."

CHAPTER 28
PAVEL

Who could you trust? No one. In short, our plan for me to dress up like a chorister and blow up the Tsar was found out. Stupid people. Evil snakes. There were spies everywhere, all of whom could be bought for a ruble or two. Or just a jug of *samogon* — home brew — the worst vodka made from the nastiest of potatoes. The Russian peasant — he was a lazy good-for-nothing, loyal to neither master nor collective, only to liquid spirits, no matter how bad.

It had seemed like such a good plan, to strike right at the heart of the beast — oh, how glorious it would have been if I'd succeeded in blowing up Nicholas the Bloody and his kin in his own home, and right before Christmas, no less! I would have been such a hero, so famous! Why, it would have been like hurling gas on a fire, for that was our goal, not simply to kill or maim but to incite revolution, to spread it fast and furious. And if I'd succeeded it would have done so much good for our cause — the chaos would have spread so quickly, burning and burning, and how the people would have risen up against the oppressors!

But *foo* . . .

Some pathetic soul informed on a handful of our comrades, and these men were promptly arrested. Within a matter of days a kind of tribunal was set up, all of ours were found guilty, and that very day, within a few hours, they were hung. All of them.

Of course, following this we searched long and hard for the right target, not merely as revenge but, again, to move the people to action and help them liberate themselves from the chains of the capitalist and tsarist masters. And this target we did not find until the spring of 1906, and he was called Pyotr Stolypin. I actually never saw the man until that fateful day when we took action against him and his, and by then our bloody Tsar had seen fit to make this Stolypin the very top man, some kind of big minister. Some said we chose Stolypin as a target simply because he was so high up — supposedly, the bastard controlled everything from the security forces to the censors and even the passports — while others claimed we needed to get rid of him because his reforms were doing too much good and therefore soothing the masses and making it easier for them to tolerate the Tsar and his money-grubbing hounds. But really, I think, it was because of how many of us he killed. Yes, that was the immediate problem. It was this Stolypin who continued — no, made even bigger — the program of catching and immediately convicting and killing our people. Within a matter of months, thousands of good revolutionaries were hanging and dangling in the wind from Stolypin's so-called neckties. Because we lost such a lot of comrades and so quickly, too, the call to action came fast. It was either do something or dwindle into dust and blow away, the hopes of the downtrodden forever ruined.

We all knew that to keep the Organization alive we had to get rid of this Stolypin, and I was ordered to return to the capital, and there I was to work as a spy. And this was my duty: to track the comings and goings of this Mr. Minister, who settled not really in Sankt Peterburg but just outside of town in a comfortable country house on Aptekarski Island. I took a job across the lane in another house, nothing special, just minding the garden, but it gave me plenty of time to watch. In this way, I learned and reported the rhythms of the Minister's house and when he himself, the big *sheeshka* — pine-cone — came and went, as well as who actually lived in the house, who guarded it, and so on. He and his wife and their brood of four children lived in this big wooden dacha with lots of rooms, and there were many servants and lackeys running this way and that, all bowing without end, and there was, too, a pleasant garden out back for them to stroll in and the children to play. There was lots of fresh air, of course, and greenhouses as well. I was told the Minister himself liked this fresh air and plentiful exercise, too. Watching their pretty lives, I couldn't help remembering how poorly my Shura and I had lived, there in the corner of a basement, four families sharing a kitchen and one filthy toilet, the air so disgusting. There were millions upon millions of comrades who lived like that, too, and yet here was this bourgeois family living so sweetly in the country air, such a good place for the little ones. Yes, while the rest of us suffered in filth and cramped quarters, here was Mr. Minister who was waited on hand and foot by a herd of uniformed lackeys. I was sure that he and his were eating as much meat as they wanted — even as much white bread, when all that the *narod* — the masses

— could afford was black. What pigs. How we suffered so they could live such a nice, fat life.

One of my jobs was to count the number of carriages attached to the house, because they would be useful when the uprising finally came. We could use them for barricades.

It was by my calculation that every Saturday Stolypin stayed at this summer mansion and received all sorts of people, petitioners from all sorts of classes wanting this or that from him. And when I made my report of this we quickly decided that it was on such a Saturday that we would kill him.

"The perfect time for us to get directly into the house," one of my leaders reported.

There lived with Stolypin an old maid, Annushka, who was not quite right in the head but was devoted to her master. I learned that Stolypin had brought her from his large estate in a distant province. This Annushka was short and ugly and gray, and had been attached to the family forever — she'd been born a serf to them — and though the Emancipation had been long ago, the poor woman didn't understand that she was free. She would not step one foot beyond the edge of her master's property. Her only job was to sweep the front steps, and there she stood all day long, sweeping with her twig broom after each and every visitor mounted the steps and entered the house. She swept with such determination that soon she scratched away all the paint and the steps had to be repaired.

Anyway, though Annushka wouldn't leave her master's territory, I met her several times at the rear of the garden, there by a wicket fence. I asked of her master, of her master's beautiful dacha, and she told me many things freely and without hesitation. She was all innocence, that one, and through her I learned that Mr. Minister Stolypin's study, cloak room, and two reception rooms were all downstairs, off to one side, while off the other way was one parlor and the dining room, the kitchens too. Upstairs were all the bedrooms and a parlor.

"And that's where my mistress sits, up there in that big window, you see?" Annushka told me with a near-toothless smile. "She sits up there in her parlor and does her needlework. She makes such pretty things, sometimes even aprons for me!"

From where we stood, she pointed to all the windows of the big dacha, telling me where her master worked, where his children played, and generally making sure I understood her household and how it operated.

She was very proud to belong to the family, and it was from this simple Annushka's description that we made our plan — how we would enter the house, where we would find Mr. Minister, and precisely where we should throw the bomb. I begged desperately to do the deed, but was not allowed. My face was already known in the neighborhood, and it was feared I would be blocked from the property altogether. New comrades were needed who could come in disguise and not be recognized.

After much talk, we finally decided on a particular Saturday, and when that day arrived it was warm and sunny. Lots of people came to see the Minister and beg his help. Some were important people with official petitions from banks or other cities, some were ordinary folk with hungry children in tow, even a few priests. By late morning, I had counted almost fifty souls who had entered the house, Annushka sweeping the stoop after each of them passed.

It was about then that I saw our two comrades coming up the lane in an open carriage. They were dressed as policemen, helmets and all. They didn't look at me, and I pretended not to see them, even though I wanted to cheer them on. Really, it was so exciting. How could they not succeed?

When they turned onto the property of the dacha, a guard immediately stopped the carriage, demanding, "What business do you have here?"

One of our men, a tall, thin comrade who did not look quite comfortable in his police uniform, for it was too small for him, replied, "We have two portfolios to deliver to Mr. Minister Stolypin."

"Hand them to me and I'll make sure he receives them," demanded the guard.

The other comrade, who was shorter and smarter, too, quickly called from the carriage, saying, "We would gladly do so, my friend, but we carry important papers — official government ones at that — and our instructions are to place them only in the hands of Mr. Minister himself."

With a shrug, the guard, who that morning had already heard so many sad stories from those wanting to get in, thought nothing of it and opened the gate and let the carriage pass. This was all according to plan, and the carriage with our two fake policemen rolled onto the Minister's property.

But within seconds, just after they had passed through the gate, things started to take a nasty turn. The house was not too far down the drive, but suddenly I heard shouts and saw men running after the carriage.

Someone, a soldier, was demanding what kind of police our two men were, where they had come from, who had sent them, and what exactly they were carrying.

"We're here to deliver two portfolios to Mr. Minister Stolypin, that's all!" shouted our tall policeman with a nervous grin.

"I demand to know who has sent you!"

And then a real policeman appeared from the side of the house, and demanded, "Hey, why aren't you two wearing the new helmets?"

One of our comrades said, "Please, my friends, just let us do our —"

"But why aren't you wearing the new uniforms? All uniforms were changed two weeks ago, and you should be wearing the new uniforms and the new helmets!"

Fearing that they had been discovered, our fake policemen cracked the whip and the carriage bolted toward the large wooden dacha. From all around came screaming and yelling.

"Stop! Stop right now!" cried the Minister's guards.

But our fellows, dedicated to the Revolution, would not slow, let alone stop, and they steered the carriage right toward the front entrance of the house. I hurried across the lane, and with my own eyes saw all the commotion — the racing carriage, the soldiers and guards hurrying to apprehend our comrades. I even saw two of Mr. Minister Stolypin's own children — a young girl and a much younger boy — come running onto the balcony above the front entrance, for they were eager to see what all the excitement was about. And when the carriage reached the house itself I watched as our fellows, still clutching the portfolios, leaped down from the carriage and rushed toward the entrance of the house and up the steps. The former serf Annushka was there at the door as always but, riled by the commotion, she didn't greet the men with her toothless smile or even get ready to sweep away their filth. Instead, she took her twig broom and started swinging it at the men in an attempt to beat them back.

"Go away! Go away!" she screamed.

But our brave men swatted her like a fly, flicking her right off the stoop and into the bushes. The next moment they were charging inside.

Yes, in one second our comrades disappeared into the house, two very able men quite determined to put an end to this Stolypin. And then in a flash they were dead and gone, blown to pieces, because there came — oh! — what an explosion! I never saw such a thing, never heard anything so loud!

Certainly they must have thrown the bombs down in the entry hall, right onto the wood floor. Perhaps there were more guards blocking their way. Perhaps they realized they could go no farther — it must have been this — and when they realized they could not reach the Minister and toss the bombs at his feet they smashed them there on the floor. First the front door blew right off its hinges, shooting out some forty paces, followed immediately by some poor soul who came hurtling outside, head over heels, flying through the air like a rock. And then the entire huge summer house seemed to lift right up off its foundation. Yes, right before my eyes the whole house jumped upward, but actually it was the front of the house that took it the worst, for the entrance was blown clean away and even the balcony with the children on it exploded into the sky. Wood and doors and glass went flying everywhere, and even the horse that had pulled our fake policemen was lifted up into the air and thrown against a tree.

And then there was an odd quiet, but not complete quiet, for as the explosion reverberated through the neighborhood I could hear pane after pane of glass breaking in all

229

the surrounding houses — later I heard that all the windows in all the houses on the island were broken or at least cracked. Even when the explosion was finished there was an odd kind of noise, a strange rain of sorts, as pieces of wood and glass and stone and even shoes and children's toys began to fall down right on me. A huge brass samovar came tumbling out of the sky, landing not on my head but right at my feet.

My ears ringing, I ran toward the house, couldn't stop myself. As I made my way up the drive, there were bodies everywhere, arms and legs, too, just like a real battlefield. For another minute or two there was silence, and then all of a sudden there was one scream, then another, and finally an entire chorus of agony. I looked around in shock. There, off to the side, buried in debris, was the body of Annushka, legs and arms twisted this way and that. She was quite dead, probably killed instantly. And there a gardener, his head blown off, and two women piled on top of each other, their faces ripped away and chests carved wide. *Radi boga,* how many had we killed here today? How many had given their lives just so we could eliminate the Minister who was so determined to stomp out the uprising of the oppressed?

I realized then that not just the front of

the house had been ripped away but all the rooms in the central part too. Hearing someone cough, I looked up and saw a woman standing there at the top of the main staircase, of which only the top two steps remained. Looking like a ghost, this woman was completely covered in a white dust of plaster and limestone, and she surveyed everything, calmly and evenly. Then downstairs, off to the left, a door was pushed open and a large man stepped through the doorway and into a room that no longer existed. I recognized him as none other than Mr. Minister Stolypin. His office had been missed completely, and he emerged unscathed except for a large blue ink stain on his shirt — the worst that had happened to him was that his inkpot had spilled against his chest, dumping ink all over his fine white shirt.

The woman at the top of the stairs looked down at big Mr. Minister and in a flat, even voice, she said, "Thank God, you are alive."

"Yes, my dear, as are you," he said to this woman, who was obviously his wife. "And the children? Do you have them?"

"I don't know where the two little ones are."

Not knowing what I did — that the young ones had been on the balcony above the front entrance — the two parents turned and went separate ways, disappearing toward the back of the house. I nearly called out to them, nearly shouted, "No, your children were on the front balcony, looking at all the excitement. They must be lying out this way, out front — look this way! The force of the blast must have hurled them out here, into the front garden!"

Instead, it was I who went searching for the children.

I stepped over a body, broken and bent in a very strange way, and made my way over a pile of shattered wood. The carriage that had brought our fake policemen was heaved on its side and mostly destroyed, and the horse that had pulled the carriage hung there in its harness, stabbed in the side with a board and bleeding like a river. If the poor creature wasn't already dead, it would be in a second. Noticing that there was something odd about the horse, I looked closely and saw that stuck to its side, right there on the hide, was a person's ear. Two steps beyond was a man, lying facedown and moaning. I stooped by his side, listening as he tried to speak. I couldn't understand a thing, and simply watched as he took a deep breath and then expired, blood pouring from his mouth. A little gray cat came running out of nowhere, frightened and excited, and scampered over the dead man's back.

Off to the side I saw some scraps of railing and clambered in that direction, and there, under the debris, I found the two youngest children of Mr. Minister Stolypin. Lifting up a large board, I first found the boy, who was perhaps three years old, certainly no more than four. He was lying quite still, his legs twisted in opposite directions — broken, I was sure — and he had a gash in his forehead. At first I thought he too was dead. When I brushed the grime and debris from the child's face, however, he blinked twice and looked up at me sweetly.

And with a faint smile, the boy managed to utter, "You're a nice uncle."

Fighting back something — just what I didn't know — I managed to say, "Don't try to move."

The boy thought for a moment, and replied, "I can't."

Trying to make sure he was comfortable, I pushed everything aside as best I could, leaving him lying there quite calmly. Just a few paces away lay the other child, the girl, who was perhaps a teenager. She lay beneath a large piece of wooden furniture, which I grabbed and hurled aside. There were rocks and some other things covering her too, and these things I quickly pulled from her body. Looking for injuries, I could see none until my eyes came to her feet, both of which seemed to have been all but blown off.

When I lifted part of a desk off her arm, her body quivered, and she opened her eyes and gasped, "What kind of dream is this?"

"It's not a dream, my child," I replied.

"Oh." Coming quickly to her senses, she asked, "Can you tell me, please, does Papa live?"

As much as I wanted to deny it, I could not lie, and said, "Yes."

"Thank God. And thank God it's me who's hurt and not him."

Her devotion touched something long forgotten inside me, and I knelt by her side and took her hand and held it and said some kind of comforting words, something even religious. I had seen enough bad accidents in my village to know she might actually live, but I was likewise certain that if she survived she would definitely be maimed for life. Glancing down at her damaged feet, I was sure she would never walk again.

As I crouched by the girl, holding her hand and soothing her, I suddenly felt a firm hand on my shoulder. Turning and looking up, my heart leaped when I saw that it was none other than the bastard, Mr. Minister Stolypin, bearing over me in his ink-stained finery. My first thought was that I had been found out and he himself had come to do me in. But rather than punching me or ripping out my throat or stringing me up from a tree, he looked at me gratefully.

"Thank you, my good man, for finding my daughter," he said, tears of relief filling his eyes.

I should have shot him right then and there and finished the job, but of course I had no gun. It occurred to me that I should have shoved him back and strangled him to death, but he was a bigger, stronger, mightier person than me. In fact and quite oddly, I realized that there was not a crumb of strength left in me. I felt completely drained, and it was all I could do to stand.

And so as I rose directly by his side I nodded toward his daughter's mangled feet, and quietly offered but one thing, perhaps the only piece of village wisdom that I, a peasant, could give to such a highly placed Minister, saying, "The doctors will want to amputate — do not let them."

This man, nothing more at that moment than the most devoted of fathers, gasped in horror and half fell against me, clutching my arm for support. Despite all that I had been taught by my comrades and the hatred that burned within my own heart, I steadied Stolypin, hanging on to him until he regained his composure.

Then finally dropping to his knees by his daughter, Stolypin gently said, "My beautiful Natasha . . . do not worry, my sweet one, everything's going to be all right."

"You're here, Papa, and not hurt."

"Not in the least, and I won't leave your side."

I disappeared then, traipsing off through the mayhem completely unnoticed, not a soul suspecting me of my role in this messy affair. I walked all the way back into the city and across the Troitsky Bridge, where I paused midway and stared across the vast waters of the Neva River. From there I proceeded through the Field of Mars, eventually finding my way into the much less glorious corners of the capital, where my comrades took me in. They tried to feed me tea, but I refused. I told them everything — excepting how I had come face-to-face with our number-one enemy, not to mention the human words we had exchanged, which became the darkest secret of my life.

Yes, and although we had failed to eliminate our target, I later heard that thirty people had been killed immediately by the blast, and that many more died in the following days. It was a pity that so many had to give their lives for the cause, but such was the price. And while we failed to eliminate our main target — the Minister himself — news of the attack spread through the Empire so that everyone learned of our determination to help the downtrodden and needy. In that way we succeeded greatly, and in that way we were more greatly feared than ever.

I heard, too, that when young Natasha was rushed to the best hospital the chief doctors were, just as I had guessed, determined to cut away both of the girl's feet, certain that that was the only way to save her life. With tears streaming down his big cheeks, Stolypin, perhaps heeding my words, pleaded for the doctors to wait at least until the next morning, and to this, despite their fears of gangrene setting in, they agreed. The girl, I was told, survived the night without incident, and the doctors waited another day after that, and then another. Much to their astonishment and the joy of father and mother, the child began to improve almost miraculously, and her feet, though forever maimed, were saved. I heard, too, that a peasant from the Tobolsk District had a very strong desire to bless Stolypin's injured daughter with an icon, and he was granted entry and came to her and prayed by her side. Perhaps this was why she recovered so well. This peasant — his name was Grigori Rasputin.

That was the first time I had ever heard the name.

As for the youngest child, the boy, in the following weeks I went to great lengths to learn his fate, and found out that both of his legs had been broken, as well as his hip. However, a medical sister told me that I mustn't concern myself, that both he and yet another of the Minister's children, a daughter whose kidney had been torn by the blast, were recovering just fine.

Soon after the bombing the Tsar moved Stolypin and his entire family into the Winter Palace, placing them behind the tall iron gates and thick doors of the imperial home. They hid them there, the best soldiers guarding them day and night, and each time the Minister left the Palace he snuck out a different door, and with great secrecy too. As for the exercise and fresh air that Mr. Minister Stolypin so greatly craved, he was forced to pace the paths laid up there on the roof of the Winter Palace, and I think I once saw him up top, going around and around among the decorations along the edges of the roof.

Because of our failure to kill him, the hangman Minister lived and pressed on, more determined than ever to string up as many members of our Organization as he could, and he nearly succeeded in this, nearly wiped us out completely. Unfortunately, we did not succeed in assassinating him for another five years, not until 1911, when one of ours, the Jew named Bogrov, shot Stolypin with a Browning revolver at the Kiev Opera House, there in the presence of the Emperor.

That finally brought the end to "Stolypin's neckties" and to his reforms, and in this way we hoped to speed up the struggle of the Oppressed.

CHAPTER 29
ELLA

Honestly, I was quite taken aback when a family battle broke out to prevent me my plans, to frighten me about the difficulties — all with great love but with utter incomprehension of my character. More than once I had to assure Nicky dear that I had not fallen under the influence of a *prelest duxha* — a charmed spirit — and that I alone, without any outer influence, had decided this course. And poor Alicky. In the beginning she was quite disturbed, for she worried that my steps toward chastity and poverty would demean the Family. I knew she imagined I let people call me a saint — she told one of my countesses this — but good gracious, what was I, no better and probably worse than others. In any case, people never said such exaggerated things to my face, for all knew I hated flattery as a dangerous poison.

So I wrote to the two of them, Nicky and

my sister:

My Dearest Ones,
Forgive me, *both of you*. I know and feel
alas, *I worry you* and perhaps you don't
quite understand me, please forgive and
be *patient* with me, forgive my mistakes,
forgive my *living differently* than *you*
would *have wished, forgive* that I *can't
often* come to see you because of my *duties here.* Simply with your good hearts
forgive, and with your large Christian
souls *pray* for me and my work.

Only my older sister, Victoria, in England,
understood my need — it was only she who
from the start thought it was right that I fill
up my life with good work. As to those of
proper society who said I could definitely
do more good in my previous role, I could
only answer that I didn't know if they were
right or wrong, only that life and time would
show, but certainly God who was all love
would forgive me my mistakes, as He certainly saw my wish of serving Him and His.
In any case, for me the bitter bite of gossip
had long lost its sting.
Suffice to say that during all this time I
felt calm and at peace, really it was so, even
with so many momentous decisions. I never

had one moment of despair or loneliness, surely because the living and dead were near me and I didn't realize entirely the earthly separation.

Within short years I had accomplished much. I arranged for Maria a marriage to the second son of the Crown Prince of Sweden, for by family law she was of course allowed only this, marriage to another royal, and this match seemed reasonable. Too, I built them a palace in Stockholm, and saw that Maria was set with a proper dowry. As for her younger brother, Dmitri, I took him to the capital, where he was enrolled in the cavalry school to prepare him for his life in the Horse Guards.

Content that my duties to the children had been discharged, I set about my project with even more energy. Day and night I devoted myself entirely to the study and establishment of my *Marfo-Marinski Obitel Miloserdiya vo Vladenii Vlikoi Knyagini Elisavyeti Fyodorovni,* otherwise to be known in English as the Martha and Mary Convent of Mercy Under the Direction of Grand Duchess Elisabeth Fyodorovna. It seemed quite a daunting name, but the idea was clear, for it was to be inspired by Christ's own simple words: "I was hungry and you fed me, sick and you cared for me." The territories that I had purchased for my community along the cobbled Bolshaya Ordinka were most satisfying, spacious and green and abundant with fresh air.

Little did I know, however, that my plans, all of which were intended for charity, would be taken nearly as heresy by the Holy Synod.

First upon my list of things to do was the complete closing of my court, whereupon I let go my dear ladies, who had been all service and kindness to me. Likewise, my servants were released, all with good pensions, and finally I shut up altogether my apartments in the Nikolaevski Palace, leaving behind my icons as gift. From there I moved into modest rooms none too far from my future community, which by 1908 was then in the midst of planning and soon under construction, too.

I still maintained and visited every day my hospital for soldiers — such dear men — and soon I also saw great need for a house of death for women. Such a place I opened in an old house that I had bought from a peasant on a side street, Denezhni Pereulok, and into this house we welcomed a never-ending string of consumptive women. These were the poorest of the poor, most of whom had worked as the lowliest charwomen, only to be turned away from their work when they could no longer hide their illness. When even the hospitals refused to take in these suffering ones and they had nowhere else to go, word got about and they came to my doorstep. I was especially devoted to them all and considered it my duty to offer them a bed of comfort as they prepared for their solemn change of lodging. I had written my sister of the sufferings of these women, for they were always coughing and spitting and had such little appetite and, too, such a nasty taste in their mouths. Responding in all kindness, both Alicky and my great friend, Princess Yusupova, regularly had grapes sent from their Crimea estates, making sure that we were never without.

Upon my orders I was always to be notified when one of the women was close to end, and one day word came round of one such case. With a basket in hand, I hurried to my house of death, and in one of the white rooms found a woman, Evdokia, unable to open her eyes and struggling desperately for each breath. It was clear she had but hours. Sitting by her side and clutching her hand was her husband, Ivan, who had a large beard and wore torn, dirty clothes. He worked in a smelter, operating the bellows.

Upon my entry he looked up at me with tear-stained eyes and recognized me immediately, for it was all true, as much as I wished for incognito, everyone in these parts knew that I was a member of the Ruling House. But rather than greeting me with even a modicum of courtesy, he glared at me with something akin to hatred, and I perceived that this Ivan would rather have brought his wife anywhere but here . . . and yet there was nowhere else. It fazed me not, however, for all that mattered was the comfort of the dying woman and the proper care of her soul.

"May I join you, sir?" I asked.

Ivan said nothing, simply turned back to his wife, whom he clearly loved so very dearly. I sat down as well, and my first task was to take a damp cloth from a nearby enamel bowl and mop the poor woman's feverish brow.

I had never and would never consider it my duty to mislead any of my patients with false hopes of recovery. No, none of the women who entered these doors were ever told otherwise. In other words, we placated them not with lies or glibness or false cheer but with the truth that their earthly end was soon to come. In this they all found not fright but peace, and in this way we were able to prepare them for their sacred voyage.

From my basket I took a handful of grapes, which had been chilled deep in the cellar, but as I reached to place them into the woman's mouth her husband's thick, gnarly hand suddenly came up. As fast as a pickpocket, he grabbed my wrist.

Not releasing me, Ivan demanded, "What are you trying to do, eh, Princess, kill her? What is that?"

With no great ease, I opened my hand and exposed the small fruits. He looked at them but still there was no trust in his eyes, only confusion at best. Had he never seen a grape before, or did he think my intentions purely evil?

"They are grapes, sir, pure and simple, and I only mean to put your wife more at ease," I said. "She can no longer swallow, but these grapes are cool and wet, and if you'll allow me I'll pack them gently in her cheeks. Within a short time they will begin to crack and slowly release their juices, thereby moistening her tongue."

"But . . . but . . ." he muttered, wanting, perhaps against his better judgment, to believe me.

"Do not worry, no medicament of any sort has been added to them." And seeing that he still feared I meant her harm, I reached with my free hand into my other — the one he held so tightly — and took a grape and popped it into my own mouth. "They're sweet and refreshing. Would you care for one, sir?"

He shook his head and, with a nod to his wife, softly said, "Go on."

Yes, Ivan let me place grapes in each of his wife's cheeks. And an hour later, when those were smashed of wetness, he let me remove them and place fresh ones into her mouth. I did so another hour after that, and yet an hour later, too, which is to say that this Evdokia lasted nearly another four hours before ascending to the Giver of all life. Finally, when she'd breathed her last, the poor man fell upon her body sobbing like a child. I crossed around to him then, placing one hand upon his shoulder as I said a prayer for this newly departed servant of God.

A short time later it was brought to my attention that this man had no financial means to see to his wife's funeral, and I told him not to worry, that coffin and prayers and all would be taken care of.

I explained, "We will transfer your wife to the small church across the street, where Psalter will be said over her."

"Yes, but at whose expense? Whose?" he asked. "Yours?"

Of course it was, but I said, "That is of no importance." And wondering if he was all alone, I queried, "Have you children, sir?"

With some degree of difficulty, he replied, "We had two young boys, but they both died from diphtheria. So now you see, it's just . . . just me . . ."

"Both my mother and young sister died of such," I confessed, taking both his hands in mine. "Just remember, you are never alone."

"But . . . but for me there is no one else . . ."

"Yes, you have God, and you have us here. Please, just come back later today for prayers, and any other time for a meal as well."

Without replying yea or nay, he turned to leave, then almost as quickly spun back, bowing deeply and firmly grasping both of my hands in his.

"Thank you, Your Highness," he said, kissing my fingers. "Thank you for caring for my wife and . . . and thank you for the fruits you fed her."

"It was both my pleasure and my solemn duty. As for the grapes, though, please do not thank me. This batch is from my sister, sent to us here out of concern and mercy for these suffering women."

"Your sister . . . the Empress . . . she sent the . . . the fruits?" he gasped, unable to hide his shock.

"Yes."

His face quickly reddening with rage or embarrassment or shock — I couldn't tell which — he quickly turned and made for the door. Just as quickly, he stopped.

Looking over his shoulder, he quietly confessed, "I would not have become a Communist if I had met your kind before."

"Please, just don't forget this afternoon's Psalter," I said.

Without replying, he fled out the door, whence I did not doubt he disappeared into the Khitrovka, the worst slums of any city quite round the globe.

As I suspected, the man did not return for prayers over his wife's coffin. The reasons were of no importance, all that mattered was that ordinance be followed, so later that afternoon, dressed in a fresh white dress free of any contagion, I went to the church. And there I took it upon myself as duty to read the Psalms over the woman's open casket, thereby aiding her soul as it passed through *mitarstva,* the toll gates.

Work on my community continued apace,

and with great excitement too. I gathered every book relevant to my scheme, reading in English, German, and French about foundations where prayer and work were braided as one. In my native Germany I visited the fine Kaiserwerth Diakonissen training schools, where nurses and teachers were instructed in the care of young and old. Upon my visit to England, my sister Victoria led me to both the Convent of the Sisters of Bethany and, of course, the Little Sisters of the Poor. By studying these good institutions I was able to more finely perceive what was being asked of me and how I might improve its birth. In short, I understood that I was meant to reawaken a slightly modified order of deaconesses whose goal so closely matched mine, which was to aid the sick and the poor. To me the concept seemed simple and pure, but it came as quite a revolution within our Orthodoxy.

With the sale of my personal things and also an estate in Poltava, which had been left to my husband for the purposes of charity, I raised considerable sums. And with these moneys I was not only able to purchase a proper site but also to hire the artist Nesterov, whom Sergei so liked, and, upon Nesterov's own suggestion, the architect

Aleksei Shchusev. It soon became clear that we would be able to remake four of the original buildings on the property and plan for a church, tying all together with a beautiful whitewashed wall that would be covered with vines. At the center of my complex we planned a quiet, peaceful garden that would be planted with white lilies — my favorite — and sweet peas, lilacs, and fruit trees, too. To Nesterov I assigned the eventual task of painting the interior frescoes of the church, along with some icons, while Shchusev proposed a most beautiful white church that artfully blended the beauty of old Russia — complete with onion domes — with a hint of Style Moderne. Both my beloved Kostya and even Nicky dear, along with a host of others, certainly, came to the laying of the cornerstone of the Church of the Protection of the Most Holy Mother of God. Even the fearfully holy icon, The Iverian Virgin, was brought down from the Kremlin by old carriage for the ceremony. It was a very powerful day.

By midwinter of 1909, even though work on the church continued, enough was otherwise done that I was able to move into my house, one of the little buildings that had been remade and incorporated into the plan for my *obitel.* In all I had three rooms there, airy and cozy, so summerlike, and all who saw them were enchanted. In my sitting room I placed summer furniture of English willow covered with blue chintz, and a desk too. There was my prayer room, the walls of which I covered respectfully with many icons, and also my simple bedroom, in which was placed only a few things, chiefly a plain wooden bed with no mattress or pillow, only planks. In truth, I was sleeping less and less, usually only some three hours, for I was often called either to prayers or to the bedside of the sick.

And yet I had by this time not received the veil, and because of this we few who were there in the early days were required to begin our operation under the guidance of our spiritual father, Father Mitrofan, the kindest and most devoted of confessors, and a real presence with his long hair, big beard, and broad forehead.

Still I pressed on, and after much time and deliberation I conceived a formal plan for the formation of my order, a plan that I in turn submitted to the Holy Synod. I knew this would be no easy feat. Since centuries Russia had operated her centers of religion under the Basilian Laws whereby nuns lived a most cloistered life, all but permanently shut away from the world around them; they lived a life of prayer and contemplation, venturing beyond the walls of the monastery only in extreme cases, to beg for alms, for example, and then only with a bishop's permission. But I wished for more than that. I envisioned that my sisters should reach out to a community in need, for despite my great respect for such cloistered institutions of prayer and devotion, I saw a different need and felt a different calling.

Appearing before the Holy Synod, I was faced with many heavy faces, a panel of men in great vestments who took great umbrage at my request.

Hermongen, Bishop of Saratov, clearly disliked my proposal, saying, "I'm afraid your request is quite contrary to our canons. The order of deaconesses was done away with by decree centuries and centuries ago, and that decree was quite definitive."

"If Her Imperial Highness finds herself in need of a religious vocation," voiced the most stern Metropolitan of St. Peterburg, "I would suggest that all must be based on our strict Basilian laws."

"Yes, either that or submit yourself to any other of our fine women's monasteries, of which Russia possesses a great number," suggested another of these religious leaders.

I understood immediately where this was headed, and I knew I was completely done for the moment Hermongen began mumbling that my plan for a group of active sisters smacked of "Protestant leaven." These words, craftily chosen, lit the fire of opposition under still others, and there came grumblings that the whole idea was not Orthodox enough, simply too Western, and these complaints even drowned out the support I had from the powerful Metropolitan Vladimir of Moscow. In short, it was a complete rout, and I and my petition were summarily dismissed as near-blasphemy.

I was vexed, there was no doubt of it, and discouraged, too, but I set right about reworking my rules.

I spent the ensuing months studying my books, and with the consult of important clergy, from Vladimir's own suffragan to others, I altered my plan, borrowing much from St. Vincent de Paul. Quite some time later I was back before the members of the Holy Synod with a different proposal. Once again, I was met with doubt and dismiss, and they questioned much, and did so without hiding their displeasure, either. Long had I known the obstacles of Russia, but I was determined to both innovate and invigorate, drawing inspiration from my own mother and all the daring good she had done for her people, from hospitals to clean bathing water.

Upon the second visit to the Synod, one of the first questions asked of me was: "Our Orthodox sisters have always worn square-toed boots, robes of black, and a *klobuk* upon their heads, not to mention a long black veil. Why is it, then, that you wish for this . . . this combination, a pale-gray habit and no head gear excepting a mere veil?"

Looking calmly at the Metropolitans and Bishops alike, I replied, "It is my intention that my sisters will be active in hospital work, busy with caring from morning into the night. With this in mind, I have proposed garments that would be more suitable for this busy work. My sisters will need to move quickly and ably without being constrained."

Hermongen groaned with suspicion, then stared upon me, demanding, "But why meat? All of our true Orthodox sisters have always gone without such. True, from time to time they are offered fish, perhaps, but never meat — *never.*"

"Please understand," I began, for I had expected this question and prepared for it, too, "that since years I myself have not eaten meat of any sort, not even fish. Only milk and vegetables have served me. But I intend for my sisters to be young and full of energy. I wish them to eat a healthy diet, including meat, so that they may be better able to serve those in need. It is for their strength. You see, I feel that work is the foundation of one's religious life — to give one's whole strength to God — and prayer and contemplation its final reward."

On and on the questions went, and I had to explain so much, why I proposed taking only sisters between the ages of twenty-one and forty — "So that they will be full of energy" — and why I would require all to take an annual holiday — "For their refreshment."

Again, Hermongen threw an unkind remark here and there, such a pity for he had not seen our place and the good we were already doing. And again it was implied that my Order sought to imitate Protestantism, which was completely unjust. Really, it came as no surprise that the Holy Synod refused me again.

All would have been lost, too, had my brother-in-law not soon stepped forward. Nicky and I corresponded at length, I took his consult to heart, he understood my intent, and finally by Imperial Decree he established the Order of Saints Martha and Mary. With one swoop the whole thing was done.

And what joy it was when my new life in the church began. It was as if bidding good-bye to the past with all its faults and sins, all with the hope of a higher goal and a purer existence. As the official day approached I wrote Nicky dear, asking him to pray for me, for taking my vows was even more serious than when a young girl marries. How interesting it all was, what turns my life had taken. I had come to a dazzling court in a new land as the young bride of a mighty Romanov, and now I was espousing Christ and His cause, hoping to give all I could to Him and our neighbors.

Finally and at long last by 1910 all was scheduled, and the night before the ceremony an all-night vigil was held there on our territories. Just after sunrise, as the early spring sun began to show its bashful face, I gathered my sixteen sisters about me there in the garden. How eager they were, how earnest and yearning of good deed. Collected, I surveyed them with pride, noting there were sisters of every walk, from nobility to the lowest rung, and yet we were of one now. Especially eager to join was Varya, my young lady's maid, who of her own accord had chosen to follow me from the Palace and down this profound path of self-denial. Soon to be known as Nun Varvara, she would serve the community and Him with as much devotion, I was sure, as she had once served me at Court.

To all these beautiful faces, I said, "I am about to leave the brilliant world in which it fell to me to occupy a brilliant position, but together with you I am about to enter a much greater world — that of the poor and afflicted."

We were then led into our chapel where Bishop Tryphon tonsured us all, shaving the tops of our heads during a liturgy written especially for us. And finally we were offered the veil.

And, with a booming voice, Bishop Tryphon proclaimed, "This veil will hide you from the world, and the world will be hidden from you, but it will be at the same time a witness of your work of charity, which will resound before the Lord to His glory."

The very next day, Metropolitan Vladimir of Moscow, who had always been my supporter, came, and during Divine Liturgy he elevated me to the position of Abbess. From that day on I was known to all as Matushka Yelisaveta — Mother Elisabeth.

And our community flourished.

CHAPTER 30
PAVEL

We finally got rid of this Mr. Minister Stolypin, but the truth, we soon realized, was that killing him really didn't help the Organization or the cause. By then it was too late, and I have forever felt guilty for this, that I didn't try to kill him with my own bare hands that day he survived the bombing of his dacha. Simply, by the time one of ours shot him at the Kiev Opera, Mr. Bloodsucking Minister had already killed too many of us, some said as many as two or three thousand revolutionaries strung up all across the country. In that way, by the year 1911 we had become an army with not enough soldiers.

But what was strange, what bothered me most, was how quiet things had got. In short, the anger of the people was not like it used to be. The strikes had stopped. There were no more marches. And the people were no longer screaming for food. It turned out that the so-called reforms of this Mr. Minister had begun to work. I heard more and more about peasants even way out there in the back of beyond who owned land for the very first time, and I even heard about a new kind of peasant, the *kulak,* who not only owned big tracts but could afford to hire people to work for him. In the cities, too, you could see the prosperity, and not just on the street where merchants were driving carriages with four horses, just like real nobles. No, you could see it in the air, too, smell it even, for the factories were belching smoke day and night. Sure, Russia was booming in a way no one had ever seen, which meant, much to our horror, Mr. Minister Stolypin had done it, defeated the oppressed and saved Russia for the capitalist hounds. He and he alone had relieved the pressure, for he had successfully let the steam out of that boiling cauldron which had been so ripe and ready to explode.

Poor Russian slobs, they were happy with so little. They had been thirsty and Stolypin had seen to it that they got a drop, and this single drop had been enough to satisfy them. Who would have guessed that in the end the beaten-down peasant could be so loyal to the Tsar?

I know my comrades had wanted to bypass

capitalism altogether, to go straight from the chains of autocracy to the freedoms of socialism and even all the way to Communism in one single leap. That was the goal. Now, however, they licked their wounds by saying perhaps it would be necessary to pass first through the hellish fires of capitalism before true Communism could be built, such was the natural progression.

All I knew was that within a few short years my comrades were either dead, sent off to prison in Siberia, or packing their bags and heading abroad. One of my last comrades, an educated guy who had in his day killed seven or eight government officials and blown up three banks, packed up and took a boat all the way to America.

The last I heard he had changed his name and was teaching mathematics at a university in some northern city called Dakota.

Chapter 31
Ella

All were surprised at how quickly we grew — all except me, for I had long sensed the need to reach out and knew how well we would be received. There was much suffering in Moscow and so many who needed our help, which my sisters gave with boundless joy and love. I had long felt that Moscow was the hope of Russia, and wealthy Muscovites, long wanting to help, opened up their hearts to us, giving of money and materials to a most generous extent. Yes, our success spawned more success, and was felt by all, for while my community was part of the old Russia, we belonged at the same time to the new Russia, with our new interests and new ideals, not to mention our young sisters, who were so full of energy and strength.

Such was the need that soon my *obitel* quickly grew to thirty sisters, and within three years' time there were 97 of us serving in many obediences. Some were employed at the apothecary shop that provided free medicaments to the poor, others at our hospital that had an operating theater and twenty-two beds and which itself was served by thirty-four doctors who could be called at a moment's notice, still others could be found in the kitchen, bakery, refectory, or the administrative office, and in many other areas as well. Each and every day we served over 300 meals to poor working mothers, and, too, there was my orphanage for girls. Also, I had recently established a home for beggar boys, where they were bathed and clothed and fed, and then apprenticed as messenger boys — these little chaps with red bands around their caps could be seen delivering letters all about town or standing outside Moscow's best stores, taking parcels from fine ladies and delivering them to their homes. I was most proud of them and hoped so dearly for their bright futures. We taught them how to read and kept close attention to their development so as not to lose their souls.

In short, we grew tremendously, our operating theater became known as the best in the city, and every day my community was full of useful activity. I was determined that though I and my sisters had taken the veil, we would not be dead to the world, and in 1913 alone we saw almost 11,000 patients in our outpatient clinic, and more than 12,000 petitions came across my desk. I personally went over each and every petition, of course, and with my work at the hospital and elsewhere, not to mention prayers, I found not much time or need for sleep.

We had then at our hospital a most horridly burned cook, injured when an oil stove had spilt all over her. From head to foot nearly her entire body was covered with burns, and gangrene had set in by the time she reached us — that such a dire case was brought to us wasn't surprising since we were often given the most hopeless cases. I knew that there were those who quietly said it might be better if the poor suffering woman passed from this world, but my reply to that was, "God willing, she will not die here." So determined was I that I personally changed her bandages twice a day, which took well over two hours each time. Oh, the poor creature, she really was in such pain. The change of bandaging was hideously uncomfortable for her, and she cried out at the slightest touch, yet we dared not chloroform her, so close to death was she. Too, the stench of gangrene was unbearable for nearly all, so penetrating that after each session I had to remove my garments and have them aired.

I had just changed into fresh robes after one such session when Nun Varvara came to me, quietly saying, "Matushka, there is a woman from America to see you."

"Ah, yes, that would be Mrs. Dorr, the journalist."

"A woman working as a journalist?" asked Nun Varvara, unable to hide her surprise.

"Yes, and why not? She has written at length about woman's suffrage all across America and Europe, and she has come to tell me about some model education plan in the American city of Gary."

"I see. And how is our patient, the cook?"

"She suffers greatly, but I sense improvement already. Mark my words, we will be singing a Te Deum to her within a month's time."

"Slava bogu." Thanks to God, said Nun Varvara, crossing herself.

A few minutes later I went to my parlor and found a woman standing there. Her dress was pale blue and her hair brown, and one couldn't help sensing her determined but pleasant air. Admiring a bunch of my favorite flowers, white lilies, which were arranged in a vase, she stood near my desk, which was piled with papers.

Entering the bright room, in English I said, "I am so happy to find that I have time to meet you today, Mrs. Dorr."

"Your Highness speaks English?" said the woman, turning to me, her eyes wide with astonishment. "I thought we might be conducting the interview in French."

"Well, my mother was English, after all."

"Forgive me, I had forgotten."

Motioning her to sit, I added, "I welcome any opportunity to speak English, because if one is wholly Russian, as I am, and especially if one is Orthodox, one hears hardly anything except Russian or French. When I was a child I always spoke English to my mother, and German to my father, such were the ways of our household." My furniture of English willow creaked loudly as we sat down, and I asked, "Tell me, what do you think of my convent?"

"It's beautiful — the vines on the walls, the verbena along the paths. It's all so warm and welcoming that I feel as if I've stepped back into the romantic thirteenth century."

"That is just what I wanted my convent to be, one of those busy, useful medieval types. Such convents were wonderfully efficient aids to civilization in the Middle Ages, and I don't think they should have been allowed to disappear. Russia needs them, certainly now more than ever — yes, we need the kind of convent that fills the space between the austere, enclosed orders and the life of the outside world. Here in my community we make a point of trying to understand what is happening around us. My sisters read the newspapers, we keep track of events, and we receive and consult with people in active life. We are Marys, but we are Marthas as well, and we are most hopeful of building up a strong, new Russia."

Mrs. Dorr took out a small notebook and wrote something down, and said, "Well, things are looking quite well in your country. Of course, the entire world knows of your riotous and bloody events of a few years ago, and, quite frankly, I wasn't sure what to expect when I arrived last week."

"As one of our noted politicians recently said, just ten more years of steady, hard work and Russia will be saved. You see, the Russian people are good and kind at heart, but they are mostly children — big, ignorant, impulsive children. If only they would realize they must obey their leaders — only then will we emerge into a wonderful nation. Everyone is trying so hard, and I pray daily for the Emperor." The bells of our church chimed the hour softly, and I paused to cross myself. "Now tell me about those wonderful public schools of yours — I hear there is quite a model system being established in your city of Gary."

"Yes, in Gary, Indiana, actually. What has begun there is something called the Gary Plan, or platoon schools, which is a system of dividing schools into separate platoons, so to speak, for more efficient use."

The American plan for education was all most interesting, and for nearly three quarters of an hour I listened as this very able woman explained the plan for improving the lot of each and every child via stimulating education. The standard curriculums were being expanded upon, explained Mrs. Dorr, and schooling during the summer months had even been added. Most interestingly and strangely, educational services were even being made available to the adult worker, which I had never heard of before. As I listened I couldn't help admiring what the Americans were doing — making education more natural and based upon the child, and more democratic too. Mrs. Dorr told me it was an exceedingly expensive program, but it had proved so popular that it was being accepted as far away as New York.

"America is simply stupendous," I finally exclaimed. "How I regret that I never went there. Of course, I never shall now. But, to be perfectly frank, to me the United States stands for order and efficiency of the best kind, the kind of order only a free people can create, the kind I pray may be built someday here in Russia. Truly, it is wonderful, and I can scarcely help envying you sinfully."

"May I quote you, Your Highness?"

"Yes, by all means. Think of America — a great, young, hurrying nation that can still find time to study all these frightful problems of poverty and disease, and to grapple with them as well. I hope you will go on doing that, and still find more and more ways of helping children, you must never let go of that. Too, I am entranced by the way you are trying to bring education and beauty into the lives of your workers. After all, how can you expect workmen to have beauty in their souls if they toil all day in hot, hideous factories or on remote farms? The poverty of our peasants and the poor working conditions of our workers are for us a great, great problem that we must quickly resolve."

We talked more about the Gary schools, which I was eager to see here in Russia, and about American women and their welfare work, especially for the tubercular and anemic. It was my belief, I remarked to my

269

visitor, that if a country were to thrive, women would have to play a role equally important and equally prominent as that of men. I'd always had a special devotion to Jeanne d'Arc, I explained, and believed she had been inspired by God, just as so many other women had been called by God to do great things.

"In America," said Mrs. Dorr, "we would say you are a good feminist — and to me that is the greatest compliment. I can't tell you how much I admire your convent for its beauty and even more for the ease with which you are reaching out to those in need. Everyone seems so happy and content here."

"I'm so glad that you like my little *obitel*," I said as I rose to my feet. "Please come again and see all that I hope to accomplish in the years ahead. We have great plans to help a great many."

"Thank you, Your Highness, I would love to return. Your convent is one of the brightest stars in the new Russia, and one that it can least afford to lose. I wish you all the best success."

Yes, all that my lovely adopted homeland needed was a few more years of peace and hard work. We were so close. Our industries were flourishing, our scientists had become known throughout the world, and our crops were so bountiful that we had left our famine years behind and become Europe's breadbasket. Indeed, we were such a rich country, wealthy in oil and gold and diamonds, and finally we were on the verge of being able to exploit all of this for the good of the entire Motherland. Even our writers and painters and musicians — such as Tolstoy and Dostoyevsky, Repin and Kandinsky, Chaikovsky and Rachmaninoff — were becoming known around the world. If only we could keep moving forward, not leaving the poor behind but embracing them and bringing them along and raising them up.

Perhaps we didn't even need ten years, perhaps only another five. In any case, we were never to find out because the peace and harmony that we so desperately needed was shattered by the outbreak in August, 1914, of that hideous war: the Great War. Within so short a time millions of our people were killed as war engulfed the whole of my beloved country, gushing over all like a waterfall of flame and leaving everyone, victor and vanquished alike, horribly maimed.

CHAPTER 32
PAVEL

When the war broke out, well, that was when I thought the Revolution was absolutely lost forever and ever. On all the streets there were crowds waving flags and singing "God Save the Tsar!" and everywhere there was this joy, this sense of pride and love for the Motherland. I couldn't believe it, couldn't believe that the oppressed would feel such passion for the Tsar and his lying ministers who had done nothing but walk all over them for centuries and centuries. Why, even the lowliest of workers were tripping over themselves as they rushed to enlist in the Tsar's army. How was this possible? How could they not see what my Bolshevik leaders did, that this stupid business was simply a war of kings and empires, namely German, English, Austrian, and Russian? Sure, it was nothing but a stupid imperialistic affair spurred on by the capitalist warmongers who would make big profits from the sale of guns. And who was going to do the actual fighting? The nobles themselves, those princes and counts who for centuries had bought and sold us pathetic serfs? The rich factory owners who would grow fat and rich from the sale of their guns and bullets? Absolutely not! No, it was the poor and downtrodden who would be out there on the front lines, massacred one after another, their bodies crushed into the mud.

The last of my leaders were so discouraged that they had all left by the time war broke out. They said that new guy, Lenin, was in Switzerland and that that writer, the famous one, Gorky, was off sunning himself in Italy. But not me. I had nowhere to go, no one to see, so I just disappeared into my own country, sleeping in haystacks or train stations, stealing food from here, there, and what did I do when I needed a ruble or two? Why, that was easy, I just robbed someone, the old babushkas were the easiest, the donation pots in the churches a cinch, too. Actually, I never went hungry because fortunately it was a great sin to refuse bread to a beggar. And I begged a lot.

Oddly, one fall day in 1915 I found myself outside her white walls.

I didn't know quite why I decided to walk halfway across the city, let alone how I had got back to Moscow in the first place, but suddenly there I was, staring at the thick vines creeping up the walls of the Marfo-Marinski Obitel. Yes, just standing there, my belly empty, admiring how the leaves on the vines were so yellow and orange and red. So pretty. But sure, these colors meant it would be winter before too long, and I wondered if maybe the sisters would feed me here today, or at least offer me a cup of tea with nice sugar. That was what I really wanted, hot tea and a sugar cube I could hold in my teeth as I drank.

I certainly never expected to see her, but I had been skulking about outside the women's monastery for, who knew, an hour, maybe more, when not the large carriage gates but the small brown side gate suddenly swung open. First came two sisters dressed in long gray habits, which was strange to me because I had never seen anything like this, a sister dressed in anything but either all black for regular days or all white for feast days. And yet here were these freshly scrubbed girls in something so different, so modern — imagine, gray robes! — and with white cloth around their pink, healthy, and plump faces. Even that was strange, for all the other sisters I had ever seen were all pasty and pale, as if they barely ate and never saw the sun. But not these two! Accompanying them, hanging on to their arms, actually, were two men with bandages over their eyes. I knew the story of these men immediately, as did anyone from the country — these two had been soldiers fighting in the dirty war and their eyes had been burned away by gases in the trenches. They were everywhere in the country now, thousands of blind men like them, and I watched as the two young sisters escorted these men along, either getting them out for fresh air and a stroll or, perhaps, teaching them how to get about town with no eyes.

And then to my astonishment Matushka herself came through the small gate as well.

I couldn't see her face at first, but of course it was her, my heart knew it immediately, for even though she too was draped in long gray robes, the figure was as tall and elegant as a real *dama.* Sure, and a moment later she turned slightly and I saw the lovely face that I had glimpsed only once but would recognize anywhere, for I had seen it time and again in my dreams. Like the young sisters, she wore not a scrap of black, which was so strange. She was carrying a basket, too, and just as she pulled shut the gate a slight wind came up, catching her garments, and even I was touched, really it was beautiful, this vision of her, so light in such dark times. Somehow she was set apart, so different, but then again, that was the way she had been when I'd seen her sitting in that carriage all dressed up in her fine clothes and all those expensive stones. Yes, though her clothing was now completely different, clearly marking her as a bride of Christ, there was something that was absolutely the same about her. Perhaps it was those eyes, so soft, so sensitive and kind, and I remembered that night when she had looked out the carriage window right at me, how her gaze had disarmed me, and how in that way she had saved her life and those of the two children as well. Again today she glanced my way, and again I lost my breath, stunned by something, I really didn't know what. She seemed to smile at me, but no, it wasn't at all possible that she remembered me from the night when our fates had passed each other like desperate boats in a violent storm.

People up and down the street, upon recognizing the Grand Duchess, stopped and bowed and crossed themselves.

"Good morning, Matushka!" cried two or three of them almost in unison.

"God bless you and your work, Matushka!" hollered a man, a knife sharpener who'd set up his grinding wheel on the corner.

"Thank you, Matushka!" called an old woman, bowing at the waist as she marked her forehead, stomach, right shoulder, left. "My son lives because of you!"

There was only one comrade, a one-legged man balancing on cracked crutches, who looked at this royal abbess as if she were nothing but a dog. He was leaning against a tree just a few paces from me, and he turned his dirty, worn face to me.

"You know, don't you, that that bitch of a woman and her sister are nothing but dirty German whores?"

I quietly replied, "So I've heard."

"It's true, I tell you, and it's only because of them that we're losing the war!"

Obviously he'd been a soldier, and nodding toward his missing leg, I asked, "When?"

"Last winter." He shrugged, and added, "I suppose I'm one of the lucky ones — I was wounded, they pulled me back from the front, and a week later all my comrades were wiped out, every last one of them. I should be dead like the rest of 'em, but instead I'm just a gimp."

I should have said something, like maybe

talked about the Organization and the need for revolution. I should have grumbled about the bourgeoisie, about exploitation of the lower classes, or, really, about any of the things I had been taught. I'm sure the soldier would have listened eagerly, but I couldn't take my eyes off the beauty in robes, the wind and the light curling around her as she stood there across the street. In reply to all her well-wishers, she simply and meekly bowed her head in thanks and hurried on, quite alone, basket in one hand while with the other she pulled her robe close to her face as if hiding herself, as if the last thing she wanted was to be recognized.

I didn't know why, but as soon as she started off I knew that I would follow her. I mumbled something to the one-legged comrade and then hurried along until I was some twenty or thirty paces behind her. All these questions were tripping through my mind. Where was she going, what was she doing, and, most important, was there food there in that basket that I might take from her? Or was it money, eh? After all, she was heading north on Bolshaya Ordinka, so perhaps she was headed straight toward the Kremlin, perhaps she had taken a basket of money from her church and was giving it over to the ministers. Yes, that was likely, and it occurred to me then that I could kill her now, thereby finishing the job I'd neglected so long ago. I could jump on her and beat her and make myself rich at the same time, too.

But then she veered off the wide cobbled street, soon crossing Solyanka Street and weaving her way through a maze of lost alleys, ducking through one archway, past the falling-down house of a half-ruined noble, and eventually emerging onto another street. She continued up this way and then cut to a boulevard. What was this all about? By then I could tell she was not hurrying toward the Kremlin, so what in the name of the devil was this holy princess doing? Where was she headed, this sly cat? Perhaps instead of taking money to the Kremlin she was delivering a basketful of rubles to German spies. Now, I thought, wouldn't that be wonderful if the stories passing from tongue to tongue were really true! And how great it would be if I caught her in the act, right in the middle of a secret meeting! Ha, I could report it and maybe then the people would get so mad that finally and at long last they would rise up!

Trailing her, I couldn't stop, didn't dare.

She had remarkable energy, that one, for

she was moving so quickly that I had to trot along to keep up with her. She was all business, and yet people smiled and nodded at her as they passed, perhaps not recognizing how high and mighty she really was, only seeing the strange light robes and knowing that she was from there, that community that had become so well known and, too, so well loved throughout Moscow. Pure and simple, she was a vision of Godliness to all who laid eyes upon her, that much I could tell. Or perhaps she was just a simple reminder that some still believed with all their hearts in a better world. And yet still I couldn't tell what she was doing, just where she was going in such a rush.

I wondered of course if she had some kind of business in Kitai Gorod, the Chinese town, but after we crossed a *kanal* and turned to the right, it was clear she wasn't going that far. No, we were descending into the lowlands in and around the Yauza River. And from the mist in the air and the stench that soon filled my nose, I understood that this stupid, foolish woman was heading straight into the Khitrovka, the famous slums of Moscow, which sprawled around a dangerous market selling rotten food and stolen goods, not to mention young girls, even young boys. *Bozhe moi,* my God, this was the most hellish corner of the country, and even I wanted to run up and tell her, No, stop, it's too dangerous! Don't go in! Word was that ten or twenty thousand pathetic souls lived in this Godforsaken area, a collection of thieves and robbers, beggars and murderers. If anyone escaped the labor camps of Siberia, they didn't stay out in the forests. No, they snuck all the way back here, because both the police and the soldiers were too afraid to go into the depths of the Khitrovka and flush them out. Even my revolutionary pals told me that if I was ever found out, if I was ever chased, this was where I should run, straight into these slums. Of course, the lowlifes in and about might cut my throat for a ruble or plunge a knife in my back for pleasure, but at least the police wouldn't catch me, oh, no!

But the nastiness of the Khitrovka seemed not to faze her in the least. In fact, the misery ahead seemed to draw her, and this sister of the Empress, this princess who had once danced the mazurka on the finest parquet floors in the greatest palaces, this greatest of European beauties, stepped through an open sewer along which slowly ran human waste of the nastiest sort. When she came to the corner of a crumbling building, she turned left, obviously certain of where she was going. Wasting no time, I hurried along, turned the corner, and nearly ran into her and three big, thick policemen, for there she stood, this woman in robes, talking to the giant men.

"Please, Matushka," said one of the uniformed ones, "in a block or so you'll enter the heart of the Khitrovka, and this is as far as the three of us dare go. We ask you again and again, please, no farther! If something happens in the streets ahead, we will not be able to go in to help you."

"My dear men, you are always too kind to me and I so appreciate your good thoughts," she replied in the gentlest of voices. "But, once again, I am needed in these parts."

"Yes, but —" began another constable.

"Please, my boy, do not worry. My life is in God's hands, not yours."

With a kind wave and smile, she pressed on, going where certainly no princess had ever gone, deep into the filthy Khitrovka. I myself thought of turning back, but curiosity had hooked me, and I tailed her into a dark alley where the sun was all but blotted out. I couldn't help wondering, if those policemen back there on the edge of the Khitrovka knew her by sight, just how often did she come here and what in the name of the devil was her business? Might it not be with spies and Germans?

As I traipsed after her, nearly losing her from sight, I heard screaming, then breaking glass. From another direction came drunken laughter and crying children. As I passed a *traktir* — the cheapest of taverns — its doors were shoved open by two men, laughing and stumbling, and a stinky cloud of stale beer and boiling cabbage overwhelmed me. A few steps later I came to a man slumped against a building, lying in a puddle of his own vomit. All this I saw, and a woman with a painted face who stood in a doorway marked with the required red lamp. When I glanced at her she pulled open the top of her dress and showed me her huge naked breasts.

"Right this way, handsome," she called, licking her lips.

I looked away. This place was nothing but a pile of roaches feasting on one another, and like an insect myself I scurried on. Rounding a corner after the princess nun, I watched as she proceeded down a lane of disgusting shops, this one selling something that was supposed to be sausages, another grimy bread, and there, a guy chopping chickens on a huge stump and throwing the carcasses on the floor. Next I saw a handful of tailors working frantically away as they transformed stolen fur capes and coats into unrecognizable hats and muffs. Up and down the passage were gathered clumps of men, too, and great wafts of smoke from *papirosi* — the cheapest cigarettes — curled into the dark air, mingling with the scent of sour sunflower oil that came from every kitchen. Time and time again they greeted this lowly Romanov not with a sneer or snarl or the least bit of coarseness — let alone a threat of any kind — but with a simple and polite nod of the head.

"Good afternoon, Matushka," these forsaken souls called one after another.

A row of five fat, toothless babushki sat upon huge iron pots of *lapshi,* and though the old women didn't rise — their one and only job was to sit tight on the pots so that their big thighs and thick skirts would keep the pots of noodles warm — all of them bowed their heads to the princess nun and crossed themselves. When I passed by, however, the women and every questionable guy about gazed at me the way a starving man stares at a hen. I pulled up my collar and wrapped my arms around myself, and probably the only reason they left me alone was how ragged I looked — it was obvious to anyone that I had nothing to offer, not even a dirty kopeck to my name.

Up ahead I suddenly saw a boy appear out of nowhere, a filthy street urchin covered from head to toe in grime. The princess stopped and greeted him, they exchanged a few words, and the boy pointed in one particular direction. The little one then reached up with his dirty paw, and she, not hesitating in the least, reached out with her clean white hand and took it. Obviously nervous and scared, the boy quickly led her off through a series of small streets that got narrower and dirtier with each step. I pushed on, for neither of them suspected that someone, namely me, was following.

A few minutes later the boy and the nun came to a crumbling grayish stone house and disappeared inside. When I approached the building, I saw the name "Petrov" written in faded, peeling paint, and guessed that this place was like the one where me and my wife had lived, and entering I found out, sure, I was correct. This Mr. Petrov, who owned the building, rented out small corners, measured perhaps by the *arzhin* — the length of an arm or two — to the poorest sorts. Coming to one grimy curtain, I slowly pulled it back, seeing nothing and no one, only a couple of wooden bunks and some torn clothes. Drawn by voices, I moved on past the stairs and in a nook found myself staring at three men who, like me, looked as if they hadn't been to the *banya* in months. Gathered around a wooden crate, they were munching on sunflower seeds, and scattered around them on the floor lay what looked like a rug of dead beetles but was actually a carpet of husks. There were cards strewn in front of them, and off to the side was a jug of cloudy vodka. They stared up at me like wild dogs ready to pounce, and one of them reached down for a knife sticking out of his boot.

"Well, what of it?" demanded one, tugging on his long, tangled beard.

The words simply fell out of my mouth. "Did you see a sister in gray robes? Did she —"

"Back there," said another man, motioning the direction with his chin. "She went to take care of the whore Luska."

With a nod of my head, I quickly moved on, weaving between tattered curtains that divided one small room from another. It was then that I sensed it, heard it — soft but pained crying, a mourning that came from deep within someone's soul. Following the sound the way a hunter follows the moon, I soon came to the rear of the Petrov slum house, where one of the tattered

286

curtains glowed with the soft light of a kerosene lamp. Besides the soft crying, I now heard another voice furiously chanting.

"Lord Jesus Christ, Son of God, please have mercy . . ." repeated Matushka over and over.

As quietly as I could I edged forward, sensing beyond the curtain not just one but two figures huddled around something, a bed perhaps.

"I begged Ludmilla not to do it!" sobbed a woman, referring to the whore Luska by her full and respectful name. "I begged her to just go ahead. And she promised . . . she promised . . . !"

"You did all you could, my child."

"But she said she wouldn't and then . . . then she came back right here and did it herself . . . oi, *bozhe moi!* She was just so afraid . . . afraid that if she looked pregnant the men would turn away . . . and . . . and afraid to bring a new life into this disgusting place!"

"Even if I'd gotten here sooner, I wouldn't have been able to help her. She lost so much blood so quickly."

As quietly as I could, I inched my way around, searching for a crack in the curtains, when all of a sudden — *Gospodi!* — something reached out and grabbed me by the arm. I nearly shouted out, nearly jumped right out of my skin! Looking over, I saw not a thug about to slit my throat but a smiling brat — that kid, the filthy one. Grinning, he put a finger to his lips and then tugged me the other way. I shuffled to the side, and then the urchin pointed to a hole in the curtain. Understanding, I bent over and peered into a makeshift room, and there, sure enough, was that Romanov as well as another, a woman with loose clothing and wild hair. A prostitute, it was obvious. The two of them, the sister in robes and the sister of the night, stood on either side of a plank bed, and all I could see on the bed between them was a pair of legs spread wide, the feet turned out. Clearly, someone was dead. It was only when the Romanov sister bent to the side, reaching for her basket, that I got a clear view of the bed and nearly threw up. Lying there was a naked woman, most definitely dead, the black hair between her legs absolutely soaked with the darkest blood I had ever seen. Her thighs, a yellowed sheet, and everything else were covered with this blood, too, and, worse, lying between her legs was a still bloody lump of something. What in the name of the devil had come out of her womanly parts? What had she cut away? A growth of some sort? Some kind of tumor? But no . . . dear God, no. In horror, I watched as this so-called Matushka leaned over, a clean white towel in hand, and carefully picked up the lifeless form, wrapping it gently in the folds. And it was then that I saw the smallest arm drop out of that lump.

"It's a beautiful little girl, and she's merely crossed over to a better world," said the Romanov in the kindest of voices. "And now she will rest for eternity in the arms of God."

The other prostitute, the living one, had turned away now, sobbing uncontrollably as the sister tenderly wrapped the towel around the aborted child. The Romanov mumbled a soft prayer over the small body and then lowered it into the willow basket and slowly drew the lid.

"Now, young woman," said the sister to the prostitute, "you must get me some more clean towels. Oh, and a sheet or two as well. I will need some help cleaning the body, for with your permission I would like to take both mother and daughter back to my *obitel* for Psalter and a proper Christian burial."

"Yes . . . please . . . take her far away from this place . . . !"

As the prostitute rose to her feet, I turned away, stumbling backward. I wanted to run straight from that rat hole of a building, to run far away. Instead I managed just a few steps, where I yanked back a half-torn curtain and slumped into another little corner and dropped down onto a bed of planks. Some lazy slob was asleep on the top bunk, and I lowered myself onto the lower one. Bent over, my head in my hands, I stared at the floor, not moving for the next hour, maybe more. All the time I was aware but wasn't aware of the two women working away, washing the body and then wrapping it, too, in a sheet or something, perhaps just another torn curtain. I heard the sound of rags being wrung, lots of drops falling into a pan of water. And the soft chanting of hymns being sung as well.

Sometime later, I heard Matushka say, "I'll take the infant in the basket with me now, and I'll pay the men out front, the ones who were playing cards, to bring the body. Now, young woman, what about you? What can I do for you?"

The prostitute mumbled, "Nothing . . . nothing at all."

"Will you come to services for your friend Ludmilla?"

"Well . . ."

"Yes, please come tonight to my *obitel* on Bolshaya Ordinka. And after you've prayed for Ludmilla, let's have a talk. Perhaps I can rent a sewing machine for you — the efficient kind with a foot pump. I've done this for others, and they've set themselves up in business. Perhaps that would be of interest, or perhaps one of the classes that we've just started for adult workers. Do you know how to read?"

"But, Matushka, I'm not worthy of such kindness. I'm just a woman of the night and . . . and I'm not good enough for . . . for . . ."

"Nonsense. God's image may become unclear, but, my child, it can never be entirely wiped away. Please, just come see me." The princess nun then said, "As for the young boy who led me here, to whom does he belong?"

"Little Arkasha? He belongs to everyone . . . and yet, as far as I know, to no one."

"Just as I feared. Hopefully he's still waiting somewhere for me."

Listening through the curtains, I heard the creaking of the willow basket, the swoosh of long clothing, and then gentle steps. Moving on the other side of the curtains, I saw her, too, or rather the essence of her, for as the Romanov nun moved along, the tattered fabric walls of all the corner rooms swirled and swayed as if a spirit from another world were passing. A moment later, another set of steps moved quickly after her.

"Matushka, wait!" called the young woman.

She stopped right in front of the corner where I sat, only an old piece of hanging material separating us, and said, "Yes, what is it, my child?"

"I just wanted to tell you not to pay the men out front until they get there — you know, until they bring Ludmilla all the way to you. Otherwise, they'll just take your money and do nothing."

"Oh, I'm not worried about that," she said with a soft laugh. "Do not fear, they'll not fail me."

And in this Matushka was absolutely right. Without a moment of hesitation, she went right up to the three card players and paid them generously in advance to carry the body of the dead whore up to her *obitel.* She then proceeded onto the street, looked for and found the urchin Arkasha, and when I peered out the door of the Petrov slum the last I saw of this Romanov was her flowing gray robe as she walked away, carrying the basket with the swaddled dead baby in one hand and, with the other, holding on to the boy's dirty paw.

Not bad, I thought, for while that day this

Matushka had fished two dead souls out of the Khitrovka, that of Luska and her stillborn child, this strange sister had also managed to take with her a live fledgling, young Arkasha. She led him straight out of this hellhole and to her home for beggar boys, perhaps saving his life. And as for the drunken card players — such unruly comrades — they didn't disappoint Matushka, either, for not even thirty minutes later they gathered up the dead whore Luska and carted her off on their shoulders, delivering her, just as promised and paid for, to the Marfo-Marinski Obitel.

All this I know because I helped too. At first the card players wouldn't let me, all three shouted *"Nyet!"* and told me to be off. But I told them I didn't want any of their money, and though at first they grumped and threatened me, in time they let me lend a hand. Holding Luska by her right leg, I helped the three comrades carry the corpse away from that pathetic house and all the way up the Bolshaya Ordinka and eventually right through the brown wooden gate of the *obitel.*

And though I didn't take a kopeck for my work, in the end, after we delivered the body behind the white walls and into the chapel, I did get paid, though not in rubles. Upon the orders of Matushka herself, the young novices of the monastery led us into the dining hall and fed us all a large hot bowl of meat borscht with some fresh black bread and heaps of butter, plus two cups of good, strong caravan tea. They even gave me two cubes of sugar, and sitting there like a squirrel getting ready for winter, I drank my tea with one cube of sugar packed into each of my cheeks.

It was a heavenly moment shattered by something quite like a bolt of lightning.

"Do I by chance know you?" asked a voice. "Have I seen you somewhere before?"

I turned sideways and looked up. None other than Matushka herself was staring down upon me, her beautiful face, framed by the wimple of her order, more than just puzzled. On her lips rested a smile as fragile as a fine teacup, while in her eyes I could clearly see some kind of demon — either that of pain or dark anger, just which I couldn't tell.

Panicking, I didn't know what to say, but in the end I did what Russian peasants have always been so good at, and I shook my head, and muttered, *"Nyet, nyet."*

But she didn't believe me, I understood that by the way she continued to stare harshly upon me. I could almost hear her thinking: Who is this man, what kind of prickly thorn has he been in my path of life?

"Well," she said, "enjoy your tea . . . and come back to see us again."

But she wasn't as good at lying as me, her voice was just too flat and her eyes too tight.

CHAPTER 33
ELLA

Our initial, glorious victories were, so tragically, only short-lived, and what we all expected to be a short war soon appeared otherwise. Our Second Army was all but wiped out in the Battle of Tannenberg — 100,000 taken prisoner, 35,000 killed or maimed, with only 10,000 escaping — and it was even worse for the First. Lord, I think 125,000 of our men were slaughtered out there in Prussia. Really, we could not continue for long with losses like that, so it was no wonder that I heard grumblings when I walked beyond our walls. Less and less I was greeted with smiles and more and more with wicked words, for the poor, tired souls were angry at everything German, including me simply because of my ancestry.

"Hessian witch!" the nasty few would mutter behind my back, though in truth it did not hurt.

As incredible and ridiculous as it seemed

even then, there were rumors about that I was sending gold to my native lands — yes, supposedly I was hoarding Siberian gold right there at my *obitel* and sending it by the nugget via secret courier to Germany to help in the war efforts against my beloved Russia! What tittle-tattle, what evil tongues! What no one knew was my intense dislike of the Prussians, who'd all but overrun my native Darmstadt, or, for that matter, that I'd never been fond of my own cousin, the Kaiser Wilhelm, who had once so strongly sought my hand in marriage. And these dark stories weren't just the work of German spies, who were so intent on damaging the morale on the home front. Incredibly, it was also the work of those foolish revolutionaries, who came secretly flooding back into Russia, intent on undermining dear Nicky and Alicky, revolutionaries who were more determined than ever to wipe away our God-given monarchy. Black rumors swelled like great waves, passing from one tongue to the next, one claiming that Nicky was being drugged by Alicky, another that Alicky had a direct telegraph line from her boudoir all the way to Cousin Willy in Berlin. Of course, the worst of the worst was being said in and about that foolish man, Rasputin, who had become such a stain on the Throne. For the life of me I could not understand Alicky's dependence on him, and I prayed night and day for her deliverance from him.

Sadly, all these untrue stories worked like dark magic. Our people were hungry, our people were tired, and unrest amongst all the classes was frothed up as easily as a pair of eggs. Just several weeks earlier an anti-German riot had erupted in Moscow with German homes and shops looted and destroyed. Even the police did not bother to interfere.

Of course, none of this was helped by a matter that did worry me — that our military hospitals were not being filled up by our own Russian wounded but by prisoners, both German and Austrian. Muscovites didn't like that at all, even though the military hospitals were far less comfortable than the Red Cross or private ones. Nevertheless, the tongues said I only looked after Germans and even took them endless sweets and rubles. Such untruths. Yes, I did visit the wounded prisoners, for a soul is a soul no matter from what country, but I did no more than pray for them. Unfortunately, all this dark talk was put on my back even though I, perhaps more Russian than many Russians, cared so deeply for the men of my new homeland. To make absolutely sure there was no preferential treatment, however, I stopped my visits to the prisoners altogether and had a ladies' committee, with my *Grande Maîtresse* Countess Olsuvieva at the head, look into this matter.

But what should have been a great warning of the darkness to come was the incident that took place upon my return from Petrograd — yes, not long after the outbreak of war even our capital had been renamed, for to the Russian ear "Sankt Peterburg" sounded harshly German and hence unpleasant, and so it, too, was dashed. I had been there in the capital for the state funeral in 1915 of Grand Duke Konstantin Konstantinovich — soon after the battlefield death of one of his beloved sons, my dear Kostya had suffered a fatal *infarkt* — and upon my arrival home in Moscow everything at first seemed normal. At the Nikolaevski Station I descended my private railcar without incident and moved freely along the platform, perceiving no problem whatsoever. Unlike my previous days, I was traveling without a suite of any sort — neither court ladies nor guards of any sort — and while there were certainly many eyes upon me and I was, despite my robes, widely recognized, this was not unusual and

by no means threatening either. Really, hith-
ertofore in all my travels and ventures into
the bleakest, poorest corners of our vast
Empire, I had not once felt the least indica-
tion of malevolence directed upon my
person. However, no sooner had I passed
through the Imperial Waiting Rooms and
exited onto the broad, bustling street than
things began to disintegrate. A limousine
was waiting for me, and as the uniformed
driver helped me settle into the rear seat, a
most violent disruption broke about, initiated no doubt by a handful of unpatriotic
agitators.

"Look, it's the German bitch!" shouted
one man.

"It's a filthy Romanov traitor!" hollered
another.

"Get her! Down with her!"

It was shocking, really, how quickly they
swarmed around the motorcar, rather more
like a pack of wild dogs or mad beasts than
human beings. Wasting not a moment, my
chauffeur scurried quickly around and into
the vehicle, but no sooner had he shut the
door than fists began pounding the windows. In one moment there were ten men,
the next twenty, and then thirty.

"German bitch!" they cried one after another.

I clutched automatically at the cypress cross that I always wore around my neck, and I could hear my heart pounding, feel my thoughts dashing here and there. Good Lord, what was happening?

"I think it best if we move quickly on," I recommended to the chauffeur.

"Yes, but . . . but . . ." he said, motioning to the men now clambering over the hood of the vehicle.

"Just proceed," I said as calmly as I could. "Do not worry, we are in God's hands."

White with fear, he managed to start up the motor and engage the vehicle in gear. We had rolled not even a half pace when a man jumped right in front of the vehicle, his arms outstretched, his face red with rage. Immediately, my driver stomped on the brakes and the vehicle jerked to a standstill. The man blocking our way screamed something, foul words that I had never heard in Russian, and an even greater cry of anger flew through the crowd. All around, from every side, people charged closer, flaming me with fiery insults. Someone pounded on my window, and I saw a furious red-faced woman with a scarf tied around her head. My inclination was to smile gently upon her, but this woman sucked in her cheeks and with great force expelled a good quantity of saliva upon the glass. And then another man did likewise, spitting his hatred upon us. Another followed suit, and then another and another, until the windows and the windscreen were covered. The next instant, several large men took hold of the wheels and the entire limousine began to rock most violently up and down and side to side.

"Please . . . drive on . . . quickly now!" I requested, clutching the seat. "Quickly!"

"But, Your Highness, what if I hit someone?"

"God willing, they'll step aside!"

Despite all my good thoughts and all my good prayers, the fear came flooding into my heart like an evil river, rampaging and scouring my mind with doubt. How could this be? These were my children to whom I had given my entire soul and for whom I felt nothing but divine love. Where did such hatred come from? What sin had I committed to engender this rage?

I held tightly the cross upon my breast, firmly shut my eyes, and chanted, *"Gospodi pomilui . . ."* Lord have mercy . . .

No sooner had my driver pushed again on the accelerator and we began moving again, albeit ever so slowly, than something crashed against the side of the car with the most frightening sound. It sounded as if a bomb, and I screamed as I had not since childhood. All my fears whooshed back to that day when my Sergei was blown apart, and I was sure my end had now come as well. I struggled for my control, but found myself lost in that frightening memory when the center of Moscow rocked with my husband's death. But it was not a bomb hurled against my motorcar but a rock, a cobblestone, actually, pulled right from the street. There came another, and then one after that, all raining down upon my vehicle, simply pure thunder and storm. Suddenly a stone sailed directly through one of the side windows, glass exploded everywhere, and I screamed yet again, as did the driver, his voice high and terrified. Almost the next instant a huge stone came hurtling directly from the front, smashing the windscreen into a thousand shards, glass like needles tearing at my driver. From behind I heard someone pounding on the window behind my head, and I tensed and steeled myself as if I were to be shot. All around voices and the worst insults came at me like cannon fodder, wounding me not physically but heart and soul, which I felt far more deeply. To my side I saw a massive hairy hand reach for the door, and from the coarse rage I understood that the intention was to rip me from my vehicle so that the crowd could pull me apart upon the street.

And then came the soldiers on horseback with whips and sabers, and it was only in this manner that the incident was concluded as promptly as it had begun.

Yes, the soldiers beat away our attackers posthaste, and the hooligans fled, for even though the days of serfdom were fifty years past, the memory of the master's whip and knout was long and bitter throughout Russia. My driver sped hastily on, driving clumsily as he blotted the cuts on his forehead and cheeks. With tears in my eyes, I glanced back through the soiled rear window and saw a poor few continuing to fight, only to be beaten down and even trampled upon. I wanted to go back, to reach out to all of those poor souls and offer them solace, but my driver, wiping sweat and blood from his brow, sailed us through the heart of the city.

Lord . . .

By the time the motorcar reached my *obitel* and passed through the carriage gates, I had wiped away my tears. Word of the incident spread quickly, however, and some fifty sisters came scurrying out, the dear ones so concerned for my safety and shocked at the outbreak, and I did my best to calm them.

"Praise be to God for your safe return!" exclaimed my confessor, Father Mitrofan, the fear drawn all across his big face as he hurried out in his long black robes.

I did my best to hide away my shock and fear as I said, "Everything is perfectly fine."

"But . . . but look at the motorcar — the windscreen is smashed! And you, Matushka, you are so pale and . . . and . . . !"

"Let me repeat, I am fine," I said too sternly.

Father Mitrofan knew me far better, however, and he gently guided me along to my reception room.

"Please," he called to one of my novices, "bring us tea at once."

In the following days there was little I could do to control the story, and though the censors would not let it be printed in our papers, it flew all across Moscow — the Romanov nun attacked! — spreading like heathen fire. When word of concern came from the head constable of the city, I assured him that it had been only a scant few agitators and nothing serious. Indeed, many about the city were so shocked by the incident that they flooded my community with breads and vegetables, eggs and milk, as if to atone for some great sin. Wishing to quiet the worry, I forbade any and all of my sisters to speak of the matter — the sick and the wounded needed their attention, not stories of the doubters and faithless. Least of all did I want to worry Nicky and Alicky — the two were consumed by their war efforts — yet despite my best efforts an official report was made to the Emperor and his horror knew no end.

The only truly grievous result of the whole sad affair was that under Nicky's command the highest authorities and even the Metropolitan came to me and all but forbade my travels beyond my white walls, particularly and especially to such dangerous places as the Khitrovka. Deep into the night, I prayed on my knees for guidance, and though in the end I acquiesced and agreed to stay close to home — if my presence stirred up such unrest, perhaps it was indeed best I not go about and be seen — my soul ached with concern. Yes, lying at night on my plank bed, I couldn't help worrying. What of all the Ludmillas and the young Arkashas — if I were to remain essentially locked away, just who was going to reach out to them body and soul?

And though I essentially retired to my community, busying myself with prayers and care for the needy and war wounded, the world around me continued to deteriorate at an alarming pace. Under the strain of transporting all the troops, I heard of the railway system breaking down, with one muddle followed by another, and soon sugar was rationed. I was told, too, that the shelves grew emptier and emptier, not just of sugar but all foodstuffs, and one day another story came round that while the workers could barely get black bread, we at my *obitel* feasted on chicken cutlets and meat pies, not to mention fruit jams. It would have been an amusing story had I not clearly understood the danger in such lies, and all this while my diet consisted purely of vegetables, such as onions and turnips with an egg here or there and an occasional spot of milk. Sadly, too, out of the blue sky I received an anonymous letter telling me that my sister and I should return to Germany immediately because, after all, we were not Russian and our loyalties were nested firmly with the enemy. I paid it no attention, merely wished that my letter writer would come pray by my side.

With some degree of secrecy I did manage another trip to the capital and there to see my sister at Tsarskoye. There were many who had begged me to influence Alicky, who, with Nicky off at the front, ruled as essentially regent of the Empire. Her authority was understood by everyone of every class, and abhorred, too, particularly with the black name of Rasputin mentioned round every tea table and in every queue. Instead, I navigated away from any controversial subject with Alicky, and but for a few days we two sisters managed a good visit, cozy, calm, and homey. Her children, those four beautiful girls and the Heir Tsarevich, were such a delight to me, and for brief moments the horrors of war seemed distant. Despite the malicious tales otherwise, Alicky and I had always been and still were close.

Yes, I averted any difficult conversation with my sister, but upon my return to Moscow came another incident, more egregious than any other. It was said that our brother, Ernie, the Grand Duke of Hesse und bei Rhein, had been secretly sent to Russia by the Kaiser. Ernie was to negotiate some kind of shameful peace with Germany, and supposedly he'd been in hiding at the Palace in Tsarskoye. Simply preposterous. So said the tongues, however, claiming that such was the supposed reason for my recent visit to my sister. It was claimed that I, not any servant, cooked for him lest he be seen and recognized. Further, somehow disguised he was supposed to have got his way to Moscow, hiding in my railway carriage, and could now be found taking secret shelter in the depths of my *obitel*. At first I assumed this was the work of German spies, but it turned out the story was birthed quite effectively by our Russian revolutionaries. Clearly, their clever ploy was to use a deceitful story to knock away the God-given pedestal from which Nicky ruled.

It came as no surprise, then, that one morning I heard shouting and yelling from beyond the walls. I was in our hospital, attending to a serious wound on the groin of one of our soldiers, when my long-faithful Nun Varvara came running in.

"People are marching upon us, Matushka!" she gasped, unable to hide her fear. "There are men with sticks and rakes coming down the street — they're shouting the worst things!"

"My dear, I'm busy at the moment. And please keep your voice down — as you can see this man needs his rest."

"But, Matushka, I'm fearful for your safety!"

"Well, I am not. And besides, I am busy caring for this poor man. The bandages on his wound must be carefully changed."

"But what —"

"Just lock the gates, my child, and I'll be there as soon as I've finished. At the moment this man's health is more important than anything else."

Nun Varvara hurried off, and I returned to my duties of caring for the man before me. Wounded in battle, he had been brought back to Moscow and operated on in our theater just yesterday, the doctors having removed four small pieces of shrapnel. In great pain, the soldier had been slipping in and out of consciousness all morning.

As I removed the bandages and cleaned his groin with warm water, the man moaned and opened his eyes. I looked at him and smiled gently. His wound was serious, but if we kept it cleansed and covered I felt we could keep gangrene at bay.

"Who . . . who are you?" he asked, speaking for the first time.

I humbly replied, "I am your servant."

"Someone said you are a princess . . . but you are not Russian . . . I can tell by your accent. Are you a German princess? Am I in Berlin? Am I a prisoner?"

"No, my good man, you are in your Motherland. You are in Moscow. And as I've already told you, I am your servant."

From outside came shouting and yelling

and some kind of racket. Dear Lord in Heaven, were our gates being broken down?

"What's that?" said the soldier, struggling to sit up. "Are we under attack?"

I reached for some ointment and lint, and advised, "Please, just lie back down. There is nothing to be concerned about. We must attend to your wound, it must not be over-looked. Just relax."

Unfortunately, the mayhem outside seemed to grow by the moment, and quite clearly I heard someone shout, *"Nemka, doloi!"* — Away with the German woman! — but I turned my mind to all things spiritual. There was no reason to doubt, no reason to mistrust, I thought as I finished bandaging the poor man, for all was in God's hands. After all, not even a hair could fall from one's head without God's knowledge. And to calm my soldier I softly began to sing, *"Svyeta Tixhi"* — "Hail, Gentle Light." No more than ten or fifteen seconds passed, however, when I heard the disturbing sound of glass breaking.

"Will you excuse me?" I said to the soldier.

But the man had already drifted away, his eyes closed. Moving now with haste, I rinsed my hands and hurried to a small window. Peering out, I saw a mob of easily forty or fifty people, mostly men. They had breached our main gate and were flooding into the garden, rakes and thick sticks raised in their hands. Worse, they were charging after two of my youngest sisters, who were fleeing toward a side door. Right before my eyes I saw a cobblestone fly through the air, hitting one of the sisters on the back. She stumbled, the other girl took hold of her and dragged her on, and the pair frantically disappeared inside a doorway. Just as they pulled shut the door, another stone sailed after them, smashing against the wood. Then came another, and another, flying this way and that, and window after window was shattered to pieces.

"Radi boga," For the sake of the Lord, I muttered, quickly crossing myself.

Above the rabble, I heard a loud voice shout, *"Shpionka, suda!"* Bring out the spy!

"Nemka! Nemka!" The German woman, the German woman, the mob yelled nearly as one.

Without a moment's waste, I hurried off, lifting the front of my robes as I made my way from my patient's room and through a series of small corridors. I turned corner after corner, for our buildings were all linked by walkways, and when I reached the main doors of my own house I found not only a half dozen sisters frantically pushing against the door to hold it shut but Father Mitrofan throwing his weight against it as well. They had bolted the doors, of course, but the crowd outside was determined to batter their way in. Upon seeing me, Father Mitrofan and all my girls shouted their fear.

"Matushka, you must run away!" called Sister Mariya.

"They want to hurt you!" exclaimed the novice Makrina.

Even Father Mitrofan, usually so rational, frantically urged, "You must flee through the kitchens and out the back door!"

I slowed, gathering my thoughts and prayers. In all things there was wisdom, in all things there was His plan.

"Please, step aside and allow me to handle this," I said to my sisters. "One must be ready at any time to wear the martyr's crown of thorns."

At first they hesitated, but my young ones meekly obeyed, retreating as one into the next room. As the beating on the doors grew steadily rougher and harsher and the screaming beyond louder and coarser, I knew absolutely what I must do. I reached for the iron bolts and drew them open, and then I threw wide the double doors. A great cry went up from the mob, which seemed poised to run right over me, but then the advancing horde stopped, stunned by the sight of me standing there in my gray working robes.

"Welcome to my community," I said with a gentle bow of my head. "I am the Matushka of this *obitel* — is it to me you wish to speak?"

At first none knew what to say, how to act. There was some grumbling, some brandishing of the sticks.

Finally, one of them shouted, "We want your German brother, the Grand Duke of Hesse!"

"Give him to us!" yelled a handful of others.

"I, too, have heard such stories," I began, my voice strong and clear, "but I can assure you that my brother is nowhere to be found within this community. In fact, he is nowhere to be found in Russia."

"But he's hiding in the cellar, I know it!" called one.

"I'm afraid you are mistaken, for I would never permit such a thing," I replied. "It would be tantamount to treason."

"Nemka, doloi!"

"German bitch!"

"Shpionka, suda!"

"Listen to her speak — she's pure German!"

For half an instant it seemed they would rush forward and seize upon me, then ransack the entire community. I felt as if I were overlooking a kettle about to boil over, so evident was their anger and exhaustion.

"Once again," I began, my words measured, "I can assure you that my brother is not here, nor has he ever been. However, a handful of you are welcome to enter our buildings and look throughout every room. I only ask that it be no more than six of you who come in because behind these walls and under these roofs are many sick and wounded, not to mention our orphans. Please, I entreat you, do not disturb my patients and do not frighten the children, for they have already been through so much."

A voice from the back, certainly an agitator, shouted, "But I saw that German spy with my own eyes! I know he's in here!"

"He's hiding in the cellar!"

"There must be a secret room!"

"Please come in," I quickly replied, "and look for yourselves. If only you would be so kind as to put down your sticks and rakes, you may spend all afternoon with us, you may search everywhere. Only again I ask you, please do so quietly."

A man shouted, "She's lying!"

"Let's all go in, we'll get him then!"

"Nemka, doloi!"

The crowd seethed, there was obviously nothing I could do to soften them, to appease them. It was only at this moment, only just then, that I feared all would be lost, and I worried not for myself but for the others, my sisters and our sick ones. I could see these unruly brigands shift from side to side, see their sticks and rakes start to tremble. Standing there calmly, quietly, I called upon the Lord for strength.

And then I heard it, the pounding of hooves. This time it was not the Cossacks but mounted gendarmes, and they came pouring through our broken gates, fifteen, no, twenty of them. As the crowd of bandits turned to see what was bearing down upon them, I quickly shut and bolted the doors, and I stood there behind the thick wood, listening to the mayhem, the screams, the shouts, the sound of gunfire. I closed my eyes and slumped against the doors, praying that there would be no loss of life.

It was all over quickly. Not even ten minutes later, when all was essentially quiet, I opened the doors again. What had once been a tranquil garden was now a battlefield, our lilacs and laburnums broken and dashed, and everything else torn apart by

316

the fight. The sticks and rakes had been dropped helter-skelter, the rocks, too, as the people had fled, and all that was to be seen were some of the gendarmes arresting a few of the ringleaders and another handful of injured souls lying about.

"Quickly, sisters," I said, leading the way into the garden and to the wounded. "Our help is needed."

It was in this way that we tended to those who had meant us harm. There were many bruises, some broken bones, but fortunately there was no loss of life. While most of those hurt needed only some careful bandaging, there were four who remained in our hospital for more than a week, so serious were their injuries.

Later that day, I received a visit from the Metropolitan and the Governor-General himself, both of whom wanted to see what damages had been done and whether any of us had been harmed. I assured them that all were fine excepting Sister Evrosinia, the nun who had been hit on the back with the stone, for her bruise was so large that the doctors had ordered complete bed rest for a week. I felt no anger over the incident, only grief that my own people should feel that violence was their only avenue of hope. Yes, their poor lives were being stretched beyond limits — husbands off at war and being killed, impoverished wives at home trying to feed hungry mouths. How I longed to soothe their souls and fill their spirits right up with joy.

There were only two aftershocks from that day which weighed heavily upon my heart. First, the Metropolitan himself wondered if the times were so troubled that it might be best if I retired for a while to a distant monastery, perhaps even the one I'd visited not long ago up in the northern seas. I assured him, however, that my place was there in Moscow and that I would sooner die at my *obitel* than leave. Second, the Governor-General, realizing that I would not be leaving, ordered increased security be posted round our walls, which saddened me greatly, for not once had I ever wanted to be separated from the outer world and those in need.

Of greater concern, both of these men individually took me aside and pressed me on the same issue: Would I not, for the sake of the Empire and the Monarchy itself, please speak to both the Empress and the Emperor about the dark influence upon the Throne, namely, that man Rasputin?

CHAPTER 34
PAVEL

Who would have thought that in this cess-pool of wounded soldiers and overworked women the Revolution would be reborn! Who would have thought that the Russian peasants and workers, beaten down for so many centuries, would finally snap? In short, the more rotten the war made things for the people, the better things got for the Organization.

And so that became my job, to somehow make things as rotten, rotten, rotten as possible.

My revolutionary comrades fished me out of some pit, brought me back into the fold, and this became my job: gluing up posters. It didn't seem very important, but they assured me it was, and they even had a name for it: agitprop. And so they gave me a pot of glue and posters by the stack, and I put them up everywhere and by the thousands, too. Only I had to do it so I wouldn't be caught, because if I was that would be the end of me, a necktie from a lamppost!

In the following weeks I scurried around Moscow like a rat, fixing posters up on buildings, doors, walls, stairs. Usually the police ripped them down in a matter of hours, and then I had to just go round and round, fixing them up again. Sometimes I just dropped the posters on the street or left them on seats of the trams. But people saw them everywhere. Pictures of the Tsar and his religious popes riding on the backs of the toiling workers. Pictures of the capitalist pigs, all dressed up in expensive coats, licking the Tsar's feet. The laughing Tsar drinking champagne while he stood at a cannon using peasants as cannonballs to fire at the Germans.

"We must show the people that the Tsar sits atop them not as a god but as a man," explained one of my comrades, a smart fellow known only as Leon. "And that's what these posters do, they soil the image of the Emperor and bring him down from such a high level."

"Ah, so this is like flinging mud at him?" I laughed.

"Exactly."

"I like it!"

And so I flung a lot of crap, I did. I'd go

out at nine, maybe ten at night, my posters carefully hidden in a bag, and I glued them everywhere, tromping alley to alley, from the Khitrovka to the Arbat. Actually, I found the best places to leave them were the *traktiri* littered about the city, the dirty cafés of the proletariat that were packed with workers, everyone crammed along plank tables, drinking pitcher after pitcher of *kvass,* that beerlike brew made from moldy loaves of black bread.

One night I took my favorite poster, a real juicy picture, into one such *traktir,* The Seven Steps Down, with a low ceiling and a big hall, a place where coachmen usually gathered and where, late at night, there was cockfighting in a secret room. Though I wasn't a Believer, I stopped in front of the icon by the door, crossing myself just like everyone else. Every bench and table was filled, waiters in white blouses and baggy pants ran this way and that, and off in the corner an accordion player played while a Tsigane woman with a big shawl and shiny jewelry and gold teeth sang. Here they used to serve great big plates of greasy suckling pig, but no more. Meat just couldn't be found, it was getting scarcer by the day, and so it was just *kvass* and hard rolls, here and there some sausages that looked as if they'd been made from cat. There were maybe two hundred people in there, packed like sardines, mostly men with long beards and greasy hair, some loose women with flimsy skirts.

So what did I do? I got myself a tankard of drink and strolled around, smiling so innocently. And somehow I did it, I pulled my lovely pictures from under my coat and soon enough they were on a table, spilling onto the benches, and from the benches onto the floor. I acted as surprised as anyone.

"Ha!" I yelped with surprise. "Ha!"

A great roar of laughter went up and spread through the room when they saw the picture, my poster: the Empress-whore, bent over and getting fucked from behind by the monster Rasputin, with the Tsar, drunk or drugged, passed out in a barrel of money, his eyes crossed as if totally not caring about anything or anyone else, least of all us, his Russian people.

And the people loved it!

The poster was grabbed from hand to hand, ripped from one person to the next, until it reached every corner of the room. A drunk guy jumped up on a table and pulled some *prostitutka* up behind him. Taking a soup bowl, he crowned his curly blond girl queen of the hall.

"Oh, Mama Tsaritsa, I love your big German ass!" he proclaimed as he mounted his empress from behind and started to hump and hump.

Maybe two or three years before, well, this fellow would have been hauled away and beat up for such a thing, for making fun of our Empress. Either that or he would have been arrested by the police and given three. But now the whole room roared with laughter at the sight of our traitor Empress getting fucked by her secret lover, that mad beast Rasputin.

What *agitatsiya!* How good it worked! I laughed until there were tears in my eyes!

Chapter 35
Ella

In early December of 1916 I wrote to Nicky, begging an audience. He was to be in Tsarskoye for only a short while longer, and a reply came not from the Emperor but my sister, asking me to come at once. I departed the very next day. I kept hope that I would see the Emperor himself, but upon my arrival at the Palace, I found myself ushered directly into Alicky's boudoir. She was reclined there, dressed in a long white robe, a white shawl draped around her shoulders. Her hair was put up, but she wore no adornment excepting her wedding ring, and she looked exhausted and worn, so thin. For the first time I could easily see what more and more people had been telling me, that my baby sister, nine years my junior, now looked years older than I.

"Hello, my dear," she said in English, holding out her hand.

"Greetings."

As required by protocol, I curtseyed to my sister, the Empress, then kissed her hand, and only then was I able to embrace her as family. Before the war we had rarely spoken in our native language, and now of course not a word of German ever passed our lips. Had there been others in the room, we might have spoken Russian, but since it was just the two of us sisters we continued in English, the language of our mother and of course the language that Alicky spoke almost exclusively with her children and husband.

"How are things at your community?" asked Alicky.

"We are full and we are busy. With God's help I believe we are doing good work," I replied. "Among other things, I wanted to tell you that I've had reports that your four hospital trains seem to be running well."

"Thank God. There is so much suffering, so much that needs to be done. You know, of course, that I visit my hospitals here daily. Just yesterday I assisted in an amputation."

Yes, I knew that my sister, who had received her nursing certificate at the beginning of the war, was deeply involved in the day-to-day physical activities of her hospital. While some members of Court found it demeaning that the Empress should be

participating in the most gruesome opera-
tions — "Better," they said, "if Her Imperial Highness would visit all the hospitals,
her appearance granting hope to many
more" — I found it admirable that someone
so high should dare to reach so low.

I cast my eyes to the floor and softly said,
"I had hoped to see Nicky. Will he be join-
ing us?"

"I'm afraid not. He is in meetings with his
generals all day, for he is to leave tomorrow
for the Front."

"I see."

I tried my best not to hide my disappointment. Not a soul knew better than I that
my sister's health, and to a great degree her
reasoning, had been damaged by worry for
her son, who had nearly died any number
of times. Because of this Nicky was more
balanced in his approach to things, and so I
had hoped to talk with him and him alone,
for I wanted to implore him to see what was
happening around us, and to tell him what
so many important personages of the Empire had begged me to relay. Quite specifically, Nicky needed to allow the Duma to
appoint his ministers, for as it was now Alicky was essentially making these decisions,
and not just of her own accord but under
the strong influence of that man. Yes, every-

one in the Empire was fully aware that you could not rise to power without the blessing of Rasputin, and that man's wisdom on political matters was woeful at best. It was making the entire country crazy — so many screaming, Imagine, a peasant running the country! — and with all that in mind I had come, at the very least, to beg my brother-in-law to banish the man once and for all and for good to Siberia. Best would be if Nicky allowed the Duma itself the right to appoint the ministers, returned that man to the back of beyond, and, too, sent my sister off to the Crimea for a much needed rest at her beloved Livadia. That would quiet the tongues.

"Alicky, my dearest," I began, knowing that I now had no choice but to broach all with my sister, "as you know, I've long steered away from political matters, but things are worsening in Moscow, quickly so. The food lines are growing, and the people are so weary, so tired, and so hungry."

"My weak heart aches for them."

"On top of all this, in every queue and in every salon, the worst things are being said about . . . about . . ."

She shook her head in disgust, and guessed, "Father Grigori?"

"I'm afraid so."

"But it's he who just had a vision that Nicky must halt all military trains and for no fewer than three days allow only food to be transported into the cities. You know he was against the war in the first place, and you know how much he cares for the common people."

"My dear, the stories about him are simply horrible. And it's not just in Moscow but here in Petrograd. Kiev, too, and Pskov. Really, all across the Empire."

"Surely you're not like the others?" said my sister, unable to hide her anger and disappointment. "Tell me you don't believe the gossip and calumny as well?"

"All I know is that he no longer occupies himself with matters of your family, but with politics, and —"

"Ella, he is a man of God!"

"But have you not become too dependent upon him?"

"Can one become too dependent on the wisdom of the Lord? I seek Father Grigori's counsel on many matters because of his spiritual closeness, because of his connection, to the God Almighty. Besides, even you know the greatest religious leaders of their time have always been attacked by petty politicians and connivers, not to mention the courtesans. As mother of this country, what concerns me is the well-being of my people, nothing more, and how I seek counsel is therefore my business. I must remain above the petty minds, you know this all too well. Nicky and I have oft been attacked, but we must stay above all the squabbling and seek the right, Godly direction for our nation. You know very well that all true countrymen say that a constitution would not simply be the ruin of Nicky but of the true Mother Russia."

"Yes, but . . ."

And so it went, round and round. My dear sister was nothing if not powerful in her beliefs, and it was her conviction that they must not surrender any power to the bickering politicians who sought to pull Russia this way and that. God had placed Nicky on the Throne, and through God's wisdom he would find the correct path. Our conversation was intense and deep, serious but not hateful. And yet all the same it broke my heart.

"Really, my dear," said Alicky, rising at the end of our conversation, "my own position on Father Grigori is quite immovable. I hope I have made myself clear."

"Yes," I said, coming to my feet. "I'm sorry to have disturbed you. Perhaps it would have been best had I not come."

"Perhaps," she said, kissing me on both cheeks. "But I always relish your visits. Can you not stay for lunch? I know the children would love to see you."

So discouraged was I that I begged, "I'm sorry, but I have so many matters awaiting me in Moscow."

"Then at least the girls and I will see you back to the train station."

Some twenty minutes later, Alicky and the older girls, Olga and Tatyana, and I stepped out into the bitter cold, quickly climbing into a limousine. As we set off for the station, I sat right next to my sister, holding her hand the entire way, which was our little custom, and yet this time, rather than chatting as usual, we rode the short distance in silence. We were both exhausted, both fearful, perhaps, of the months ahead. If only our soldiers could hang on until the spring, then victory would be ours. Just a few more months . . .

I loved my sister so, as she did me, and though I protested that it was too cold, Alicky and the girls saw me through the station's Imperial Rooms and onto the gusty, cold platform. As the winter winds swept around us, I tenderly kissed my nieces.

"Such beauties," I said, touching each of

them gently on the chin. "Now promise me you'll take good care of your mother."

"Always," replied the oldest, Olga, with a sweet smile.

"Of course, but you have to come back soon!" beckoned Tatyana. "And write us often!"

"I will," said I, feeling older than I ever had.

Though I had failed in my mission, I embraced my sister more tightly than I had perhaps since we were children. From whence came this sense of desperation? What was it that I so feared? We lingered longer, too, in each other's arms, and I for one couldn't help being silently grateful that at least that awful man had not separated me from my beloved ones.

I kissed my baby sister, Empress of all the Russias, and we parted without another word. With the assistance of a footman, I climbed into the private carriage at the rear of the train and took my seat, whereupon I stared out at my dear sweets. Pressing the palms of both of my hands against the glass, I bid them a silent, bittersweet farewell. As the train started off with a forceful heave, it took a great deal of thought to hold back my tears.

And worried though I was over the course

of the Empire, I could not even imagine the horrors that were soon to overwhelm the Empire. It all began with a trickle of blood — the murder of none other than Rasputin himself, which, strangely, took place just a few short weeks after my visit to Alicky. I know how much this pained my sister, but even I realized what hope his end gave to so many, for the murder of Rasputin was all anyone talked about. There was rejoicing in the streets, talk that the government could now move forward, that the war would now come to a victorious end, even rumors that Alicky was to be sent off to a distant cloister whilst things calmed down.

Yes, with the black stain of Rasputin removed from the Ruling House there was so much hope. And yet . . . within barely three months the trickle of that man's blood turned into a rushing, crimson river as revolution washed away not only all of us but Great Russia as it had forever been known.

Dear Lord, how it pains me to say I have not seen my Alicky since that moment on the train platform, and even today I doubt we two sisters shall ever meet again in this earthly world.

CHAPTER 36
PAVEL

The spark that made the country blow up like a big, bad bomb was a lie, a lie we told everywhere and to everyone. And the lie we told all over that February of 1917? It was simple: no baked bread! And this made people get real mad and go real crazy! And it worked! Just to make sure, though, I even liked adding something more, because peasant that I was, I knew what would make the people really panic: no flour!

Ha!

There was plenty of flour, but it was stuck way out there in some railway cars, way out of the city, so much flour that I even heard it was rotting. But the *narod* — the masses — didn't know this. All they knew was that the bread lines were getting longer and longer, and their lives more and more miserable as the war dragged on and on and on. They could live with sugar being rationed, they could live with just a few scraps of meat in their soups. But bread? *Radi boga* — for the sake of God — how could a Russian live without bread, be it white, black, or even that gray crap, eh?

"We're fighting for the Romanovs and they won't even give us a few pieces of stale crust!" I grumbled in one breadline after another throughout Moscow. "What do they think we are, animals? To hell with the *burzhui!*" I added, using the nasty word for the bourgeoisie. "I hear our masters have not only all the bread they can eat but even sugar and salt."

"Well, one thing's for sure — our German whore Empress has plenty of bread!" complained another of my comrades, who was always planted near me. "But maybe she's not giving us any because she's angry she no longer has Rasputin's sausage!"

The crowd roared with laughter.

Rasputin, that damned dog, had been killed a few months earlier, which in truth made our job harder. We couldn't let the political scene get easier or softer for the Tsar, which meant we had to stretch the shadow of that Rasputin as far as we could and agitate, agitate, agitate.

Just like a worm, I started whispering, "I've been to two other stores this morning and they both ran out of bread. Now I hear there's not enough at this one, either. Look, the store's about to close! They're running out of bread everywhere!"

Even I was surprised at what happened next. Even I was shocked at how quickly things blew up, just like a match thrown into a barrel of kerosene. No sooner had the words passed my lips than some guy pitched a rock at the window of the bread store. And poof! The glass exploded into shards! And the crowd didn't cower away but cried out and surged forward!

"Xleb!" Bread, screamed nearly every soul!

"Give us *xleb!*"

"We are hungry!"

I'd never seen anything like it — it was like a call to charge the enemy. One moment there were a hundred souls standing in line, long-suffering folk who had never complained, just poor people in felt boots and foul coats, always submissive to master and Tsar. The next moment every last one of them, right down to the old babushkas with their scarves tied round their heads, were fiery rebels! It was magic! Like one giant flame! The crowd burst to life, surging forward, breaking every window of the bread store and piling in, frantically grabbing all the loaves from the shelves, then pushing and shouting and shoving their way into the back and emerging with sacks of flour.

There was only one voice of protest, the shop owner, a short man with a waxed mustache, who shouted, "Stop! Stop, you fools!"

But the only thing that was stopped was him, this owner — two ruffians grabbed him and pitched him right through the broken window, right outside, where he landed with a thud on the cobbles. Blood streaming down his face, he struggled to get up, making it only onto one knee.

"You've been hiding bread from us poor people! They say you've been hoarding bread and waiting for the price increases — shame on you!" shouted one *staruxha* — old woman — as she kicked the groaning man. "Shame!"

That was all it took, one kick from an old woman's worn shoe. It was like a signal. And then everyone was upon him, kicking and beating him, ripping at clothing and limb. He lived one more minute, no more. Their fury surprised even me. Like a lid finally blown off a boiling pot, the deep Russian instinct for revenge suddenly blew wide and could not be contained. People beat on the poor man as meanly as if they were finally beating on their serf-master who had beat on them! Yes, this was revolution, great revolution! Hurrah!

Turning away from the pulp of that man's body, I saw a nearby restaurant that was famous for its wine cellar. Well, that would make people break in there — free drink! — but I, devil that I was, thought of something worse, something that would make them real crazy. Officially, there had been no vodka for sale since the beginning of the war.

"Comrades, I hear they're hiding some 'national treasure' in the cellar of that restaurant!" I shouted, grabbing a rock and hurling it at the window of this other place.

The idea of getting their hands on some vodka wasn't just a spark and a little flame, it was a big explosion! Suddenly people forgot all about bread and ran to the restaurant, splitting it as wide as a watermelon. And suddenly, too, other people came running, charging from everywhere, from this way and that. Within moments there were several hundred comrades, and moments after that several hundred more. Incredible! All of a sudden I saw a dead body thrown out the window — the owner would have been smarter to run out the back! — and then I saw some waiters run out, covering their heads as they fled for their lives. A few moments later proud people emerged, one after another carrying bottles of wine. With no way to open them, however, the folks smashed the tops on the stone curbs and then started drinking from the broken bottles, red wine and blood dribbling from their smiling, cut lips. There was no vodka, but who cared as long as there was free wine! Free wine!

And I shouted the slogan we were told to shout everywhere: *"Grab nagrablenoye!"* Steal what was stolen!

"Grab nagrablenoye!" repeated an unseen soul.

"Hurrah!"

And soon enough those very words were echoed up and down the street, shouted by one comrade after another as they broke into shop after shop, stealing not only bread and wine but eggs and milk, then pants and fur hats and fine ladies' dresses, too. It wasn't too long, either, before I saw real flames licking one storefront, toasting everything in their path. There were cries of pain mixed with shouts of joy.

Then in the distance came the sound of hooves, and the crazy crowd quieted for just a moment — the Cossacks? We all paused to listen, pondering our fates. Had they come to mow us down with their silvery sabers? Come to chop off our heads like tall poppies?

But what appeared around the corner wasn't the feared Cossacks on wild ponies but our Russian troops, some thirty or forty Russian comrades on horseback, one old officer at the head. With clouds of steam pouring from the snouts of their horses, and with not sabers but rifles and pistols waving overhead, the soldiers charged right up to us. We, the poor masses, stood as one, knowing that within seconds half of us would fall dead.

But then something so strange happened . . .

"Xleb!" cried one toothless babushka, staring up at the soldiers. "We are hungry! We just want *xleb!*"

Yet again, that was all it took, just one old peasant woman calling out the obvious, and one by one the soldiers lowered their rifles until there was but one last gun raised: that of their old commanding officer. But he wasn't pointing his pistol at us. He was pointing his gun at his own soldier boys.

"Raise your guns!" he commanded his men. "Prepare to fire!"

But not one of his soldiers did as he was told. They just stared defiantly at the officer, their brooding eyes saying it all: These are our own people, we will not fire upon our own brothers and sisters!

"I command you to take up your weapons and prepare to fire!" shouted the officer, his face bursting red as he trained his weapon on one particular soldier, a boy with blond hair. "Raise your weapons or I'll fire upon —"

Suddenly there was a crack of gunfire, a noise so sharp that everyone fell silent. And gasped. At first I thought he'd done it, that the bastard officer had fired upon the blond lad, but no! One of the other soldiers had taken up his own weapon and fired on him, the officer! He shot his commander right in the face! For one long, shocking moment no one said anything, no one could guess what was going to happen next — would soldier start firing upon soldier, would they all fire upon us? — and we simply watched as the old officer, his white beard glistening with red blood, tumbled off his horse and fell to the ground dead as a log.

And then another of the soldier boys held his rifle high in the air and, in one long, glorious shout, cried, "Hurrah!"

The soldiers crossed over to the people, and in that second Russia changed completely. All the soldiers cried out in joy and the crowd whooped with delight, calling out to the soldier boys, welcoming them with bread and wine and brotherhood! Yes, it was mutiny, absolute mutiny! I shouted with joy, cried out with happiness! Unable to believe what was happening, I watched as one by one the soldiers leaped down from their horses and the people rushed toward them and embraced them, smiling and laughing.

Da, da, da, it was incredible, miraculous! I didn't understand what was happening, and yet I did, I understood it all. This wasn't like the revolution of twelve years ago when we the people had been battling the police and the soldiers, and the Cossacks, too. No, this was different. We were one, soldier and people and everyone else, united as one against the capitalist pigs and the warmongers and the tsar and his whore wife who sat upon all of us, the people! It was the Revolution, and this time I knew we would win!

Long live the Uprising of the Oppressed!

Chapter 37
Ella

If one had pondered the war figures, one would have gone insane with worry: 1,500,000 of our brave men killed, 4,000,000 wounded, 2,000,000 taken prisoner. It was no wonder there was such despair, such rabble-rousing. It was no wonder, too, that riots akin to those of twelve years past broke out all over my beloved Moscow. By the end of that February, 1917, gunshots could be heard throughout the day and from every direction. Electricity ceased, as did the trams everywhere. The post and telegraphs as well. Worse, they said the prison doors all across town had been thrown wide open and that the homes for lunatics had been emptied as well. In quick speed almost every factory went on strike, and the streets themselves became totally derelict and frightfully dangerous, and while I forbade my sisters to travel beyond our walls, I refused to close and lock our gates. I was determined that all those in need should be able to reach us, that we must not cut ourselves off. Of course there were those who said I should take shelter once again behind the Kremlin walls, but I would not leave my sisters, for I had not decided those long years ago to leave the Kremlin only to be driven back to it by anarchy.

Word from the outside world was sparse at best, and though I sent letter after letter to Alicky, I doubted that any of them reached her, and certainly I received not a word from her. Yes, it was perfectly clear we were in the revolution again, right where we had been in 1905.

When the chaos late in the month was at its height, Countess Tarlova, one of my ladies from days past, somehow managed to make her way to my community, not arriving by carriage or motorcar but on foot and in simplest dress. I knew she had been in Petrograd and yet she had somehow managed her way here, despite the railways having halted.

It was she who brought the monumental news, she who delivered the blow.

"Well, what of it?" I desperately asked, rising to my feet when this faithful woman was shown into my reception room. "Did you

343

see my sister? Is there any news of Nicky?"

In that instant, tears bloomed in her eyes, and in French she muttered but a single word: *"Abdiqué!"*

It was a knife to my heart — Nicky had abdicated! — and instantly I began weeping. "But . . . but . . ."

I could not walk, could speak no more, and were it not for this good Countess I certainly would have fallen. My confusion was immense. How could Nicky have been pulled from the Throne? What trials had the Lord Himself hurled upon poor Russia? For a good long while I could find no wisdom, no understanding, and my lady held me tightly, steadying me as my tears came aplenty, whereupon I somehow managed my way to my private chapel. Sinking to my knees, I fell to the floor and bowed before the altar and my icons, pressing my head down upon the stone. Even in my prayers I could not restrain my tears, and there I stayed well into the depths of the night, chanting and bowing and searching for the wisdom of the God Almighty. My sorrow knew no depth — what lay ahead for my dear, dear Russia? — and I took relief only in the Jesus Prayer, chanting it over and over, some three or four hundred times, in Church Slavonic: *"Gospodi Isusye Xristye*

Siin Bozhii pomiloi mnye greshnuyuu." Lord
Jesus Christ, Son of God, have mercy on
me, a sinner. Yes, as I had been taught, I
prayed without ceasing, hoping to find
humility, hoping to bring my mind into my
heart, hoping to reach a greater understanding.

Sleep came eventually but reluctantly, and
I rested a mere hour, perhaps two at most.
The monumental news of Nicky's fall
reached the city the following day, but
instead of bringing appeasement it only ac-
celerated the chaos. There were reports of
palaces and homes of every sort being
plundered and burned, and all around us I
could see it, too, gray plumes of smoke rising into the wintry sky. Desperate word
came round as well of murders of every
sort, that merchant so-and-so had been
gunned down and his clothing store plundered, that sundry princes and even princesses had been butchered in their own
homes, and, unbelievably, that almost all
our faithful soldiers had mutinied and shot
officers here and there all about the city.
My heart was breaking, and I sent telegram
after telegram to my sister, but they all came
back, not one delivered, and it would be
some time before I learned that Kerensky,
head of the Provisional Government, had

placed Nicky and she and all the children under arrest there at Tsarskoye, their own home having become their own prison. Russia it seemed had come right to the edge of a dangerous precipice and not turned away but thrown herself head over heels into the dark waters below. For months thereafter I could not speak of my sister without weeping.

And while for days I could take no food save tea, I soon forced myself to find strength, for I had my sisters and our sick ones to watch over, and to all of them I repeated, "There is nothing to fear. The Lord watches over us, and no harm will come our way unless it is His will."

But such harm did in fact come to us, passing right through our very own gates.

I was out in our garden, standing in the shallow snow and enjoying the light of the morning and, too, a kind of quiet we had not experienced in weeks. God willing, perhaps the bloodletting of the revolution had passed, perhaps in the spring months ahead our country, like the wondrous lilacs and laburnums of my garden, would wake from its dark sleep and bloom once again in splendor. Indeed, in the distance I heard not the sound of gunfire but of singing. At first my heart filled with both joy and relief

— perhaps we could all get down to what Nicky himself had only wanted, the lifting of his people to a better life — but then the voices came closer and louder, louder and closer. It was then that I recognized the tune being sung: the "Internationale." My spine tensed, for I was quite sure where those voices were headed. Hearing the determined song as well as the sound of approaching motor vehicles, a handful of sisters came scurrying outside, for despite my best efforts they had all become so protective of me.

"Matushka," ventured my Nun Varvara, breaching protocol that it was I who knew best, "perhaps you should retire to your reception room."

"No, my children, I shall handle this alone," I said as not one but two motor lorries sped right up to our front gates. "I will directly meet whatever fate awaits me. Now all of you inside — be gone this moment!"

"We will pray for you in the church, Matushka!" called Nun Varvara as she and the others hurried off.

"Pray for us all!" I replied.

I wanted to beseech my sisters with the words of the Gospel: "Ye shall be hated of all men for My Name's sake." There was no time, though, for the lorries had come to a halt, and rather than have them start back up and barge through our premises and cause any sort of trouble, I went directly to the large main gates and pulled them open. Looking out, I saw that in the backs of the two vehicles stood thirty or forty dispirited souls, singing and shouting, laughing and smoking. Like our previous visitors, most of them were men and they had red ribbons pinned to their coats and many were waving red banners — Freedom and Bread! Peace and Land! All Power to the Soviets! Practically each and every one of them had a rifle hanging from his shoulder and a coarse cigarette dangling from his lips. Upon seeing me standing humbly there in my gray robes, their craggy music all but faded away.

As an odd silence settled upon us, I gently asked, "How is it that I may help you?"

"We're here to arrest the Matushka!" shouted one, the apparent leader, who wore a large mustache. "Where is she?"

"Right before you," I replied, with a bow of my head. "I am she, the Abbess of the *Marfo-Marinski Obitel.*"

"And just what is it that you do here? Now that you're no longer 'Her Imperial Highness,' who are you, eh?"

"I serve the sick and needy, that is all."

"Well, you're going to be put on trial as a

German spy!" he said.

"That's right, we're going to take you away and toss you in prison!" came a shout from the truck.

"Down with the Romanovs, all power to the people!" shouted another.

"Hurrah!" came the voice of the mob.

Their leader, the one with the mustache, jumped down from the back and said, "We have orders to arrest you, but first we have to search the convent. We're going to arrest all the German spies you're hiding and take all the guns and ammunitions you have as well."

It seemed that half of them flew off the backs of the lorries, leaping to the ground and swarming toward me. But I would not be so intimidated, and standing there in my work robes I held out the flat of my hand.

"My good people, we have never hidden any spies or prisoners of war within these walls, nor have we ever, ever possessed armaments of any sort," I said in a most firm voice. "To do so would be a most grievous breach of our pledges to the Lord. But to satisfy yourselves you are more than welcome to search anywhere and everywhere." As with the previous incident, I stated, "However, I ask that there shall be no more than six of you who enter, for under these roofs we have many wounded soldiers and sick patients, not to mention our orphan girls and beggar boys, and I will not have them disturbed or worried. Their well-being is my only concern."

"Well . . ." grumbled their leader.

"Further," I continued most forcefully, "it will take me a few minutes to issue instructions for the care of all our dear ones, and I must also bid my dear sisters farewell. Once I have accomplished these things, I will gladly go with you."

This threw them into an unexpected muddle. I supposed they had come, fully certain to find what all the tongues had told them lay here: a nest of German spies and guns aplenty, perhaps a pile or two of gold nuggets as well. They seemed determined to find all this, and quickly so, and had planned, too, on ripping me away, screaming and flailing.

Stepping into their confusion, I asked, "But first, my friends, would you be so kind as to join us in church? I would like to gather my sisters and have Father Mitrofan perform a Te Deum for my journey."

Not knowing if they would follow, I turned and proceeded across the flagstones toward my church.

Russian peasants, I had come to learn in

my years here, were a peculiar sort, one moment all politeness, bowing and submissive, next angry and so violent, not afraid to kill. But such were the shadows, the hangovers, of their recent serfdom, when these poor people had been traded as not much more than slaves. Warm, loving of family and friends, and hardworking — I had found all this in my adopted people. All that they lacked was a proper sense of self-worth and a literate, educated manner in which to express their frustrations. Simply, they were still so afraid of their master's whip, for without education, without intelligent words, the only way they could do battle against that whip was to resort to sheer violence itself.

Oh, I pondered with the heaviest of hearts, had we but ten more years of peace our Russia would have made it, we would not have come to so destructive a time. God save and protect Russia, I silently prayed as I walked along, my head bowed.

Despite the rifles slung over their shoulders and the harsh words that escaped their lips, these were essentially good men here today, not evil, merely fearful, their fear having been churned to an evil frenzy. Which is to say that they did in fact follow me to my sweet church. Without turning, I walked on, wondering what they might do. Then I heard their booted steps behind me, proceeding if not with respect, then neither with immediate threat. Reaching the double doors of my church, I looked back and saw that there were six men, not one more, just as I had asked. All the others were waiting just beyond the gate.

And upon opening one of the large wooden doors I nearly tripped over a handful of novices and sisters, all huddled there in the dark, shocked and worried.

To two novices, I said, "Will you young ones please fetch Father Mitrofan, for I am about to go on a journey and I would like him to perform a service. The rest of you, would you please gather all the sisters here for the service, and, please, light all the lamps and candles, too?" Addressing the men, who stood outside, I politely asked, "I would very much appreciate it if all of you would join us here in the church — I assure you that we will be brief. After that, Father Mitrofan will escort you through our buildings, and you may search hi and lo to suit your needs. Yes, yes, please do come in, but I ask you to leave your rifles just outside here, for weapons are of course not needed in the house of the Lord."

Though they were hesitant to abandon

their guns, one by one they did as I requested, shrugging off their rifles and propping them up outside. They then stepped into our haven, pulling caps from heads, and bowing their heads ever so respectfully toward the iconostasis. I was pleased for their souls.

Father Mitrofan, my tall, round, bearded confessor, vested himself quickly and, fastening up the last of his garments, appeared more than startled upon the ambo. His big, wide face was red, his eyes darted about with worry, but I smiled gently before him, determined to remain calm, for there was naught that I could do but accept my fate. I fully expected to be taken away by these men, yet I tried to exude a kind of calm as my sisters poured into the church, for I had no wish to sow anxiety among my loved ones.

"There is nothing to fear," I said, slowly moving through the clouds of incense and smoke toward the front. "And, please, I will tolerate no tears."

Reaching the altar, I stared upon the beautiful images lining the iconostasis and crossed myself. As gracefully as I had once curtseyed before king and queen, I then dropped to my knees, bowing all the way over and pressing my forehead upon the cool, soothing stones. It was there that I remained on my knees throughout the brief service, repeating the prayers, crossing myself, rising and falling over and over in humility and devotion. My sisters in the choir sang like angels, and this, too, gave me strength.

With the conclusion of the brief service, I came to my feet, and kissed the gold cross which Father Mitrofan held before me. One by one all my sisters did likewise, and as I stepped aside I was more than pleased to see the revolutionaries do likewise. Good village boys that they had once surely been, they each received Father's blessing. This also warmed my heart and gave me a kind of hope that one day Russia would heal itself.

With the Te Deum concluded, I turned to these men, and said, "Father Mitrofan will now escort you about my buildings. I ask you to please look wherever you wish and to take however much time you may need. When you have finished your search, you will find me in my reception room, and from there I will go with you, just as you have requested."

I could see in their eyes that these men had been softened by the service, that something no longer burned within their souls, or at least not as hotly as before. Or was it a kind of reluctance, was that what I sensed? Not one of them moved, not one of them met my gaze.

Finally, the leader, the one with the mustache, rather sheepishly said, "The truth is that if we take you today, Matushka, we will have no place to keep you, no prison. So . . . so, I think, yes, perhaps, it would be best if you stayed here. But we must do our search. We still need to look everywhere."

"Most certainly," I replied with a warm smile. "Please look wherever you wish. It is my hope that you completely satisfy yourselves."

They headed off and were gone a good long while, verifying, inspecting, and checking virtually each and every room of the *obitel*, from the orphanage to the operating theater, the kitchens to the apothecary. An hour later I was called out from my reception rooms, and there, in my snow-covered gardens, I found the six men.

"Are you satisfied that you saw everything?" I asked.

"Yes," replied the mustached one, as several of his compatriots nodded in agreement. "We found nothing, so we are leaving now."

"Very well."

Of course they hadn't found anything, neither Germans nor spies, bullets nor guns. Such things were anathema to all that I and my work stood for. The search was nevertheless important, because now, perhaps, the story would go round that a group of revolutionaries had had a thorough look-see through our community and found virtually nothing of interest. Hopefully this time the truth would circulate instead of all those awful black lies.

I escorted the men, and as we neared the gates, I quietly said, "Thank you for allowing me to stay where I am needed."

There was not a reply from one of them, and they, perhaps a touch embarrassed, filed silently past me and onto the street, where their two lorries awaited. Upon seeing the search committee emerge from my gates, the mob burst into excited song, this time the "Marseillaise." But the song quickly fell away, for the search team was emerging with no screaming princess, no spies, and not a single weapon.

As sole explanation, the mustached one loudly proclaimed, "This is just a women's monastery, nothing else!"

All boarded the lorries and off they went, singing yet again with revolutionary fervor. Once they were gone, I tightly closed the gates. For a moment I paused, wondering if now was in fact the time to lock the gates and barricade ourselves from the outer world. I reached to do just that, but decided quite otherwise. Beyond our walls there were so many in such great need.

Turning around I saw my dear Nun Varvara, her hands clasped at her waist, standing there and looking supremely relieved.

With a large smile upon her face, she said, "Very well done, Matushka."

I smiled as well and with a light shrug, boasted, "Once again it seems that we are not yet worthy of a martyr's crown."

CHAPTER 38
PAVEL

We pulled the tsar by his prick from the throne, and it was a big surprise what happened after that: the Germans sent Lenin back to Russia. It was true. They put him in a sealed train, they gave him hundreds of thousands of rubles to make a revolution, and they snuck him through Finland and back into the country. Which meant Lenin was the only real traitor, financed by none other than our enemies who wanted only one thing: to get Russia out of the war.

All this I found out at a secret meeting that fall in Moscow. The Comrade Trotsky told me everything, that all the rumors were true. He also told me that if I talked about it at all, if I spread word of it, they would shoot me like a dog, a bullet in the back of my head. Without saying anything, I thought how funny this was — everyone had gone after the ex-empress because they said she was working for the Germans, but in fact it was our man, Lenin, who worked for them. I understood all this but it didn't bother me. I didn't care how Lenin had come back from his hiding in Switzerland.

"All I care about, Comrade," I told Trotsky right to his face, "is three things: Land to the peasants! Factories to the workers! Peace to the soldiers!"

"Exactly! Kerensky and his Provisional Government are keeping us in the war, but we have more important things — we haven't finished the revolution of the proletariat!"

No, we hadn't. There was lots more to do. Many, like Trotsky, were even calling for complete equality for the *Zhidki,* which was just what Trotsky was, one of them, a Jew man. Such interesting times.

Those months were chaos, the capitalists demanding one thing, the socialists another, and then that summer Lenin even had to flee again because suddenly Kerensky sent his men to arrest him. But our hero got away, he slipped right out of town. No one knew quite where he went — had he run all the way back to Switzerland? — but later they said that he'd scurried toward the Finnish border, where he dived into a haystack. They said he stayed hidden there almost all the way until the real Revolution but I think maybe he lived somewhere else, in a hidden dacha or something.

Da, da, da, and finally that fall a great miracle happened: The Great October Revolution!

The second Revolution was so different from the first, the February Revolution. The second, the October Revolution, was much wilder. In Moscow there was shooting from the roofs and battles on the street, us Bolsheviks trying to kill as many Kadets as we could. From everywhere you could hear the *rat-tat-tat* of machine guns, and there was one big, long battle near the Arbat where there was a military academy and where so many of the wealthy bastards lived. Villa after villa was burned, and there were bodies lying everywhere. For the first time tank trucks rumbled the streets, too.

It was during this time and on one great day that they gave me a big, important task. More than anything the Revolution needed two things: weapons and money. That was why on one particular morning they sent a group of Red Guards marching on the Kremlin. At the same time they sent me and four comrades to one of the big banks that did, they said, all sorts of business with the warmongers and foreign capitalists. My instructions were very clear: *Grab nagrable-noye!*

Not too very long after it opened we went into this bank. Actually I went first, dressed all special in a black leather coat that they gave me and instructed me to wear. They didn't want me to look like the peasant that I was, they didn't want me to look suspicious. So they made me look pretty good, and in I went through the big brass doors and into the main hall that was all covered with dark wood. Only one of the clerks, a pale man with a small, neat beard, looked up at me with any interest. It was just before ten, which meant the bank was still pretty empty, just workers and only one customer, a short old man with a cane. Not thirty seconds later, my other four comrades came in, two of the men posting themselves at the big front door, one at a side door, and another, Sasha, coming up by my side, all according to plan.

I whipped out a revolver, held it high, and fired two shots right into the ceiling. There were screams and some chunks of plaster came down on my head.

As loudly as I could, I shouted, "All of you on the floor! In the name of the Proletariat and the Revolution, we are seizing this bank! Get down on the floor! All the money in your vaults now belongs to the people! Death to the exploiters! Glory to the Revolution!"

I had thought the bankers and all the clerks in their white shirts would do nothing and give up like schoolgirls. But they were rather tough. A man with glasses, who turned out to be the director general, came out of an office, a small pistol in hand. Without hesitating, he aimed at Sasha, my comrade, who was standing right next to me, and shot him in the left shoulder. Sasha, a big guy, groaned in pain but just as quickly let out one shot and then another, killing Mr. Director General, who toppled over, landing with a juicy thud. That was all it took, actually. I turned this way and that, saw all the clerks now practically throwing themselves on the floor and covering their heads with their hands.

And then it was quiet, but only for a second. That poor Sasha. I heard another groan, turned, and saw blood bubble and flow from his lips. He looked down, as did I, and it was then that I saw a long, razor-thin sword poking out of his stomach. *Gospodi,* he'd been stabbed from behind! Sasha glanced up at me, tried to say something, choked on his own blood, swayed, and fell over. Behind him stood that old man — a sword had been hidden in his cane! And he had stabbed Sasha in the back, running the sword right through my comrade!

Purple with anger, the old man said to me, "You fucking Reds can go to the devil!"

Knowing full well what would happen next, the old shit quickly crossed himself, and I waited, I let him finish. Once he'd made his sign to a god I was sure didn't exist, I did the deed. I fired a bullet right between his eyes. When he hit the floor a black velvet bag fell from his hands. I ripped it open, and in it were twenty *brillianti,* all about the size of my thumbnail, and some fifteen or so big red and green stones, too. I quickly understood that the old man had probably just removed these things from a storage box there in the bank. He was probably taking his jewels and getting ready to run away, to leave the country. Good, I thought. All I had done was stop an enemy from taking his riches out of Russia.

We only had to kill one other person, a woman clerk who tried to sneak out the back door. One of my comrades shot her in the neck and stole her gold rings.

It was about then that we heard and felt a distant explosion that was bigger, well, than anything I'd ever experienced. Ha! I thought with a smile. Ha! Our Red brigand had succeeded, they had blown up the Kremlin gates! They were storming the Arsenal!

Yes, it was a very good day for the Revolution. Me and my comrades seized almost five million Kerensky rubles from the bank, the Red Guard had got piles of weapons and ammunition from the Arsenal, and by nightfall our red flags were flying from the Kremlin towers.

A very good day for the people, indeed: Glory to the October Revolution!

CHAPTER 39
ELLA

In the months after the Bolshevik putsch there were many who came to see me, first those hoping to protect me, second those seeking to spirit me altogether out of Russia.

As to the first, I begged them to give up all efforts of protection, for it was simply too dangerous to stand up for me. A devil had been born in the blood of the revolution, and its name was the Cheka, the All-Russian Extraordinary Commission for Combating Counter-Revolution, Profiteering and Official Corruption. The stories that reached my ears were simply too unbelievable — thousands upon thousands put to death, pushed into furnaces, scalped, some even skinned alive. I wept morning, noon, and night, particularly when came news of the clergy who were crowned with barbed wire and crucified, later taken down and thrown half-dead in pigpens for the beasts to eat. One heard tell of informants every-where, so much so that no one trusted anyone.

In truth, I was sorely tempted by the second, those who sought to take me away from this chaos. I longed for my family abroad, Irene and Victoria, and sweet Ernie, who were so sadly caught up on the German side of the war. How I wished to see them all and linger in their laughter, as I had done in my youth.

As to my dear ones here in Russia, I was totally cut off. I had virtually no news of Alicky and Nicky and the children, but I continued to write three or four times a week, though I doubted any of my letters made it through. I believed nothing I read of them in the newspapers, and soon enough the newspapers ceased altogether. Lenin and his Reds had seized control of all the press, and when the revolutionary papers started appearing their words were nothing but cheap promises and exaggerated lies.

Once even the Swedish Minister came to see me, greeting me in my own reception room with the blunt words, "I am here to inform you that I have both the means and the permission for your safe transport to my country. I urge Your Highness to leave Russia immediately, if not today, then tomorrow."

It was quite apparent whose permission this emissary had — both that of Cousin Willy, the Kaiser, and of none other than Lenin himself. But how could I be saved by these men? Willy himself had done so much toward the destruction of Russia, not simply by declaring the war in the first place, but recently by sending that hideous Lenin back into Russia so that the Fatherland would be defeated from within. Just unbelievable! Years earlier some of Nicky's officers had come up with a plan to foment revolution in Germany, but while war was one thing, Nicky would have nothing to do with devious attempts to topple a seated emperor.

As for Lenin, I knew his thoughts were anything but of my safety. Simply, I understood that he wanted to be rid of me. It was said that he was afraid to arrest me because of my good work and the warmth most Muscovites felt toward me and my sisters. It was said, too, that I was the last of all the Romanovs living of free accord. Apparently the rest of us — nearly seventy members of the former House of Romanov — had been taken by the Reds. Could that possibly be? Dear Lord in Heaven, one only had to recall the fate of Marie Antoinette and Louis XVI, not to mention the barbarism of the French Revolution, to fear what thorny path lay ahead. I had had secret word, however, that for the time being the Widow Empress, Ksenia and her brood, Olga and her new husband and baby, and others were still living in relative safety in the Crimea. I prayed this was true, I prayed for them morning, noon, and night.

But, no, I would have nothing to do with this offer of fleeing abroad, for the idea of dealing with such hatefuls as Willy and Lenin was simply impossible. In any case, how could I possibly abandon my aching Russia at the hour when she needed me most?

"Thank you for your kind thoughts, Mr. Minister," I said, rising and thereby signifying the conclusion of my audience. "But my place is here within the walls of my community and in my beloved country. I have many sisters and countless patients to watch over, you know."

"I feared such a reply," he said with a respectful bow.

"But tell me, have you heard any word of . . . of . . ." No, I could not bring myself to refer to them as the ex-Tsar and ex-Tsaritsa. ". . . of my sister and her husband?"

"Only that they have been transferred to

Siberia, nothing more."

"So I have been told. I have written to them numerous times, but I doubt that my letters have reached them."

Ominously, he said, "I fear for your country, Madame."

"Please, I beg you, pray for us."

The gentleman then quietly left, and as the door closed behind him I felt at peace, for my ultimate wish was now forever established: my fate was Russia's fate. True, much later Willy again tried to get me to quit Russia — he sent his Count Mirbach twice to see me, but each time I refused him an audience, so despicable was the thought that I might be rescued by our German enemies.

For a while longer things continued as before, patients were brought to us, we were allotted enough ration cards, even the good people of Moscow brought us foodstuffs whenever they could. Soon, however, things began to change, quickly so. Many from the outside world stopped coming to see us, fearful, I was sure, of being associated with me, a Romanov. Then the city's wooden sewer pipes broke and the water of Moscow became entirely contaminated, typhoid broke out, and everything from drinking water to lettuces had to be boiled. Worse, it became impossible to obtain any medicaments except the simplest, quinine and iodine. Still we made do, stretching our soups as far as we could. I spent many an afternoon tearing bedsheets into bandages.

To be sure, my great Russia was gone forever, and yet I took comfort in knowing that Holy Russia existed as never before. As I wrote to one of my countesses, "If one realizes the sublime sacrifice of God the Father, Who sent His Son to die and be Resurrected for us, then we sense the presence of the Holy Spirit, Who illumines our way; and then happiness becomes eternal, even when our poor human hearts and limited earthly minds have to go through moments that seem terrible."

Yes, it was true, God's ways were a mystery and perhaps it was a great blessing not to know where we were going and what the future had in store for us. All our country was being snipped into little bits, all that was gained in centuries was being demolished and by our own people, those I loved from all my heart, truly they were morally ill and blinded not to see where we were going. One's heart ached so, but I had no bitterness — could I criticize or condemn a man in delirium as a lunatic? I could only pity and long for good guardians to be found who could help him from smashing all and murdering all whom he could get at.

I tried to keep this in mind, but like so many others I fell ill and became so thin and exhausted. There were weeks when all that I could manage was to sit on my willow chaise and knit some bandages or, if my eyes felt strong enough, sew some padded dressings. Then in March came the heartbreaking news that Willy had stooped so low as to sign a separate peace with Lenin and his bloody cohorts. Simply unbelievable. I felt so ashamed for all.

And finally came that day that I will forever look back upon as the very darkest. It was the Feastday of the Iverskii Icon, and on that third day of Pascha, spring 1918, things at first seemed calm and we were able to forget awhile the sufferings around us.

Divine Liturgy had been served by His Holiness Patriarch Tikhon, who came to us and comforted us, and I tried to fill myself with the wonderment of our most important holiday. However, toward late afternoon, not long after the Patriarch had left and just when all seemed calmest, there came the ringing of the bells at our gates — yes, sadly we had started keeping the gates locked, particularly as night fell. There were marauders everywhere, people thieving everything from bread and potatoes and sugar and salt to such valuables as silver and jewels, which were oddly becoming less valuable simply because they provided no nourishment.

At first I wondered could it be a person without home or food who'd come to us for sustenance? Or could it be a mother with a sick child desperate for help? Such types often came to us these days, but when the ringing of the bells went on and on, and so loudly, too, I understood this was no weak soul. I understood that the worst had come directly to our gates.

At my insistence, it was I alone who went out, crossing my cherished courtyard in the dusky light. Out in the street I heard the rumble of a motorcar and saw a glimpse of it, too, as it sat there.

"Coming!" I called in answer to the bells, which rang and rang. "I'm coming!"

Moments later I reached the small side gate, unlocked the bolt, and swung it open. Standing there was the kind of man all Moscow had come to fear most, a brooding man wearing a long black leather coat and a tight cap. He looked every inch the *komissar* that he was, big mustache and all, while behind him stood four soldiers in the drab green uniforms of the Red Army and with rifles slung this way and that, definitely not from the right shoulders as in olden days when our soldiers were properly disciplined. Smiling humbly, I quickly glanced around and appraised the situation. There was in fact not one motorcar but two, and these men who had come to us stood there calmly and quietly with a distinct and obvious task at hand. Undoubtedly Lenin had sent them at the end of services and at the end of the day when the streets were emptiest and quietest. I surmised, and correctly so, that this hour had been chosen as the least likely to cause disruption and protest. They were to do this as quietly and secretly as possible.

"How is it that I may help you?" I kindly asked the one in the leather coat.

"I have orders for the removal of the abbess," he replied, his voice deep and flat.

"I am the Matushka of this *obitel.*"

"Then you are to come with us."

"I see."

Yes, I did see, and I did understand, quite thoroughly so: I was being arrested. Glancing briefly at the *komissar* and the four soldiers, I knew there was nothing to be done. These were not unruly peasants, not a mob gone wild on vodka, there was no way to convince these men otherwise. These were members of the Red Guard on an official mission, and that mission was to take me away, presumably out of Moscow and quite possibly into the depths of Siberia, where so many others of the Family had been sent.

"Can you tell me, please, will I be returning here tonight?"

"For your own protection, you are being transferred."

"Yes, but —"

"For your own protection, you are being transferred."

So the answer was no, I would not be returning here tonight and would most likely never see this dear place again. Lowering my eyes to the dark ground, I choked back a sob that welled deep in my being and threatened to explode. How was this possible? What of my wounded soldiers, my tubercular women, the orphan girls and my beggar boys? Looking up, I wanted to tell them how much work I had left to do, how sorely I was needed here. Too, I wanted to beg where I was being taken, how far, what then . . . I wanted to turn away and flee, to cry, to seek safe shelter.

However, I knew that my path, the one God had chosen for me to carry my cross, lay not in desperate flight but in submission to His will, His plan.

"I see," I said. "May I kindly request several hours' time to bid farewell to my sisters, appoint a successor, and visit one last time my ailing patients?"

"We will take you in thirty minutes."

I gasped silently, mournfully, and with a simple bow of my head, replied, "As you command."

I turned and in a daze made my way back. Needless to say, word of my impending removal spread madly through my community, and my sisters came dashing from the hospital, the orphanage, and the kitchens, up one set of stairs, down another. The sobbing and the wails could be heard rising in the air like a painful song, yet all knew what to do: gather in the church. Wasting not a moment, I returned to my chambers, where I collected but several changes of underlinens and another set of robes. My hands shaking uncontrollably, I looked around here, there — my desk where I had reviewed so many petitions, the willow furniture where I had sat with so many visitors and taken tea, the photos on the wall. Picking up the hem of my robes, I hurried into my private chapel, where I had sought and found so much peace and come to love and appreciate every moment and every soul. My eyes flying over the myriad of icons, I spotted one, The Mother of God, and quickly pulled it from the wall. I could not abandon it, and She could not abandon me.

With my small leather valise in hand, I made my way from my rooms, out the doors, and into the courtyard. All about me was chaos, my sisters running this way and that, Father Mitrofan yelling and even cursing, but somehow I had already begun to detach, to realize how futile was any path but that of acceptance. I had to submit or break down, and I chose the former. It was the only way. And so in a manner I was oblivious to my dear ones. I did as was needed for those in need. I entered my church, weaving amongst my weeping sisters, and stopped at the front, whereupon I looked over all as they knelt on the floor and bowed their heads over and over, pressing their worried brows to the stones. I led them in prayer, and concluded by making a large sign of the cross over all.

And I ended by saying, "Please, my dear ones, do not cry. I have confidence we shall see one another in a higher world."

There was not time for individual farewells, not a moment to bless this sister or that or kiss this novice or that orphan goodbye. It took all my strength to dam my tears, to remain as I wished all of these dear ones to remember me: strong and confident in the love of the Lord.

As I passed back through the candlelight of the church and through the doors, the sisters swarmed frantically after me, bowing and clutching at my robes and pressing the cloth of my garb tightly to their lips. I stepped through the gardens, and the sisters, all ninety-seven of them, gathered around, their wails shrieking to the heavens as one hideous choir.

"Matushka, you cannot leave us?"

"Matushka, what will become of us all?"

"Matushka!"

"Gospodi pomilui!" God have mercy!

Only one person did I cling to, and that was Father Mitrofan, whose big cheeks and white beard were soaked with tears. I reached out for his black robes, clutching his arm.

"Please, I beg you," I said, my voice stony with shock, "do not abandon this place."

"Never!" he said, choking on his words.

"Watch over these children and our patients."

"Always!"

"And continue with services for as long as you are able."

"Until death!"

As I approached the gates, I saw not only the *komissar* and his soldiers standing there but two of my cell attendants, my forever-faithful Nun Varvara as well as Nun Yekaterina. Each of them held a small valise.

"We have received permission to accompany you," said Nun Varvara.

"But no, you mustn't, you can't —"

"We will not abandon you, Matushka. We are coming," replied Nun Varvara as forcefully as a princess herself.

I did not want them to come, to bear any unnecessary tribulations, but, truth be told, it was a relief, a cushion. So be it.

Just steps from the gates, I turned and looked out over my beloveds. All at once, in a great wail, every last one of them fell to their knees, their sobs piercing my heart like divine swords. I could not speak, could not find words. I felt light of head, that I might topple. All that I could manage was to raise my trembling hand and once again make over them a large sign of the cross.

Adieu, I cried inside. Adieu, adieu . . . adieu . . .

I turned then, and the *komissar* took me brusquely by the arm, leading me to the first motorcar. I asked, "Can you tell me, are we being taken far?"

But he did not reply, merely pressed me into the rear of the vehicle. Without a word he led my Nuns Varvara and Yekaterina to the second motorcar, whereupon he pushed them into the back.

In a daze we motored off, passing down the Bolshaya Ordinka and quickly leaving the white walls of my beloved *obitel* behind me. I could not bear to glance back. As we crossed the great river, I did look across the waters at the mighty Kremlin. The double-headed eagles of the Romanovs had been ripped away from the wondrous towers of the ancient fortress, and there instead, flapping in the early night sky, were the crimson banners of the Reds.

And, as I had suspected, we — that is, I and my good Nuns Varvara and Yekaterina — were driven directly to one of the main stations, where we were placed on a train heading east. The four Red Guards accompanied us, making sure no one came to our need. Soon the engine, belching smoke, made a slow lurch forward, and we were off, lumbering through the night. But I could not rest, could not sleep. Rather, I stayed up the entire night composing a letter, which by the grace of God I was able to post the following day.

To all my beloveds at the *Marfo-Marinski*

Obitel, I wrote:

God Bless You,
Let the Resurrection of our Lord give
you strength and solace. Let Saint Sergei, Holy Dmitri, and Saint Evfrosinia
of Polotsk guard us all, my dears. All is
well on our journey. Snow everywhere.

I cannot forget this day, all those dear,
kind faces. Lord, what suffering was
marked on them, how it hurt my heart.
You have become dearer to me with
every minute. How can I leave you, my
children? How can I give you strength?

Remember, my dears, everything I
have told you. Also be not only my
children but also my obedient pupils. Be
closer to each other, be as one single
soul, wholly devoted to our Lord, and
say, as did Saint John Chrysostom:
"Glory to God for everything."

I will be living in the hope of soon being with you again and I should like to
find you all together. Read together the
Acts of the Apostles, besides the Gos-
pels. You older sisters, do your best to
keep all the young ones united. Ask
Patriarch Tikhon to take the "spring
chickens" among you under his protective wing. Make him at home in my

middle room. Use my cell for confession and the big room for visitors.

For God's sake, don't lose heart. The Mother of God knows why her Heavenly Son has sent upon us these tribulations on the day of her Feast.

Lord, I believe, help Thou mine unbelief. God's designs are inscrutable.

I cannot express how deeply moved I am by your farewell. Over these years you have made me so happy. And I know that all of you without exception are trying to live in the way I have so often spoken to you about.

Oh! What progress you will now make toward salvation! I can already see a good beginning. Only don't lose heart and don't weaken your lofty intentions, and the Lord, Who has temporarily separated us, will strengthen you spiritually. Pray for me, a sinner, that I be worthy to return to my children and that I perfect myself for your sake, and that we all think of how to prepare ourselves for eternal life.

You remember how afraid I have been that you relied too much on my help to find strength to live, and how I used to tell you: You must get closer to God. The Lord says, *My son, give me thine heart and let thy eyes observe My ways.* If you accomplish this, then you can be sure that you've given everything to God because you have given Him your heart, and that means your very self.

The peace of our Lord Jesus Christ be with you, and my love to all of you in Jesus Christ. Amen.

Your loving Mother in Christ, who prays for you all,
— Matushka

CONCLUSION

Solovetsky Islands, White Sea, USSR
October, 1936

Pavel picked up a stick and started poking at the yellow flames, moving reddish embers one way, a moist, sizzling log another. He stared into the fire, seeing not burning wood but her. Yes, he remembered her completely, that gentle smile, that beautiful face, those long robes. Rarely had a day gone by that he hadn't pictured her. Or recalled her voice. Or gone back over the events of her life.

"So . . . that's what we did in those last days, the last two or three of her life," said Pavel, glancing first up into the dark night sky, then across the fire pit at Vladimir. "We told each other our stories. I was supposed to be guarding her, but really I was following her from the garden behind the schoolhouse, into the small classroom that served as her bedroom, and out to the kitchen just so we could talk. I told her everything — about my beautiful wife, Shura, and how she'd been gunned down, and how that had forced me into the revolutionary movement. And I told her about all my killings of the little men here and there, not to mention my part in blowing up her husband. And . . ."

Across the way, Vladimir tugged on his long white beard, and asked, "And . . . ?"

"And I told her what I'd done after I heard she'd been arrested, how I went all over Moscow and used all of my connections to be transferred to Alapayevsk. My comrades said I should stay there in Moscow and stick with the real business of the Revolution rather than watching over a bunch of 'formers.' The Revolution needed me, they said, but I suppose you could say I needed her more."

"Why?"

"Because . . . because I wanted her to understand . . . to understand all the things I had done."

"You mean, you needed to confess to her?"

Pavel looked up, a mocking smile on his face. "Perhaps. But the odd thing was that, in a way, she did the same thing to me. She told me of her life of excesses as a princess and she told me of her life of repentance.

That's what I meant when I said we told each other our stories. As much as I wanted her to understand my life, it seemed she wanted me to understand hers as well."

"So . . . did you come to understand her?"

"Vladimir, my friend, I came to much more than that — I came to love her."

"As did everyone, apparently." Vladimir glanced at a large brick wall some fifty paces away, then turned quickly back, saying, "You said something about how the most interesting thing she told you was also the strangest. What was that?"

For a while Pavel said nothing. He remembered how kindly she'd said it, even naively. How wrong she'd been.

"Well," began Pavel, wiping a tear from his eye, "when we'd finished our stories — this was that last night, just hours before her . . . her end — she looked up at me and she said . . ."

"You know, Pavel, you and I really aren't so very different."

I looked at her sitting across from me, pulled my rifle over my shoulder, and laughed. "What in the devil do you mean by that?"

"Well, the two of us, you and I, have been working and traveling toward the same goal, albeit on very different paths."

"Yes, but . . ."

With a twinkle in her eye, she said, "Trust me, for if we look into the life of every human being we discover that it is indeed full of miracles."

Vladimir exclaimed, "Really? She said that?"

"Yes, but she was wrong. She was wrong about everything. While she was traveling a path of charity in the hope of redemption of all people, I was following a dark path of anger with one and only one goal: revenge."

With a wide gesture, Vladimir said, "You know she was here, don't you, that she visited this place?"

"What? The Grand Duchess Elisavyeta Fyodorovna came all the way up here to these lost islands in the White Sea? You're kidding me. I had no idea."

"Yes, she was here. One of the great pleasures she took in her religious life was visiting as many monasteries and holy sites as she could." Motioning over his shoulder toward the crumbling onion domes of the Cathedral of the Holy Trinity, Vladimir said, "Yes, before . . . before that cathedral was converted to our camp toilet, she prayed there inside. You should have seen this place then, back before the Revolution. When this was still a working monastery, it was a masterpiece of Orthodoxy — of its architecture, of its righteous isolation, and most certainly of its faith. In this harsh climate and on these stony islands people found true faith, I tell you. Thousands of pilgrims came here, including her, Matushka. In fact, she came all this way with Prince Feliks Yusupov to pray for a successful end to the war."

"No wonder fate has brought me here."

And that realization, rather than making Pavel bitter, warmed him in a very real way. Perhaps there was a plan, perhaps it was in fact not the revolutionary committee that had ordered him here but her spirit so that they might meet again in a better world. Pavel glanced over at the decrepit cathedral and of what was left of the old Church of Saint Onufry. Then he looked toward the monastery's old cemetery, which had been all dug up, coffin after coffin dumped out, the holy relics of revered saints spread over the earth.

And then his eye was caught by the faintest of blue in the dark night sky. It would be morning before too long. He had not much time left, for his solemn change of lodging would come with the first light.

"My friend," said Pavel, "I need to tell you the rest. I must . . . I must, for of course I was with Matushka right up until the very last minutes of her life." His head fell. "But how do I tell you, how do I make you understand, when for me there is no understanding at all?"

"Go on, my son, and perhaps you'll find what is needed."

He took a deep breath, gathered the strength he needed to push through, saying, "Well, as I told you, because of the killings I had done, because of how much I had done for the Revolution, I had some good connections. And that is why I was able to get the transfer I needed. They arrested her that spring and sent her to Siberia, eventually imprisoning her with five other Romanovs and a few of their retainers in the former Napolnaya School there in the town of Alapayevsk. It was a small brick building, built on a field on the edge of town, and because of my connection I was able to get myself sent there. I explained how I had helped kill one Romanov — her husband — and I was ready to kill more. They needed someone to carry out a difficult job, and they knew I could do it. I had proven myself. And I arrived there toward the end of June and was immediately assigned as one of the guards. Immediately we made things more difficult for them. We took almost everything from them — their money and gold, of course, but also their clothes and shoes, linens and pillows. We left them with, I think, just the clothes they were wearing and one pair of shoes. Also, all the retainers were sent away — only two were kept, Nun Varvara,· who was Matushka's cell attendant, and a servant named Fyodor Remez, who served one of the grand dukes, the older one. From that time forward, I was involved in the planning of the events of July 17."

Vladimir said, "So tell me of that night."

"Well, we had already told the prisoners that because of disturbances they were going to be transferred to the Upper Sinyachikhensky Works. We said this was for their own safety, since the Whites were approaching and there would be fighting. Usually they ate at seven in the evening, but we told the cook, Krivova, to speed things up. The grand dukes were fed some horseflesh stew, but the Grand Duchess had received special permission for other foods — she didn't eat meat — so she got milk and some boiled turnips and she ate in her room, just like she always did. In those last weeks she spent much of her time alone in there, either drawing or praying. Mostly praying. It was the corner room and it was very plain, just two iron beds with hard mattresses and no pillows. She shared the room with Nun Varvara. And so later that evening . . ."

I looked at the clock, saw that it was almost eleven, which was the time for us to begin. With a nod to Yuri, one of the other guards, a big, strapping comrade with dark hair, we started down the corridor and went into her room. Both Matushka and her cell attendant, Nun Varvara, were there, kneeling and praying before an icon of The Mother of God.

"It's time for us to move you to a safer place," I said.

I kept my voice calm and low because I didn't want to excite or scare them. We needed to quietly take them out of town so as not to attract attention, for our instructions direct from Moscow were to dispose of them secretly. No one was supposed to find out.

The two women quickly finished a prayer, and then rose to their feet, their gray robes flowing to the floor. I looked at them, this tall, pretty Romanov woman dressed from head to foot in her religious clothing, and her short, devoted friend, and I felt a kind of sorrow for them. They didn't know what I did, what was to happen tonight, or at least they didn't know exactly how it was to come to pass. In any case, they had no idea what had happened just the night before — that not too far away in the town of Yekaterinburg the ex-tsar, the ex-tsaritsa, all of their five children, and four attendants had been shot to death in a small basement room.

Matushka said, "We don't have many things — shall we bring them with us?"

"No, we need to move quickly tonight. Your things will be brought to you tomorrow," I lied.

Her eyes held mine, searching for the truth. And I was sure she found it. She and I had talked so much these last days, I had told her so much of my life, so she knew how to read me. Yes, in my eyes she saw the truth of what was to come.

"Please, follow me," I said, heading out of the room.

Earlier I had told the other guards that I wanted to take the Romanov woman and her attendant first because they would be easiest and not rile the others. In truth, I wanted to take them at the start because I didn't want Matushka to get upset, I didn't want to have to shoot her or her friend there in the school. That was the least I owed her, to give her as much peace as possible.

"Of course," replied Matushka.

Without any resistance or hesitation, she and the little sister followed me down the dark hall and out the back door of the school. We were very quiet. I don't think the other five Romanov men and their one servant even heard us. They were in their two rooms at the other end of the small school and their doors were shut. Perhaps they were asleep. The plan was that they would be brought out after we left.

It was a very nice night. As soon as we stepped outside, the Grand Duchess looked up with a smile. The sky was beautiful, the stars so bright, and she stared up at the heavens for the longest while.

"What glory!" she gasped.

Yes, of course she knew.

"We have a cart out back for you," I said, leading the way through the garden.

I led the way with Matushka, then Nun Varvara following me, and finally the guard Yuri behind us all. We passed through the rows of vegetables that Matushka and her compatriots had planted with their own hands. They had heard of the famine and cholera sweeping through Sankt Peterburg and Moscow, and so they had taken it upon themselves to plant carrots and cucumbers, even some potatoes. I was surprised by this — that they could think of the future when not even the next moment was certain — and I was surprised how much Matushka herself knew about such things. She oversaw the planting work and taught the Romanov men about working in the earth.

She now asked, "Pavel, do you think we'll be back to eat from our garden?"

Of course I knew the answer. Of course it was no. But at first I didn't know what to say, how to reply.

I managed only to mutter, "I . . . I don't know."

"Well, if not, make sure it goes to some needy family, will you?"

"Certainly."

From the back of the garden we passed through a grove of apple trees, and there, just after that, we came to a small horse and cart. A comrade I'd never before seen stood there, holding the horse by its bridle. All was just as we had planned, and in the back of the cart I found two pieces of material and two pieces of rope.

"We're taking you to a secret place so we need to cover your eyes," I said kind of like it was nothing.

Neither of the women said anything. They were so docile. So accepting. Like lambs. They did nothing as Yuri and I took the cotton material and tied it around their eyes, blindfolding them. In fact, they even bowed their heads to make it easier for us. They did nothing, either, as we took the rope and tied their hands behind their backs.

"We are going to seat you in the back of this cart," I said, explaining. "My comrade and I will sit up front."

That was all I said, and calmly, easily, they

let us help them up into the back of the small cart. I showed them the seat in the back, and Matushka and her Nun Varvara sat down. It was kind of awkward, and when Nun Varvara blindly stepped on the hem of her own robes, I helped her, I lifted up her garments to make it easier.

"Spacibo." Thank you, she said in clear appreciation.

Yuri and I climbed up in the front of the cart, and the comrade who had been standing there released the horse and saluted us a farewell. Off we went into the darkness, following a narrow dirt lane that passed from the edge of town and into the fields. The old horse pulling us seemed to know the way. Once I looked back and saw Matushka raising her head.

"The air smells so delicious," she said, delicately sniffing the air, "just like wild strawberries."

And, yes, there was a sweetness wafting about us. I hadn't noticed it.

"Wild mushrooms, too," I added.

"Oh, yes . . . you're quite right, Pavel. There's such a soft, loamy smell," said Matushka, carefully smelling the air. "We must be nearing a woods."

"Just ahead."

Within a few moments we reached a forest

and there, in the trees, we waited for the others. It was decided that we would do this, leave town in small groups rather than one big one, and gather there in the woods. The hope was that this way we would be less noticeable. If all of us left together someone might notice and an alarm might be sounded.

"We will wait for the others here," I said.

Sure enough, about ten minutes later the next cart arrived, carrying two of the Konstantini brothers — Prince Igor and Prince Konstantin. They too were blindfolded, and their hands were likewise tied behind their backs. Not too long after that came a third cart carrying two more, Prince Ioann and the young poet, Prince Vladimir. After them came the last of our prisoners, Grand Duke Sergei Mikhailovich and his servant Fyodor Remez. All of them were blindfolded and their hands bound behind their backs, but I noticed that the Grand Duke's arm had been bound up with something.

"He hid behind one of the cupboards and wouldn't come out," whispered one of my comrades to me, "so we had to shoot him in the arm."

Apparently the Grand Duke Sergei had put up quite a struggle, screaming that he knew we were going to kill them. Now, however, all of them were quiet. There was no crying, no screaming. And so we set off toward Sin-yachika. Somewhere along the way Matushka started singing "Magnificat," and Nun Varvara and several of the young princes joined in. Later they sang "Sviete Tixhi," and their voices were soft and pleasant in the dark night.

We saw no one else, we passed no other carts. Along the way we crossed through a large pine wood and when a wind came up you could hear the needles whistling.

The trip took almost two hours.

Of course we didn't take them all the way to the Upper Sinyachikhensky Works. That was just a story. Instead, our destination was the Nizhni Seliminski mine shaft, where they used to dig for coal or ore or something, but which had long been abandoned. The mine itself was just a big hole in the ground, and it was very deep, which was why we had chosen it as the perfect place.

Quite some time later, all according to plan, we came to a small clearing just off the side of the road, and we pulled the carts in there, one after the other. The night air had cooled pleasantly, and now it was I who looked up into the sky, searching for something but unable to see it, to find it. There was nothing there. Did that mean it was just as Marx said, that there was no god and religion was just the opiate of the people?

"We've reached our destination and will walk the rest of the way," I said, trying to keep my voice from trembling.

Yuri and I climbed down from the front of our cart, went around and helped Matushka and Nun Varvara from the back. Meanwhile, two other guards went quickly ahead — they were supposed to wait for us there, on the edge.

"We have to walk about two hundred paces," I said, taking Matushka by the arm. "I'll guide you."

"Spacibo," said Matushka as I took her by the arm.

We were first, Matushka and I, and after us came Yuri guiding the short nun. Their eyes were still blindfolded and their hands still tied behind their backs, of course. The path was narrow and kind of rough, but I did my best to steer Matushka, warning her of a rock, a turn, a hole.

Almost halfway there, Matushka said, "Tell me, Pavel, is the night still clear? Can you still see the moon and the stars?"

"Yes, it's perfectly clear," I replied, even though the clouds were moving in.

"Good, then I'm happy."

I had the sense we could have uncovered her eyes and untied her hands and she would not have protested or screamed out or tried to get away. I guessed that she would even have knelt for us. And I wanted to do this for her, give her the chance to see her fate, but of course we had long ago decided otherwise. I led her along the path, but as we walked I couldn't help wondering why we were doing this? What had driven us to this point? I thought maybe I should run away, at least with her, Matushka, but it would have been impossible. They would come after us both.

So why were we doing this? Oh, yes.

As one of my comrades had explained it to me, "You cannot go after a king without killing him."

I supposed that included all of his family too. We had to be positive there was no going back. That was the least I owed my dead wife and my unborn child, wasn't it, to make sure there was no going back?

The guards who had gone ahead of us had disappeared in the darkness, for they had hurried to the appointed spot. Meanwhile, Yuri and Nun Varvara were some twenty paces behind us, half walking, half stumbling through the dark. Looking farther back, I saw two other guards leading two more prisoners. Really, if all went according to plan this shouldn't be too difficult, it shouldn't take too long. They would go one after the other. So far, not one of the former royals was crying or calling out in protest, and that surprised me. How could the extermination of the mighty House of Romanov be so easy?

I hung on tightly to Matushka's arm as we passed around a clump of birches, and then just up ahead I saw our two comrades standing there in front of the deep pit, right on the edge. We had chosen this place not just because the mine was abandoned and not just because it was so far out of town but because of that, its depth, maybe twenty or thirty *arzhin.* Last week I had come all the way out here to check it out, and in the broad daylight I couldn't even see the bottom, for it was as deep as an old pine tree was tall. Equally important, the rocks along the shaft and at the bottom were jagged and hard and sharp.

In a weak voice, I said, "We're almost there."

I looked into her face then, that beautiful face that had enchanted so many, and saw them, her tears. One by one they were rolling out from beneath her blindfold, not a torrent but a steady flow. Her lips were trembling.

And when we reached the small platform where the other two guards were waiting, I said to Matushka, "Please . . . just one small step up . . ."

She knew the end was coming then, for her entire body started shaking, and yet she stepped up onto the platform without the least resistance. I, too, stepped right next to her and peered into the mine shaft and saw what she could not: dark infinity.

Though the words came not easily, they came with confidence as she said, "Father, forgive them for they know not what they do."

I nodded to one of the guards, who stood there with his rifle raised high, and he brought the butt of his weapon down against the side of her head in one hard blow. There was a crack of her skull, and she groaned deeply and powerfully and almost immediately started to collapse.

It was at that very moment that I pushed her, and she tumbled head over heels into the pit, her pale-gray robes billowing about her until the blackness swallowed her up. I heard her hit one side of the mine shaft, the other, and then with a loud but dull noise she fell onto the rocks at the bottom.

And then silence.

Pavel stared into the dying flames of the fire, his face blank, his eyes streaming with tears. Until that night he'd never been able to get the death of his wife out of his mind — over and over in his mind's eye he'd seen her body blossoming with such red blood as she lay against the pure white snow. But ever since the night he'd pushed the Grand

Duchess Elisavyeta he'd seen something else altogether: the image of her tumbling into the unforgiving darkness. Worse, he'd not been able to get her last words out of his mind, they haunted him nearly every minute of every day.

Across the fire, Vladimir wiped his own eyes, and asked, "And the others?"

"We clubbed them all, and one by one they went over the edge. All seven of them — next the little Nun Varvara, then the young princes and the one servant. We only had to shoot one — Grand Duke Sergei Mixhailovich, the one we'd already shot in the arm. He must have heard the grunts and groans of the others, and he put up a fight, so we put a gun to his head and blasted out his brains. As for the others, we just bashed in their heads and tossed them in, one after another."

Pavel stared up into the sky, which was rapidly becoming lighter. All at once he began to sob as he never had, deep and furious, crying not because of what was about to happen to him that very morning but because of all that he'd done, the path of horror he'd left behind. How could he see it all so clearly now? Why had it been so hidden before? Falling off the log on which he'd sat, he collapsed on the ground, carried away by his deep, rolling tears.

His face buried in the dirty snow, he cried, "Father . . . how . . . how . . . could . . ."

Vladimir, his own face mopping wet, threw off the old, ratty blanket in which he'd been wrapped all night. Sitting there now in his black robes, he clutched with one hand the large brass cross that hung from his neck, and with the other made a sign of the cross over this poor suffering soul.

"Come to . . . to me, my son!" he called through his tears to Pavel.

"But . . . but Fa . . . Father Vladimir, I am unworthy! I am filthy with sin!"

"Come to me . . . ! Rise and come to me, my son! There is still time . . . you must repent! Repent!"

"I am unworthy . . . !"

"There is no crime that cannot be forgiven if you repent with your entire being!"

"No . . . !"

And yet Pavel started crawling, one hand, one knee, one after the other. He sobbed as he had not since he was a child, his body racked with guilt, with despair, with regret. How could he have done that, killed so many and especially her? Toward what goal? The tears streamed down his face and dropped into the snow. He had thought he would receive satisfaction from his revenge, but all that was delivered unto him was torment. He had thought that he had killed to keep the Revolution rolling forward, so that the sins of their masters would never be repeated, but now he saw that the fury of upheaval was doomed only to repeat itself again and again. Dear Lord . . . how he wished that he and his wife had stayed in the countryside, how he wished they hadn't gone to that demonstration on that bloody Sunday . . . how he wished he could hold his beautiful Shura in his arms and gaze softly upon their child who was never born.

"Come to me, Pavel!" called Father Vladimir.

His body heaving with sob after sob, Pavel moved on, lifting his head, seeing the cross that hung from Father Vladimir's neck. He focused on that, this bright, shiny object that might, just might, lead somewhere, a kind of home, a kind of comfort. He saw them all — the bodies of Father Gapon, the bureaucrat in Novgorod, the blood-gasping sugar baron, the director general of the bank . . . and Matushka, Nun Varvara, the Princes, the Grand Duke, the servant — and he cried with every fiber of his being, wishing for his death, which was in fact only minutes away but which could not come soon enough.

With as much difficulty as if he were scaling up the mine shaft into which he'd thrown Matushka, he crawled across the ground. Finally reaching Father Vladimir, Pavel rose back on his knees and hurled himself into the priest's lap, clutching like a drowning man at the brass cross and kissing it over and over.

He screamed, "Father, what have I done?"

Over him, Father Vladimir made the sign of the cross again and again, repeating and chanting, *"Gospodi pomilui . . . Gospodi pomilui . . . Gospodi pomilui . . . !"* The Lord have mercy . . . the Lord have mercy . . . the Lord have mercy!

They would have stayed that way for a good long while, but suddenly the two men, the sinner and the priest, were ripped apart. Before Pavel knew what was happening, two camp guards grabbed him and yanked him to his feet. A third took Father Vladimir by the arm and pulled him up.

"It is time," said Father Vladimir to Pavel, his voice strained.

"Yes, it is time," repeated Pavel, looking up and through his tears seeing the first of the daylight.

They were shoved along then, pushed and kicked by the guards toward a large hole some forty paces away. As he stumbled, Pavel was glad for this, glad that all would soon be over. Four years ago he had questioned one of his superiors, and in turn had been accused of anti-Soviet activity. For this he'd been sentenced to ten years at the Solovki Camp, which had been transformed from the ancient Solovetsky Monastery into a concentration camp, nearly the first of the USSR's many Gulags. In an attempt to get out of heavy work in a quarry, however, last month Pavel had become a "self-cutter," amputating three of his own fingers.

For that his sentence had been changed: to be shot.

Similarly, Father Vladimir, having refused to stop preaching and consequently charged with spreading anti-Soviet propaganda, had received a similar sentence: to be shot.

As they now trudged along, Pavel looked up and on the thick brick wall of the monastery saw a red banner proudly proclaiming the popular slogan: *Cherez trud domoi!* Through work you will get home! But Pavel didn't want to go home, for his home and his heart were long gone. He just wanted to escape to another world where he was sure to face eternal damnation.

A few paces later Pavel and Vladimir were led to a deep, wide hole they themselves had dug over the past week. They had finished just yesterday, and then the killing had begun.

"*Gospodi!*" For the sake of God, gasped Father Vladimir, staring with horror into the pit.

Pavel couldn't believe it, either, the sight of so many bodies dumped in there. Forced to line up on the edge of the mass grave, the first ones were shot not ten minutes after Pavel and Father Vladimir had finished digging, the bodies falling this way and that into the pit. Even Pavel, now staring down at the bodies, was surprised at how many had been killed since just yesterday — sixty or seventy men and women, and over to one side a black mound of maybe twenty priests. The killings went on and on all the way until nightfall, at which time Pavel and Vladimir were told they would be shot with the first break of day.

Yes, they had been given one more night, and on that long night Pavel had told his story not only of her, the beautiful Grand Duchess, but of the Revolution for which he had killed and which would now kill him.

Knowing that they had but seconds left, Pavel reached over and took hold of Father Vladimir's hand, and with a trembling voice

406

said, "Thank you for listening to me, Father."

The priest, turning slightly, raised his free hand and made a quick, awkward sign of the cross, saying, "Your confession has been heard."

"But . . . but I do not wish . . . I do not deserve . . . to be forgiven."

"That, my son, is not your decision, but His."

Before Pavel could say anything else, he sensed it, the hard, cold barrel at the back of his head. The tears coming to his eyes, he looked up, saw the beauty of the blue morning, the sun streaking the sky, and he wondered if her thoughts had been like this in those last moments: of fear and hope and relief. And he wondered, too, if they, the Grand Duchess and he, would ever meet in the next life so that he might bow at her feet.

And then the shot came so quickly that he didn't even feel it, let alone hear it, and his body tumbled forward, falling onto the many who had fallen before him.

It is easier for feeble straw to resist
mighty fire than for the nature of sin to
resist the power of love.
— New-Martyr Saint Elisabeth

AUTHOR'S NOTE

The city of Alapayevsk fell to the White Army in late September, 1918, and soon thereafter the bodies of Her Imperial Highness Grand Duchess Elisabeth Fyodorovna, Nun Barbara, and the five other Romanovs and one servant were recovered from the bottom of the mine shaft where they had been pushed to their deaths on July 18, 1918. While the gruesome details of what happened in those last moments are still not certain, many stories persist. The most frequently related of those comes from the only eyewitness interrogated by White investigators, Vasily Ryabov, who claimed that burning branches and grenades were thrown into the mine shaft after the bodies, and still Elisabeth and the other Romanovs lived (Ryabov claimed they could be heard singing hymns). However, months later when the bodies were pulled from the mine, the only physical damage found on their

411

bodies was severe physical trauma from being clubbed and hurled down.

A few months after the Whites took Alapayevsk they lost it again to the Reds, and during the retreat the bodies of the Romanovs were hastily removed to Siberia and eventually, in 1920, to Beijing. Soon thereafter the relics of the Grand Duchess and Nun Barbara were transported to Jerusalem and laid to rest in the Church of Saint Mary Magdalene, where they remain to this day.

In 1981, Grand Duchess Elisabeth was canonized New-Martyr Saint Elisabeth and her faithful cell attendant canonized Nun-Martyr Saint Barbara by the Russian Orthodox Church Outside Russia and, in 1992, by the entire Russian Orthodox Church. To commemorate Saint Elisabeth, who was one of only ten 20th-century martyrs to be so honored, a statue of her was installed above the Great West Door of Westminster Abbey in 1998; Saint Elisabeth's great-nephew, Prince Philip, and his wife, Queen Elizabeth II, attended the ceremony.

In 1926 the *Marfo-Marinski Obitel Miloserdiya* (the Martha and Mary Convent of Mercy) was closed and all the remaining nuns were banished to Siberia and Central Asia; the Grand Duchess's spiritual confessor, Father Mitrofan, was imprisoned in the

Gulag and later died of pneumonia. As for the convent itself, its buildings, which during the Communist era were used as community halls and warehouses, fell into extreme disrepair. In 1993 the *Marfo-Marinski Obitel Miloserdiya* was reconsecrated at its original site on the Bolshaya Ordinka, vows for 33 nuns were renewed, and its orphanage reopened.

To this day, restoration of Grand Duchess Elisabeth's beloved *obitel* continues, as does her pioneering social work.

The author gratefully acknowledges that for the purposes of authenticity many of Grand Duchess Elisabeth's own words from her diaries and letters (including her farewell letter written on the train to Siberia) were used in the writing of this novel. Similarly, other non-copyrighted historical documents, such as the letters of Nicholas II and Empress Alexandra as well as Rhetta Dorr's actual interview of Grand Duchess Elisabeth regarding education in America, were also employed. For more information, a readers' group guide, and to view historical photographs, please visit:

www.robertalexanderbooks.com

ACKNOWLEDGMENTS

Many thanks to those who helped so very much: researcher Mary Ann Fogarty, Ellen Hart, Dr. Don Houge, Robin Seaman, Katherine Solomonson, and Meri Tarlova. My deep gratitude to everyone at Viking, particularly my editor David Cashion and publicist Ann Day. And of course, thank you, Marly!

ABOUT THE AUTHOR

Robert Alexander is the author of the bestselling novels *Rasputin's Daughter* and *The Kitchen Boy.* He has spent thirty years traveling in Russia, where he has worked for the United States government and currently is a partner in a St. Petersburg company operating a number of businesses. He lives in Minneapolis, Minnesota.

For more information, visit www.robertalexanderbooks.com

The employees of Thorndike Press hope you have enjoyed this Large Print book. All our Thorndike and Wheeler Large Print titles are designed for easy reading, and all our books are made to last. Other Thorndike Press Large Print books are available at your library, through selected bookstores, or directly from us.

For information about titles, please call:
   (800) 223-1244

or visit our Web site at:
   http://gale.cengage.com/thorndike

To share your comments, please write:
   Publisher
   Thorndike Press
   295 Kennedy Memorial Drive
   Waterville, ME 04901